ALSO BY SANDRA SPEWOCK FEDER

Side Effect

ONE OF MY OWN

ONE OF MY OWN

A NOVEL BY

SANDRA FEDER

THORNWOOD PUBLISHING CO. LLC   Connecticut 2005

Copyright © 2005 by Sandra Spewock Feder
All rights reserved under International and
Pan-American Copyright Conventions.
Published in the United States by
Thornwood Publishing Company LLC, Connecticut

Library of Congress Card Number 2004098880
ISBN 1-930541-61-9

Manufactured in the United States of America
First Edition

To G.C.
and
my husband, Jack Feder

"Boo boo," she whispered.

A small hand stretched over the crib railing and touched the bloody disk on his forearm.

Cy glanced at her face, indistinct in the darkened room. Tears shimmered in her eyes—she felt sorry for him. Though Cy meant to be strong, that made his breath catch in his throat and he coughed to cover it up.

Although he wanted to pull his arm back and hide it, Cy let her look at it. He kept on brushing her wispy hair, gold even in the faint glow of the night light.

"It's all right, Clea," he whispered. "He didn't mean it. It was an accident."

But it wasn't all right, he thought. His father did mean it and he did it all the time. His eyes began to burn at the thought that he was so bad that someone wanted to hurt him. Cy knew tears were close, so he bit his lip hard.

He didn't want to upset Clea. His parents were fighting again tonight. Even through the thick walls, he could hear loud voices, heavy footsteps, crashing sounds. Clea had awakened and Cy had known, even though his room was at the other end of the long hall and Clea hadn't made a sound.

Cy always knew when Clea was frightened, and what he should do to calm her. She stood patiently now, leaning her head slightly forward as Cy drew a pink brush through her hair. The rhythm calmed her. It calmed him, too.

Now and then Clea lightly touched his arm or his face. She loved him. Somehow that made everything else bearable. If Clea loved him, he couldn't be as bad as they said he was. Cy would do anything for her.

"You go to him," she said.

Cy was startled by her comment. At night they didn't talk about these things. Somehow in the dark it was more upsetting. He couldn't look at Clea.

Cy wanted his father to love him. "I want to be close," he

said. It was embarrassing to admit.

"But he hurts you."

Now his cheeks were hot. "I know." Shame made him grateful for the low lights.

From the beginning, Cy had known he was adopted. If there was something so terrible about him, why did they take him? And if they didn't want him, why did they keep him? He pushed that thought away. It brought up other thoughts—about why his real parents had given him up. About what he had done to make them not want him. Sometimes thinking about it made him curl up on the floor, hugging his knees.

"Is that dumb?" she asked. Her voice was fainter than before.

Now Cy's cheeks were flaming."Love isn't smart, Clea," he said defensively. "It's..." But he couldn't find the words.

Cy continued brushing. Small sparks of static electricity crackled in her hair. He must have pulled too hard; she winced.

"I like to be close, too" she said.

"Not when it gets me this," Cy said with vehemence, poking at his arm. "Not when it's as hot as a cigarette!"

He was shaking his head, and suddenly he saw something on his sleeve that took his breath away.

He was wearing his good luck pajamas, the ones with spaceships all over them. With trembling fingers he probed the sleeve of his top. His index finger came through a hole burned in the fabric, right through the middle of a spaceship. Somehow that hole was worse than burning his arm. His throat tightened and his eyes pinched.

A loud crash startled him. He turned toward the door and waited, dreading the approach of footsteps.

But there were no footsteps, just low voices. Though he didn't want to hear what they were saying, he always strained to listen. Cy didn't understand all of what he heard; just enough to know his father was hurting his mother.

Cy began brushing Clea's hair again, trying to focus only on her hair and not on what was happening down the hall in his parents' bedroom.

Cy heard a door slam and his heart began to beat so hard he could hear it in his ears. He brushed Clea's hair harder. A faint buttery smell drifted to his nose—and some part of his brain identified it as ozone. By brushing her hair, he made static electricity that changed the oxygen. The air smells like before a big storm, he thought. Cy's nose quivered, and he shuddered.

When Clea made a small snuffling sound, Cy suddenly realized how hard he was brushing. "I'm sorry, Clea," he said, hugging her. He was amazed when she pushed him away with a cry, and tottered and stumbled backward. Cy looked down at the sheet on the bottom of her crib where she had been standing. The light was faint, but he knew exactly what he saw in front of her pink-socked feet.

Small, smudged dark circles.

Cy felt his breath sucked out of him, leaving a mixture of fear, anger, and nausea. His father had hurt Clea. He had burned her feet, just like he burned Cy's arm. *Clea.*

She stared at him with wide eyes. When he reached for her, she made a low threatening moan. Her legs were trembling.

The look on Clea's face sickened Cy. It reminded him of a hurt dog he had once seen. He was frightened to see her like this and he felt terrible and selfish. Why didn't I notice she was hurt? Why did I think her tears were for me?

Holding her legs stiff, Clea bent over and stretched one hand toward the mattress in her crib, groping the area around her. What was she doing? Cy wondered. And then he knew. She was reaching for a worn, flat shape of terry cloth, her comfort puppy. It was always in her crib, but it wasn't there tonight.

Cy dropped to the floor and crawled on his stomach, searching for the stuffed toy. But he couldn't find it.

Cy got back to his feet, leaned on the crib railing and miserably watched her. She didn't want him to brush her hair, and there was nothing else he could do for her. He was no longer able to hold it back. Hot tears dropped freely from his

eyes, which hurt as if someone were pinching them from inside. Clea's face swam in front of him.

Through his sobs Cy heard something downstairs. He
stopped crying to listen and heard it again. Was it the TV?
What had his parents left on this time? he worried. He always
had to go around checking the house—for burners left on, lit
cigarettes, unlocked doors. Though he didn't want to take
the chance that they would find him out of bed, he couldn't
sleep until he knew.

"Clea, I hear something," he whispered, sniffling. "I'm going to check downstairs and then I'll come back to you."

"No. Don't go," she said. She stood stiffly, reaching one
hand toward him and curling her fingers, beckoning him back.

"It's all right," he told her. "I'll be right back."

He padded quickly along the polished wood floors of the
hallway to the head of the stairs. The front door was directly
across from the bottom of the stairs. His bare feet flapped
down the wood treads, his hands slid along the banister.

But before he reached the bottom step, the door exploded
in a shower of wooden splinters and ax blades. Cy slipped
in surprise and horror and fell back hard, sliding down
the steps. Two bundled figures with masks and axes burst
through and ran for him. Heavily gloved hands grabbed
him by his arms and dragged him back toward the hole
that had been the front door.

Cy's arms and legs had lost their bones with the first shock.
His head fell back as he gaped up at them.

As they crossed the threshold, and Cy looked up under
the windows of the house, a greater fear flamed through him
and made his hands and fingers ache.

He flailed in the men's grip, his legs doing a crazy dance,
and he screamed. "No! I have to get Clea. No!"

The gloved hands didn't slow down until they dumped Cy
in the yard, where other people were standing.

"Don't shush me!" a voice said angrily. "Nothing goes up
like that. Not without help."

Cy lifted his chin in time to get scalding hot air blown in his face. His eyes blinked shut against the pain, but that made them burn more. A watery squint showed him nothing but orange-red. Then the orange-red took shape and he saw it was a house.

His eyes still streaming, Cy clawed and wriggled his way on his belly toward the front stairs. Hands grabbed his ankles and dragged him back.

Someone's long legs were suddenly in front of Cy, blocking his view. Cy struggled to get around him. The legs collapsed next to him and a hand grabbed his shoulder hard and shook him.

"Where is Clea?" An angry face with glasses was inches from his, but his eyes weren't focusing.

Cy couldn't breathe, let alone speak.

"Is she in there? Did you leave her in there?" Cy felt the fingers digging into his collarbone and he moaned.

A loud crash followed a creaking, tearing sound as something large inside the house gave way. Cy's head snapped up. He tore away the man's hand and scrambled to his feet.

"No!" he shrieked, running toward the fire.

A beam crashed with flames and sparks, showering Cy. His pajama top caught fire and he tore at his chest, screaming. In the pain he forgot Clea.

The man who had grabbed him, yanked him into his arms and threw him to the ground. He rolled Cy over and over until Cy thought he would throw up from the pain or the rolling. Faintly he heard sirens wailing. The last thing he remembered was hands lifting him into that wailing sound.

Cy awakened alone in the dark. The smell of smoke still filled his nose. Though burns on his chest and arms throbbed, what tortured him was the certainty that Clea was dead because he had left her behind. His last images of her—hand reaching out for him, pink-socked foot making bloodprints in her crib—were the worst. Sobs wracked his stomach. Pushing his fists into his eyes to rub away the sight, he found her small pink hairbrush clutched in his hand.

TWENTY YEARS LATER
WESTPORT, CT

1

"I'm pregnant!" she sobbed.

Cy held her as she trembled, her face buried in his chest.

"I'm pregnant," she said again, but her voice was muffled by his tear-soaked shirt and tie.

Cy stroked her clean-smelling hair and patted her back reassuringly. He could feel her ribs through the dress; she must have lost weight under the stress and anxiety. They would have to watch her carefully.

Cy looked over her head at the man sitting at the desk; he was still glowering. The hell with him, Cy thought. The man twisted a watch on his wrist, glanced at it, and re-crossed his legs. He was impatient every time Cy saw him. What kind of man was he?

The woman hiccuped and lifted her head to look at Cy. Her eyes were puffy, red, and mascara-stained, but they were shining.

"I'm pregnant," she repeated, in triumph. "Thank you, Dr. Cy. God bless you."

Cy smiled at her and shot another look at the husband; the man looked resentful. Cy could understand that he wasn't happy about the varicocelectomies he'd undergone—but that had been with another doctor, before they came here, and it had been nothing compared to what his wife had endured. Besides, all that was over, and now they were going to have a baby. Cy hoped the husband hadn't been lying about wanting a baby, just going through the motions. Because he almost seemed disappointed now that his wife was pregnant.

Cy led the woman to a chair and handed her a box of tissues. "We should talk a little about what comes next," he told them.

Thank God she got pregnant with the second cycle of IVF, Cy thought. He didn't have a lot of confidence in the

husband's commitment to the pregnancy—the whole process had apparently done nothing but annoy him. Cy
watched the man. He still hadn't moved—to hold her, congratulate her, whatever. One would think this had nothing
to do with him.

There was a knock at the door, and a big, square nurse
bustled in with a paper cup which she placed on Cy's desk.

"I thought you might like a drink of water," Aggie said,
smiling at the woman and at Cy. Then she left.

As Cy handed the woman the cup, her husband scraped
his chair back abruptly, loudly. Like a rabbit, she started at
the sound and shook the cup, emptying the contents all over
Cy's sleeves.

"Oh Dr. Cy, I'm so sorry!"

Her face, radiant just a moment ago, was already drawn
in what Cy thought must be a frequent mask of contrition.

"It's all right," he reassured her. "It's only water. If we'd
been celebrating with red wine, that might be different."

She leaned back in the chair and seemed to relax. Cy briefly
mopped his sleeves and then rolled them up his forearms. He
hoped the husband didn't upset her too much. Just because
she was pregnant didn't mean she would stay pregnant. The
miscarriage rate with IVF's was the same as in the general
population, 15 to 30 percent.

"Now that you're pregnant..." Cy began again.

The door opened, this time without a knock. A tall, thin
man wearing glasses and a crisp white coat stuck in his head.
He smiled warmly.

"Well?" He craned his neck to scan the room and frowned.
"Is it true—congratulations are in order?" He looked expect-
antly at Cy.

Cy hated to say anything to jinx himself, but he had to
answer the head of the clinic. He nodded yes to Dr. Wyatt.

"Ah, congratulations, congratulations," the older man said,
smiling broadly. He stepped into the room and rubbed his
hands together briskly. "Good, good."

Cy chafed at the older man's presence. Dr. Wyatt had to

stick his nose into everything at the clinic. In the past it had been a blessing, the couple of times Cy had needed help when he was green. Now Cy could handle his patients by himself. If he needed to consult, he would.

"We're so happy," the woman said.

Cy noticed that the husband said nothing, but at least he had stopped glowering.

"That's wonderful, just wonderful," Dr. Wyatt said, beaming.

Now Cy couldn't help smiling fondly at the older man. He knew the nurses kidded that Dr. Wyatt's habit of saying things twice was the reason so many of his patients had twins. They all knew the truth: pregnancies resulting from IVF are more likely to result in multiple births.

The husband stood up abruptly. "We've taken enough of your time," he said, and headed for the door.

He must have gotten the opening he wanted when Dr. Wyatt came in, Cy thought. There was more for them to talk about, but it would have to wait.

The wife silently followed her husband. After she watched him start down the hall, she turned to Cy.

"Thank you, Dr. Cy. For not giving up. For making me be a fighter. I've wanted one of my own so much, but I didn't have enough strength to do it by myself. I will always be grateful to you."

When she was gone, Cy closed the door.

Dr. Wyatt said: "She went through a lot before she came here, didn't she?"

Cy nodded. "Eight years with Clomid, artificial insemination, several laparoscopies, and several operations for adhesions."

"The second IVF cycle was successful?" Dr. Wyatt asked.

Cy nodded; Dr. Wyatt knew everything that happened at his clinic.

"Sit down," Dr. Wyatt said. "I need to talk with you."

Cy sat down, the flush of success still warming him, expecting Dr. Wyatt to congratulate him, too.

2

"You're going to put this clinic into bankruptcy."

That was the last thing Cy expected Dr. Wyatt to say to him. Cy was bowled over—not only by the abrupt change in Dr. Wyatt, but because he'd never before been criticized for the way he worked. He felt skewered behind his desk, his stomach tight as he waited to hear the rest of it. Cy knew he wouldn't be allowed to defend himself. The head of the clinic didn't entertain discussions or answer questions; he made pronouncements. Though he had lived with the older man's style for years, Cy had never gotten used to it. It still galled him and threw him off stride.

"You go more than the extra mile for each patient. That's why it takes you so much time. You're conscientious, you're a good doctor. But you have to budget your time, Cy. This is a business." Dr. Wyatt had a cheap retractable pen in his hand, and he clicked it as if for emphasis.

That stung Cy, and not only because it was unfair. This was the man who had raised him when his adopted parents were killed in the fire. Cy still found himself responding to Dr. Wyatt like a boy who wants his father's approval.

"Whether we help a patient ourselves or end up recommending an alternative, we have to budget our time wisely," Dr. Wyatt said.

Cy pushed his appointment calendar—every square was filled in—toward Dr. Wyatt, but the older man ignored it. Cy saw more patients than anyone else in the clinic. So why is he telling me this? Cy wondered.

"If we don't budget our time, we'll get to the point where we help only those couples who have money," Dr. Wyatt said. Though he chafed at the unfairness of his lecture, Cy couldn't help admiring the man's mission. Dr. Wyatt had started his clinic over twenty years ago, at a time when the concept of artificial means to get pregnant was not widely popular, and the medical techniques were far from what they were today. He had persevered in building his privately-funded clinic—there had been no government money for research—and offering his services both to those who could pay and those who couldn't. Cy didn't understand why the focus of this lecture was on money. Though he wasn't privy to the exact figures, Cy always thought the clinic was successful.

"Everyone who wants a child deserves to have one; not just those society thinks are worthy." Dr. Wyatt took off his glasses and rubbed his eyes with the heels of both hands. His hands were dry and pale from frequent washing.

In spite of the older man's criticism, Cy felt a surge of affection for him. He knew the doctor had chronic eyestrain from the long hours he put in at the clinic, his reading, and his work on the computer. Cy had encouraged him to hire an assistant, but the older man said he was so used to doing things on his own that he couldn't change now.

Cy began to wonder if the older man were tired, even ill. Maybe the real issue wasn't how Cy spent his time. Maybe Dr. Wyatt wanted to cut down the hours he spent in the clinic. God knows he worked hard. Besides the patients he saw on a steady basis, he never turned down requests from organizations like the CDC to prepare a paper or a talk for them. Even though he didn't always make the presentation himself, he did the lion's share of the work.

Dr. Wyatt put his glasses on Cy's desk, and Cy was startled at how thick the lenses had gotten. Though he didn't know why, Cy began to feel guilty.

Dr. Wyatt picked up his glasses, rubbed a lens with his thumb. "I'd like you to take over two young couples I'm seeing this morning. You'll be doing an egg retrieval from the women and getting a semen sample from the men. I want you to do the IVF yourself and biopsy the embryos."

That was so out of sync with what Dr. Wyatt had been saying that Cy didn't even question the last-minute nature of the assignment. Instead, he blurted: "You've never done that before. Why now?"

Dr. Wyatt looked at his glasses. "If your patient load is heavier," he said, "you'll be forced to spend less time with each patient—and to accomplish more in the time you have available."

Cy knew a more crowded schedule wasn't going to make him more efficient. It was only going to put him under greater pressure. A disturbing thought occurred to him. Was Dr. Wyatt testing him in some way? Though the thought made Cy's stomach churn, he didn't know what to say. He had striven to meet Dr. Wyatt's expectations for the past twenty years.

Dr. Wyatt drummed his fingers impatiently on the clipboard in his lap. He looked disappointed. "This is a business," he finally said. "If it doesn't make money, no one wins."

Cy still didn't know what to say.

Dr. Wyatt frowned at Cy. "Please change your shirt. Your sleeves are wet. I don't want my doctors walking around the clinic with rolled-up sleeves like car mechanics."

He got up abruptly and left.

Cy glared at the closed door for what seemed like a long time. Thanks to Dr. Wyatt, Cy had run the gamut of emotions from surprise to disappointment to indignation to anxiety to hurt. Right now Cy felt used up. Tired.

And frustrated enough to want to throw something. He had become a doctor to help people. If that took a lot of his time, that was his choice. He was giving the clinic everything he had. He wasn't cheating Dr. Wyatt or his patients. He always thought carefully about the course of treatments and any tests he ordered. Why the hell couldn't Dr. Wyatt trust him—after all these years—to do what he needed to do?

Cy slammed a desk drawer, shook his head. He opened another drawer to get a fresh shirt. When he reached inside, his hand closed on a small box. He knew what it was, what it contained, but he removed it and opened it. Inside was a baby's pink hairbrush, with a few strands of gold hair caught in the bristles. It was Clea's hairbrush, the only thing of hers that he had. Below the box was a bundled stack of envelopes. He took out the stack.

Cy removed the top envelope; the postmark was from a week ago. He read the message inside again:

I can't take your money anymore.

The stack of envelopes represented the failed efforts of a series of private investigators to find Clea or even some trace of her. Since the night of the fire, Cy had been obsessed with questions: Where had the fire come from? How had it spread so fast? Why had they found the remains of his adoptive father, but no trace of his adoptive mother—or Clea—in the ruins of the house?

Cy had talked to plenty of so-called authorities who insisted that the temperature of the fire had been high enough to obliterate any trace of human remains. Yet Cy stubbornly pointed out that bones from his father had been found.

By now, even the hard-bitten investigators had told Cy to give up, accept the inevitable, get on with his life. So why did he keep at it? What was motivating him? Did he really believe Clea was alive, or was he still spurred by some sense of guilt?

Cy put the small box away and pulled out a clean shirt. He pulled off the plastic bag, removed the cardboard, unbuttoned the front. All he knew was that if he had a chance to live just one part of his life over, he would relive the night of the fire. Only this time, he wouldn't fail Clea.

3

"I'm only thirty-five. Why do you want to biopsy my embryos?"

Claire Young said the last three words as if they were in another language. Her face had tightened and she looked older than she had minutes ago. With a nervous gesture she pushed shoulder-length blonde hair behind her ear and waited for the answer.

Dr. Wyatt sighed as he sank into the chair behind his desk. He was going to have to spend a lot of time with this couple—explaining things and selling them on the procedure—but it was the right thing to do for them. He buzzed Aggie to rearrange his schedule.

While he spoke to Aggie, he sized up the young woman sitting across from him. A professional with a science background. Wanted to be involved in her treatment. Asked pertinent questions—like this one; she understood there was a connection between her age and the quality of her embryos.

He got off the phone, nodded to her. "You're right. You're young and we have every reason to hope that your eggs are just fine and the embryos are healthy. But hope isn't enough. You came to see me because you haven't been able to get pregnant. You want a child and you don't want to spend any more time trying methods that don't work. I recommended in vitro fertilization to give you the best chance to get pregnant. And I want to test your embryos to be sure that only normal, healthy embryos are transferred to you. I want you to have a healthy baby."

Claire's face tightened, frightened and worried, and she said, "Can't you tell how the embryos are by looking at them?" Dr. Wyatt shook his head. "By looking under the microscope, we can only check for certain things: the number of cells in the embryo, whether those cells are a uniform size, if any of the cells lacks a nucleus or has an abnormal-looking nucleus. But that doesn't give us enough to go on. Studies have shown that while most abnormal-appearing embryos have chromosomal abnormalities, so do nearly a third of normal-appearing embryos."

Claire's husband, Tom, sat protectively near her. He reached over to put his hand on her arm. "Frankly, we're concerned that taking one of the cells might damage the embryo, and we don't want to chance that."

Dr. Wyatt reassured them. "The same technology that I've developed over the past twenty-five years to do thousands of successful in vitro fertilizations is used to safely remove a cell from the embryo." For emphasis he patted the thick album on his desk. The young couple had seen its contents: hundreds of pictures of Dr. Wyatt's 'test tube' babies.

"But won't removing the cell take away something the embryo needs?" Tom persisted.

"Absolutely not," Dr. Wyatt said. "At three days, your embryo has just eight cells. Any one of them has all the information needed to make a baby. Taking one of those cells to test won't hurt the embryo at all. But it will tell us if there is anything seriously wrong with the embryo." He looked at the husband and then the wife while he said this.

Claire kept folding and unfolding a piece of paper.

"I sense that you have more questions," Dr. Wyatt said gently. "Please ask me. Don't feel that anything is small or unimportant. I want you to feel comfortable."

Claire smiled gratefully. "I keep hearing about GIFT and FISH and PCR. What are they?"

Dr. Wyatt smiled inside. He was sure she knew the answers to her questions, but was trying to be diplomatic about asking him if there were any other treatments that he should use in addition to, or instead of, what he was recommending.

"GIFT stands for Gamete Intra-Fallopian Transfer," he said. "It means taking your egg and your husband's sperm and transferring them to your fallopian tube. The other two are techniques used to help analyze genetic material," Dr. Wyatt added. "PCR stands for Polymerase Chain Reaction. It's a way to amplify small amounts of genetic material so there's enough for us to run tests. FISH is a method using fluorescence. It helps us to quickly determine which chromosomes are present in the nuclei and which are absent. That way we can rule out any defects that are caused by the lack of chromosomes or by an abnormal number of chromosomes."

Dr. Wyatt decided to drop the heavy words here. "Like Down's syndrome."

A shadow crossed Claire's face. "I thought the chance for delivering a baby with a defect like that was about 1% for someone my age," she said.

She's done research, Dr. Wyatt thought. It indicated that she was really committed to having a child. That pleased him.

"Let me explain something," Dr. Wyatt said. "The condition in an embryo that has an extra or a missing chromosome is called aneuploidy. More than 20% of <u>embryos</u>—not babies—from women in your age range—35 to 39—are affected. The difference in percentages between embryos and babies is due to the fact that a pregnancy with aneuploidy is less likely to attach to the uterus or go to term. Most will be miscarried. We don't want you to miscarry."

The couple exchanged a glance that made Dr. Wyatt sure his explanation had hit its mark.

"Does one cell give you enough material to determine if there is a defect?" Tom asked.

"Yes," Dr. Wyatt said. "And when we're looking for a specific gene defect and need more material, we use PCR. PCR allows us to amplify—from a single cell—only that tiny part of the gene that has a mutation. If the gene is normal, that small part will not amplify."

The couple's stiff postures seemed to relax. Dr. Wyatt sensed that their misgivings were waning, and he felt gratified. Now was the moment to close.

He leaned forward and said to them: "Our genes are not who we are. As far as we can tell, they simply give us a place to live in. But we owe it to our children to give them the best home we can."

Tom and Claire looked at each other and clasped hands.

Dr. Wyatt knew he had their consent; now he wanted their signatures. "Testing can be completed within a day," he said. "Then we'll know which embryos we want to transfer back to you."

They signed the consent form. "Good, good," Dr. Wyatt said. They left, looking much happier than when they had arrived.

Dr. Wyatt sighed contentedly. The couple's embryos were already biopsied. He had anticipated their decision and the blastomeres were already on their way to the lab to be tested.

****

Aggie stuck her head in his office. "It's the CDC," she said breathlessly.

Dr. Wyatt smiled thinly, nodded. That she got excited about things like the Centers for Disease Control and Prevention calling, grated on him. What was so special about the organizations he dealt with? Didn't she realize what he had achieved with his clinic was what drew them to ask for his help, advice, cooperation?

He picked up the phone. "Let me call you back," he said. This had become standard procedure long ago, when he realized Aggie was listening in. He had been furious, but even then she had been too valuable to fire. He worked around her.

"Jim!" the voice at the other end barked. "What the hell is going on? You said you would have the samples here by today."

Even after ten years, Dr. Wyatt still resented the familiar form of address. "I sent the package to the director."

There was silence for a beat. Then: "Why didn't you tell me you were sending it to him? Why didn't he tell me?"

It's simple, Dr. Wyatt thought. Your boss didn't have to tell you because you work for him. I don't have to tell you because you're an idiot.

"He was in a hurry," Dr. Wyatt said.

"How did they look?" the voice asked. "Do you think we'll be able to use them?"

"I wouldn't have sent them otherwise." Dr. Wyatt bit off the words. What did this idiot take him for?

"It looks as if there are correlations between the new strain of papillovirus and abnormalities in the polar body," the voice said excitedly. "We've gotten samples from all over the country, but yours are the cleanest, the best to use."

Dr. Wyatt's feathers unruffled a bit at the praise. "I'm glad I could help the study."

"Are you coming down for the director's address?" the voice asked.

"Of course. I've already made travel arrangements."

"If you need a ride from the airport, let me know," the voice said. "OK?"

When Dr. Wyatt hung up, he felt like wiping the receiver. Though he knew people like the one he had just talked to were necessary, he still hated to deal with them. Despite their degrees, they knew nothing about science. Still, they managed to insinuate themselves into positions of power and money. That idiot he'd just talked to had the authority to influence, if not make, policy.

And he wouldn't know a polar body from a polar bear.

4

"Dr. Cy, I have something I think you'll want to see," the feminine voice on the line said.

Cy hung up the phone, but his hand stayed on the receiver. I know as little about her now as I did when she came here, he thought.

As Cy headed toward her desk in the office area, he considered that she was one of the brightest and most talented people he had met. Always thorough and precise, always did far more than she had to. In fact, he thought she was wasting herself here—she could get a job anywhere. But she did her work nearly in isolation, keeping herself at an emotional and physical distance from everyone in the clinic. What happened to make her this way? Cy wondered.

"Dr. Cy, can you sign these for me?"

Blocking his way was Aggie, the nurse who had brought in the cup of water. As Cy read the order on her clipboard, Aggie revealed the real reason she'd intercepted him.

"That pill she's married to, you're not going to let him foul things up, are you?"

Cy knew she was talking about the couple he'd just seen, but he paused before answering. Though the nature of their work tended to put all of the staff on a more familiar basis, Aggie pushed the envelope. Cy thought it was due equally to her tenure and personality. She waited for his answer in a freshly ironed white dress, with her hands crossed over her waist.

"We'll do our best for her, Aggie," he promised, handing her the clipboard.

Across the office, Cy saw the woman who had called him on the phone: Ham, their computer operator. And he was reminded why getting work might not be as easy for her as she deserved.

Seated at her computer with her back to him, Ham's shapeless, dark-colored outfit made her look as if her bottom might lap over both sides of the ergonomic chair. Cy knew that overweight people were at a disadvantage when competing for work. Whether employers said they were concerned about possible health problems or just thought slimmer people looked better, weight was a barrier. Though the clinic had a number of overweight patients—to the extent that there was a clinic-sponsored fertility support group—it had still taken a lot of convincing on Cy's part to get Dr. Wyatt to hire Ham.

Ham turned as Cy approached. Thick, glossy brown hair swung just above her shoulders. Perched on the nose of a beautifully classic face was a pair of black harlequin-frame glasses with rhinestones—an unexpected touch that Cy hoped meant Ham had a sense of humor.

How does she wear long-sleeved clothes in this weather? Cy wondered. She must be stifling. He pulled up a chair close to Ham.

"What do you have?" he asked, smiling in anticipation.

Ham turned her attention back to the screen. "I told you I would write a program to help you stay on top of each patient's care. Here's a sample, using one patient."

Cy watched her hands as she clicked on key words on the screen, and quickly showed him the capabilities of her program. As with many of the overweight women Cy had seen in his practice, Ham's extra pounds had not marred the beauty of her face or hands. Well, she isn't grossly overweight, he thought. Still, he estimated that she would benefit from losing forty or fifty pounds.

"You can call up the patient's visits, the tests done on that visit, their results," Ham said. "During an IVF cycle, you can monitor the drugs given: Lupron, HMG and HCG." She clicked again. "If you want, you can see the blood estrogen levels on a graph. You can also keep track of the number of eggs retrieved, how many embryos were fertilized, and how many embryos were implanted. And," she added, "the results."

She clicked and there was a picture of a baby, another

portrait for their gallery.

Cy smiled. "You did a great job," he said.

"Thanks," Ham said, eyes riveted to the computer screen. "You may want to compare values for a couple of different patients. If you click here, you can compare the charts of any patients whose names you type in. In case you want to do statistics on the patient pool as a whole."

Ham tapped the screen with her finger; she still wasn't finished.

"There's something else. Of course I've created a field for the mother's date of birth, so you can correlate her age with any of the other fields—like number of eggs, quality of eggs, pregnancy rate." She paused. "But I've also created fields for the gender and the birth dates of the children born from Assisted Reproductive Technology."

Cy waited for her to explain.

"I've read that babies conceived in the winter tend to be male; those conceived in the summer tend to be female," she began. "The idea being that male embryos need more temperate conditions to survive."

A small smile crossed Cy's face, and she must have caught it.

"Gender selection is one of the reasons people come for IVF," Ham said. "Whether we agree with it or not, it's a fact of life. People are always going to want to 'balance' their families. So why not work with nature? I've also created fields for the gender of the embryos transferred, and the dates. That way you can determine if there is any correlation between pregnancy rate and date of transfer or even embryo gender."

Cy frowned, thinking about that.

"Of course, we can only identify the sex of the embryos that undergo Preimplantation Genetic Diagnosis," she said. "But we do a lot of them."

Cy nodded. "I know." PGD involved taking one cell from an eight-cell embryo and testing it, generally for the presence of genetic diseases. But a number of inherited diseases were sex-linked, so the test also identified the gender of the embryo. Their clinic seemed to do more than other clinics did. Cy knew Dr. Wyatt was a perfectionist, but were the tests really necessary?

As Cy watched Ham guide him through the details of the program, he was struck by how ingenious it was. How did she come up with her programs? Was it just a logical application of programming rules? He was interested enough to ask her.

Ham stopped typing and stared at the screen with unfocused eyes.

"It's not that linear, nor completely logical," she said. "I've learned that I have to be willing to do a kind of inner listening. I have to be open to perceiving patterns, to respecting them and responding to them. Gradually, I perceive larger, more inclusive patterns. Patience is important. So is a surrender of sorts. I have to let it lead me in its own time, and let it choose what it wants to use to get me there."

Ham looked at Cy and smiled for the first time since he'd sat down beside her. "What is absolutely clear is when I find the solution. I <u>know</u> I have it, and there's a delight in it—every time."

Cy thought how radiant her face was when she was happy—and how unguarded. That was what drew him to her: the intelligent and earnest light in her eyes. The moment didn't last long. Her face became serious and she resumed guiding him through the program.

"There's something else I've worked out," she said, showing him a highly magnified picture of an embryo on the computer screen. "I know you sometimes want to take pictures of the egg or sperm or embryo—either for your own records or for publication or presentations. With a digital camera attached to the lab's high-power microscope, you can take pictures like this. Then the camera can be connected to a computer so the pictures can be saved on the computer or printed out with a printer. Or with another peripheral that makes regular photographic prints."

Cy was amazed. It was exactly what they needed, done in a clear and elegant way. So like Ham. "Dr. Wyatt will appreciate that," he said. "He can do everything in-house. He likes control over his work." And over everything else, Cy thought.

Cy reached toward the screen just as Ham was pointing out yet another feature. Her index finger jabbed Cy's forearm. He flinched and pulled his arm back.

"I'm sorry," Ham said. Her chair groaned as she turned to look at him. She seemed baffled by his response.

"It's nothing, Ham, a reflex reaction. An old scar that still hurts." He rubbed his arm. The old burn mark from his adoptive father's cigarette had never completely healed. More than once it had occurred to Cy that his mind was keeping the wound open, just as it was not letting go of Clea.

Ham turned to the screen again and began telling Cy other useful things he could do with her program.

But this time Cy wasn't listening. He had decided to find another private investigator. He wasn't ready to give up looking for Clea.

5

Ham had been flush with nervousness and pride when she'd interviewed at the clinic. "Don't even pay me until you see what I can do," she had said. She knew her talent had played a big role in getting her the job, but it hadn't clinched the deal. Dr. Cy had. He had fought for her to be hired; she had heard his and Dr. Wyatt's voices in another room after her interview.

Though the job gave her ongoing access to most areas of the clinic's business, she had literally sweated every day over mostly boring, routine work. Still, she would always be grateful to Dr. Cy, even if she didn't find what she had come here for.

Today was one of the bright spots, one of the occasional chances to do creative programming. Dr. Cy was a good audience; he had understood the program's usefulness and had appreciated the ingenious features she had built in. Though her demonstration had been cut short when Dr. Cy was called to an appointment, that had turned out to be lucky. Ham had found a small glitch after he left. Now she was fixing it; she was sure all she needed to do was rewrite a couple of lines in the program.

In the middle of her code writing, an image of Dr. Cy came to Ham and she stopped typing. He had the kindest eyes she had ever seen on a man. Sometimes she let herself think about it, but not often—what point was there?

Ham didn't hear the office manager until she was on top of her. She jumped a little, which made her chair groan like crazy. Why did people feel they had to sneak up on you?

"I had to come over to ask you," Jane said. "Where did you get that duster? It looks great. So much style for a large size." The stout woman leaned over Ham, as if to get a better look at the tent she was wearing.

Ham glanced out of the corner of her harlequin frames. She didn't want to be rude, but her best work came when she had clearly in mind what she wanted to do. Program writing was an art. When you got inspiration, you went with it.

With her attention focused on fixing the program, Ham answered Jane mechanically, without any of her usual filtering of what she confided. "The shopping channel. They sell large sizes."

"The shopping channel! How did you know they had stuff like this?" Jane asked. "I'm always looking for clothes that look like they belong on people and not on furniture."

Ham only half-heard what Jane asked. "Sick headache," Ham answered.

Jane laughed. "What?"

Ham was typing in new lines of program text. "Sometimes I get sick headaches that last for days and make me nauseous. At three in the morning I'm awake, throwing up in between putting ice bags on my head. I turn on the TV so I'm not alone. The shopping channel is good company."

"Sounds like tension," Jane said. "If you get too involved in what goes on here—I know how it is, you can feel for every woman who comes in here, sometimes it takes your heart out—you can make yourself sick. When I first started here I nearly went crazy between the tears and the tension. Now I try to pretend that it's like a TV program that I can turn off."

Ham didn't answer. She was focused on finishing her changes.

"That duster looks wonderful on you," Jane said. "Do you mind telling me who the designer is? I promise I'll buy something else, I won't copy you."

"You're welcome to wear anything you like," Ham said. "I think it was their house label."

Ham thought that was the end of it until she felt something tickling her back. When she realized it was Jane's hand, she whipped her head around and pushed herself away with her feet, making the casters of her chair squeal.

Jane stood with her hand in midair, as if she were surprised at Ham's reaction.

"I was just checking the name on your label," she said.

Why didn't you just ask? Ham thought.

The tension was broken by Jane's phone. Jane trundled away, but her last look at Ham was reproachful.

Too bad, Ham thought. She didn't go out of her way to alienate people, but if they couldn't respect her personal space, she wasn't going to apologize to them.

Ham reran the computer program until she was sure her corrections worked. Then she was nibbled at by worries that she'd antagonized Jane. Ham knew it never paid to make enemies. She found herself craving her usual reassurance—food. Digging into the pile of candy bars at the bottom of her file drawer, she pulled one out and tore off the wrapper.

6

They're like a couple of crows, she thought. Flapping around in dark fabric, as if loose clothes could camouflage their bulk. Why did fat women always dress at extremes? It was either dark colored tents or neon spandex. Betty Winter stood near the receptionist's desk, opening her mail with a letter opener as she watched Ham and Jane at a desk across the office space.

Ham's sleeves jiggled as her hands moved over the computer's keyboard, and when Jane lifted her arm she made her wide sleeve move like a wing. What is she doing now? Betty wondered. She knew that Ham was developing programs for the whole office to use.

How complicated could it be? Betty thought impatiently. A simple office software program should be able to take care of an operation this size. You could probably start with something standard and make minor adjustments. Why did everyone try to make things complicated?

She knew why. So they could build their own little empires, which created divisive groups in the office, which led to tension and trouble. A twinge told Betty there was tension in her own shoulders. I hate working in that kind of environment, she thought. Dr. Wyatt solo created all the tension she could handle.

Aggie stuck her head around the corner. "Dr. Winter? Your next appointment is in your office."

Dr. Betty Winter was abashed, suddenly aware of the quality of her thoughts. She hadn't realized how critical she'd been until she was interrupted. I'm not usually like that, she thought. I'm beginning to sound like Dr. Wyatt. Betty knew what it was to struggle with a problem—including her weight. Though she had managed to become—and stay—slim, she knew there was often such a thin line between success and failure.

She began to gather up her stack of mail. Her breath caught in her throat as she saw a cashier's check sticking out of the envelope she'd just opened. Oh Lord, no, she thought. Not when I'm the only black doctor they've ever had in this clinic. She turned over the envelope, praying it wasn't what she thought it was.

But it was. She had opened an envelope addressed to Dr. Wyatt. Her heart sank as she saw PERSONAL AND CONFIDENTIAL plastered in large letters across the front. Oh, there will be hell to pay when he sees this, she worried. He was as fiercely private a man as she had ever met.

In spite of her anxiety, Betty couldn't help noticing the amount of the cashier's check—$50,000—and that it was made out to Cash. While stuffing the check back into the envelope, she wondered at the choice of payment, as well as its size. In Connecticut, the law required health insurers to offer coverage for infertility diagnosis and treatment. But that just meant that insurers had to let employers know that coverage is available. There was no requirement for insurers to provide coverage, nor for employers to include it in their insurance plans. Because of these variables, the cost for a couple who sought help at a fertility clinic could be minimal or substantial. Even though Betty wasn't involved in billing—that was Jane's department—she knew that when the cost of treatment was high, most people paid in installments, by check.

Like a child who has just broken a vase, Betty looked for some place to hide the pieces. I should just give it to him and tell him my mistake, she thought. I don't want any deception. But as she walked to her office and her appointment, Betty passed the desk of the office manager—Jane, one of the 'crows' she had been watching. Impulsively, as if it were someone else's hand doing it, Betty slipped the envelope into the middle of a stack of mail on Jane's desk. Then she hurried guiltily down the hall to her office.

7

The silver-blonde haired woman was sitting in his office—
in his chair—like a queen holding court.

Dr. Wyatt was furious. No one came into his office without being invited; no one ever sat in his chair. But the uneasiness his rich patroness elicited from him always out-
weighed any other emotion.

"Good morning, Mrs. Greene," he smiled. "Did Aggie offer
you coffee?"

As if he had been relegated to a footstool at her feet, he
lowered himself into one of the visitor chairs at his desk.

Mrs. Greene shook her perfectly styled head, which wafted
some of her expensive scent toward him. "I'm fine."

"How can I help you?" he asked.

She smiled at him in a way that made him feel as if he
were sitting there with no clothes.

"I'm here to discuss adoption, Doctor."

They went through the charade of this actually being a
discussion, but she always got what she wanted. It was the
only time she came here. Whenever she said the word, he
shrank inside. But he had to face facts.

"Don't look so crushed," she said. "I know you've never
liked the idea, but we've tried it your way."

For the past twenty-five years they'd tried it his way, and
then ended up with her adoption agency when his way didn't
work.

"When they can't have a child by themselves and they still
want one, they need help," she said. "Everyone deserves to
have a child. You've said it yourself. You did the best you
could. It's that simple."

It wasn't that simple. Why couldn't he help everyone to
have a baby? Why did he fail with some of the people he most
wanted to help?

"I suppose there's no other solution?" he asked. "Maybe they could try another IVF cycle."

She shook her head. "Leave it to my adoption agency," she said. "I know what kind of child they're looking for. I'll take care of everything."

Almost everything, he thought.

"I'll expect you tonight?" she asked.

"Of course."

Mrs. Greene rose. He saw that her elegant suit wasn't creased nor was it marred by perspiration—although this was one of the hottest and most humid days of the year. Wrinkles and sweating are for the poor, Dr. Wyatt thought.

"I've always been glad you're on my team," she smiled. "You're like money in the bank."

She stopped behind his chair and brushed her fingertips across the back of his neck.

It took all his willpower not to shudder.

8

As soon as Betty stepped into her office, she knew something was wrong with the couple seated there.

The man did a quick double-take when he saw Betty. Why doesn't he just shout 'But she's black!' she thought. He must not have known. Is he going to back out?

Betty gave herself a mental kick in the pants. She should be more confident of her skills. It wasn't like when she was starting out. She had hung her M.D. diploma from Harvard directly behind her as she sat at her desk, so it was the first thing people saw when they came into her office.

Unfortunately, her insecurity still lingered, or she wouldn't worry about a potential client's reaction to her skin color. Or how the head of the clinic would react to her accidentally opening one piece of his mail.

But the man quickly recovered and introduced himself and his wife as Bruce and Rose Butler. He got up to shake Betty's hand, but the young woman sat rigidly with her legs together and her arms crossed over her chest. As if she would fly to pieces if she let go, Betty thought.

Betty walked over to the woman. "I'm Dr. Betty Winter." She would have preferred that her patients call her Betty. After all, the journey they were embarking on was one of the most intimate of all—to make a child. But Dr. Wyatt's procedures called for titles.

The young woman didn't unlock her arms or extend her hand. "I'm Rose," she said. Though her clothes weren't nearly as expensive as her husband's, she was well-groomed—but in a much more conservative style than Betty would have expected for someone her age.

Betty usually sat behind her desk while she did the preliminary interview—physical examinations and tests would come later. But today something told her to be closer to the couple. When the husband sat down, Betty leaned back against her desk, facing them.

From the first moment, Bruce Butler tried to take control of the meeting.

"We won't take much of your time," he began. "We've only just begun to try to have a baby. Maybe you can make some suggestions for timing or diet. I've also noticed that Rose's periods aren't always regular."

Rose glanced at her husband from the corners of her eyes. She hugged herself as if she were cold.

Bruce's manner was grating, and Betty was surprised that he seemed so knowledgeable about his wife's periods. Betty knew that women who weren't ovulating regularly had a more difficult time getting pregnant; they didn't know when to time their love-making.

Most women who didn't ovulate regularly had slightly increased amounts of testosterone, so Betty casually looked for subtle signs of increased male hormone production. But she saw no acne, no oiliness to Rose's skin, no abnormal body hair distribution. And when Betty's glance reached Rose's open-toed sandals, she saw no hair on her big toes.

Betty wondered if Bruce were wrong. He might be one of those men who doesn't want to hear that he needs help— even though fertility problems lay with the husband fifty percent of the time—and holds onto anything that indicates his wife has the shortcoming.

Betty sighed. So much of the fertility business was an art, not a science. Many times doctors couldn't help people become pregnant and didn't know what caused their infertility. Medicine even had a word for this kind of infertility: idiopathic. Almost as often, things worked out and doctors couldn't explain it. Given that, you'd think couples would do everything possible to succeed, and put all their cards on the table. But it didn't work that way. Even when people swore they were *dying* to have a baby, they held things back. Betty spent a good part of each appointment just watching and listening. Things came out that she wouldn't have learned any other way.

Rose coughed softly and shifted in her chair. Bruce looked annoyed and said: "I told you not to go out to lunch the other day. She always takes you somewhere where you can pick something up."

"I'm just clearing my throat," Rose said.

Bruce ignored what she said. "I don't know why you have to go out at all," he added. "There's plenty to do in the house."

Betty began to feel the same chill that made Rose shiver. She decided to arrange for a follow-up appointment where she could talk with Rose alone. But when she opened her mouth to speak, she saw something in the way Bruce looked at Rose that told her it wasn't going to happen. Betty was wondering what to do next when Bruce's cell phone rang. He looked at the number and got up and left, excusing himself.

"I'll be in the car," he told Rose. "You won't be much longer, will you, Doctor?"

When the door shut behind Bruce, Betty Winter let out a sigh of relief. She noticed that Rose's stiff posture eased, though she still didn't relax.

Immediately, Betty went back to her chair behind her desk, took one of her business cards, and wrote on the back. Sliding it across the desk to Rose, she said urgently: "Whether you make another appointment or not, please feel free to call me at any time. My cell phone number is on the back."

Rose took the card, but didn't say anything. Something is wrong here, Betty thought. While she pretended to organize the items on her desk, she tried to sound out Rose. "How long have you known him?" she asked.

Rose paused long enough to make Betty think she wasn't going to answer.

"Ten years."

Betty repressed a shudder. "Has he always been so...protective?" Betty glanced up to see Rose's face briefly twist.

"He loves me and wants the best for me."

Parrot, Betty thought. That's what he tells her. "Do you have a means of income of your own—a job, investments, that sort of thing?"

Rose's brow furrowed. "I still work, but he wants me to quit now, not even wait until the baby is born."

"Why, Rose?" Betty searched the young woman's eyes.

"He says I don't need the money. That I don't need a job." Her voice cracked.

Betty Winter had suspected abuse, and when Rose lifted her hand to wipe the corners of her eyes, her sleeve fell back to reveal large, dark bruises on her forearm. That was it. Betty couldn't hold herself back.

"How does he know what you need? How dare he tell you what you need? Rose, jealousy isn't loving, it isn't romantic, it isn't even harmless. It is pure, evil, selfishness. He wants you to exist for his benefit, and he will punish you if you ever act as if you're a human being with a life of your own."

Betty paused briefly to catch her breath and glance at Rose for some kind of acknowledgment. But Rose sat stone-faced, looking straight ahead.

"Men like him start out saying they just want to be with you and help you to make choices. Soon he demands your constant attention, tells you where you can go, and with whom. He ends up telling you what to feel and when to feel it, and he will punish you if you ever step out of line. When that happens, it will feel as if he has his hands around your windpipe, crushing the life out of you."

Betty thought she saw a flicker of fear in Rose's eyes.

"A selfish man takes everything personally because he thinks everything in the world relates to him," Betty said. "So he will grill you about everything you think, say, and do. He doesn't just sap your energy—denying you the release of your emotions is like never letting you sleep."

Rose was now listening with her eyes wide open. Like a deer caught in headlights, Betty thought.

"You will change from being a calm, loving, caring person to someone who wants to kill him before he kills you. Get away, Rose. Leave him."

At that, Rose stumbled to her feet and backed out the door. When it clicked shut behind her, Betty's whole body began to tremble.

What in God's name have I done? Her hands shook on the red desk blotter. As many times as Betty had been tempted to say something like this in the past to a patient, she had never done it. What had made her do it today? It wasn't professional, it wasn't her business. Thoughts tumbled over one another. Had she upset Rose so much that she wouldn't seek the kind of help she needed? Would she tell her husband what Betty had said? Would he restrict her life any more if he knew? Would he hurt her again?

On top of all of this was the worry—What would happen when Dr. Wyatt found out?

Trying to calm herself, Betty began to straighten her desk. When she realized she was shuffling them like a deck of cards, she threw her business cards down on the desk.

9

A knock on Betty's door made her heart jump. She was sure it was the first fallout from the meeting she'd just had with Rose.

But it was Jane, the office manager, one of the 'crows' she'd been watching earlier. Betty's stomach knotted. Had the woman seen the letter to Dr. Wyatt that Betty had opened and then hid on her desk? Betty ran a small gamut of emotions—from guilt and shame for what she had done, to discomfort at the prospect of being upbraided by her own employee.

"Dr. Winter, I'd like to start my vacation tomorrow, instead of next week," Jane said. "Dr. Wyatt said it was all right with him if it was all right with you."

Betty exhaled gratefully, so relieved not to have been found out, that she would have approved a lot more than a vacation. "Of course, it's all right. I hope you have a good trip. Where are you going?"

"To Bermuda. It's my first time there! I'm so excited. They say the food at the hotel I'm staying at is wonderful."

It crossed Betty's mind that Jane was overweight, and a place with great food was probably not the best vacation choice. But Betty said: "Have fun. Take care."

"Thank you. I'll be leaving soon, so I can catch my plane."

Almost as soon as Jane left, there was another knock on the door, followed by Dr. Wyatt's entrance. His thin face looked tired as he sat across from her and leaned toward her. Betty's heart jumped again. She wasn't lucky enough to miss trouble twice.

"I just saw Mr. and Mrs. Butler leave and I want to know how your first meeting went."

Betty didn't know what to say. If she told him the truth, she knew he would be angry that she'd alienated a patient. But if she lied and he later found out, it would be much worse.

She had to be honest and tell him she wasn't sure the couple would be back.

Apparently, Dr. Wyatt mistook Betty's hesitation for a reluctance to talk with him.

"I assume you have no objection to discussing any of your patients with me," he said softly. "I have spent twenty-five years developing the best care available. I have a vested interest in maintaining that quality. Now tell me about your patient."

Betty could have kicked herself for her bad luck. Even her hesitation was getting her into hot water with him.

Quickly she outlined what she had observed and what the couple had said during the appointment. Dr. Wyatt waited for a while after she finished, as if he didn't think she'd been forthright with him. Suddenly she remembered something. As she felt her face flame with embarrassment, she added, "Mr. Butler mentioned something else. Apparently his mother was a patient of yours—about twenty-five years ago. So he was one of your babies."

Dr. Wyatt lifted his head and gave her his first smile. "Is that so? I'll have to refresh my memory."

As he rose to leave, Dr. Wyatt told her, "Mrs. Butler made an appointment with you for next Wednesday. We'll talk again then."

Before Betty could say anything to him, Dr. Wyatt was gone.

10

"Happy birthday, Betty."

Moments after the door closed behind Dr. Wyatt, Cy had knocked and poked his head in her office.

Betty wondered how he knew, and whether Aggie had told everyone how old she was as well. The look on her face must have been one Cy could read.

"Aggie reminded us," he said. He walked toward her desk. "The present is coming later, but I brought the candles for your cake." He dumped five small boxes on her desk—about one hundred candles.

Betty burst out laughing. She had been wound so tight after Dr. Wyatt's visit, the release felt good. "So this is how you treat your friends," she said. "Woe to your poor patients."

Cy sobered, shook his head. "Dr. Wyatt thinks just the opposite. That I'm spending too much time and too many resources on them."

Betty couldn't believe it. "You see more patients than anyone, including Dr. Wyatt," she said. "Your patients rave about you. And after Dr. Wyatt, you're the biggest stickler for following clinic procedure."

"Thanks. I thought I'd been doing a good job, but to hear him tell it, I'm driving the clinic into a hole. I don't get it, Betty. All of our schedules are full, but Dr. Wyatt acts as if he desperately needs money. What's going on? I can't believe the overhead of this clinic is that bad, not with the fees we charge."

Betty squirmed inside before she spoke. "Maybe he feels the need to be more independent."

"Independent? What do you mean? He runs his own clinic."

"Maybe he would like not to be beholden to anyone."

"Who is he beholden to? "

Betty burst with frustration. "For a smart man you can be

thick as wood. Do I have to spell it out? Mrs. Greene. The woman who helps fund this clinic. The one who arrives here in a chauffeured Rolls."

Cy didn't pick up on what she said.

"After she leaves, her fragrance doesn't," Betty said. "It follows Dr. Wyatt for the rest of the day."

Now Cy looked embarrassed.

"Maybe he's trying to make enough of his own money so he can be free of hers," Betty finished quietly.

"I feel like I'm being disloyal if I notice," Cy said. "So it never occurred to me. You could be right, Betty."

"I just hope their association with the clinic doesn't hurt us," she said.

"How?"

"It seems Mr. Greene's companies are in the paper all the time. He gets contracts that other companies insist he's not best qualified for."

"Maybe it's just sour grapes."

"And maybe it's more than that. But no one's been able to prove anything."

"How could that affect the clinic?"

"I don't know, maybe guilt by association."

Cy laughed. "Being associated with big money doesn't seem to hurt anyone."

"Still, I wish the Greenes weren't so generous. Every time they donate something to the clinic, there's a metal plaque to announce it."

There was an awkward silence that Cy broke.

"What really bothers me is that you can't say anything to Dr. Wyatt. Whether or not he really believes what he says to you, you'd like a chance to defend yourself."

Betty and Cy had commiserated on many occasions. When he wanted to, Dr. Wyatt could bring even a seasoned professional to his knees. Initially, because Cy had spent so many years with Dr. Wyatt—growing up with him and then working with him—Betty had been leery of his friendship. At the least, she had expected the older man's critical nature to have rubbed off. But Cy had proven to be an exceptional friend and his humor was a bonus.

Betty nodded. "I'm one up on you. Today I managed to get into hot water by not saying anything."

"No rest for the weary," Cy said. "Can't win for losing. No good deed goes unpunished."

"You're damned if you do and damned if you don't. It's always darkest before the dawn," Betty said. She laughed; Cy helped put things in perspective.

There was a pause in their conversation. By unspoken consent they let off steam, but always stopped short of criticizing Dr. Wyatt.

Cy nudged aside the boxes of candles to reveal the cover of a scientific journal. "You're still following his career."

Betty was going to deny that she was still interested in what her ex-husband did, but she knew Cy knew better. "I read the article," he said. "He's gotten more scientists to support his claims."

"It's unbelievable," she burst out. "I've seen the so-called research. Either it's so bad you can't draw any conclusions, or the conclusions have no relation to the evidence. How does he manage it? What is the incentive for these people to support him? They're supposed to be scientists. I know it's naive, but I always thought science was the last bastion of truth."

"You're not naive," Cy said. "I feel the same way. So do a lot of other scientists." He smiled. "Don't get so worked up you let it spoil your birthday."

"I won't," Betty said. But celebrating a birthday was the last thing on her mind.

"How about dinner with an eligible doctor?" Cy asked. "His only fault is a failing memory."

Betty smiled. "Thanks. But right now I'm looking forward just to soaking my feet and watching an old movie."

Cy nodded at the candles. "Maybe I bought too few."

"When you make dinner tonight," Betty said, "add jalapeno peppers. And lots of cayenne pepper."

Cy grinned at her. "You talk tough, but you have the best

heart in this place."

He waved over his shoulder as he went out the door. "Plus you're beautiful. Happy Birthday."

Betty's thoughts returned to Dr. Wyatt and his visit. At first she had been so relieved that Rose was coming back that it more than made up for Dr. Wyatt's supervision of the case. But now she wondered how Dr. Wyatt had learned so quickly about one of her upcoming appointments.

Of course—it must be Ham's new computer program. Betty didn't want to wait for Ham to schedule a presentation—she wanted to know how to access the information she needed now.

Betty called the front desk when she couldn't reach Ham, and asked them to send Ham to her office.

"She's already gone," Aggie told her. "She went to her fertility support group."

11

"I guess he forgot about me."

The modestly dressed young woman was wringing a damp handkerchief in her hands; her eyes brimmed with tears.

Aggie had guided her to Cy's door; she still held the woman by the elbow. "Dr. Wyatt asked if you could see Mrs. Moore," she said. "He had to leave for an important meeting."

Cy knew what the important meeting was—a social event at the Greenes'—but he didn't let anything register on his face. Aggie handed him a file and frowned as she bustled away. Cy was surprised at the frown; he'd always thought that Aggie believed Dr. Wyatt could do no wrong.

"Of course, come in," Cy said, smiling. He ushered Mrs. Moore to a chair at his desk. Then he got her a glass of water and some tissues.

Cy opened the file and was surprised again. Aggie had added her own handwritten note, giving him a brief background on Mrs. Moore. Cy wondered what had motivated her to do that.

"If you give me a few minutes to review your file," he said, "I'll be in a lot better shape to answer any questions you have."

Mrs. Moore took a shaky breath, but gave him a small smile.

Cy first read Aggie's note. During the school year, Mrs. Moore was a teacher in a parochial school. During the summer she tutored and worked in a store. Her husband, a carpenter, had been out of work for the past two months after injuring his leg while working.

Cy glanced at the woman; her body was rigid, as if she were holding her breath. He got her to take a series of deep breaths with him, then he skimmed her medical file.

She had been through two unsuccessful IVF cycles at the clinic. Dr. Wyatt's notes were not encouraging, but when Cy read 'patient is not likely to be successful with a third IVF cycle,' he flared.

Cy had to control his face and stifle an exclamation. Dr. Wyatt was being unscientific, at best. Mrs. Moore was under thirty, and studies had shown that with each succeeding month the chance for pregnancy was no less in normal women who have not yet conceived than in those who were lucky enough to become pregnant in the first month. Dr. Wyatt was also adopting a negative attitude, Cy thought—completely out of keeping with the compassionate image he was famous for. Cy didn't want to jump to his own conclusions, but it seemed the clinic head was looking for excuses to drop Mrs. Moore as a patient.

A thought struck Cy. Was this why Dr. Wyatt was turning so many additional patients over to him? Not because he was trying to teach Cy to 'budget his time better.' Not because Dr. Wyatt had other social functions to attend. But because Dr. Wyatt wanted to drop these patients—because they couldn't pay as much as the wealthier or insured patients—and he didn't want to do it himself. Cy felt as if he had been punched in the gut.

Whether Mrs. Moore had seen something troubling in Cy's face, or she could no longer check her tears, she broke out in low sobs. "I know how much this costs," she said. "What if this cycle doesn't work? If I have to pay bigger installments than the ones Jane worked out for us, I can't do it. I'll have to wait—and I'll lose time and fertility."

Cy simmered at the thought that something so basic—trying to bear your own child—should have such a high price tag. It didn't have to; he knew that. He had been to enough conferences, read enough scientific papers, to know that there were doctors all over the world who were using simpler and less expensive methods to help women have babies. Why didn't Dr. Wyatt adopt some of their practices?

Dr. Wyatt knew about these techniques; Cy campaigned
for them regularly—particularly when he had a patient
like the woman in front of him. Dr. Wyatt had said for over
twenty-five years that everyone should be able to have a
child if they wanted one. So why did he hold onto his more
time- and technology-intensive methods? Dr. Wyatt said
they were safer, more reliable, more successful. But that
wasn't true and Cy knew it. After all these years, the clinic's
patients still fell into two categories: those who could pay
or whose insurance companies paid; and those who received a virtually free ride from Dr. Wyatt.

Cy was reaching his breaking point. It was one thing to
allow the older man to criticize him for imagined faults. It
was something else to allow Dr. Wyatt to stand in the way of
a patient's best interests because he chose to ignore a perfectly good course of treatment.

Fueled by anger, Cy decided to enlighten this patient
about other options. He hadn't cleared this line of discussion
with Dr. Wyatt, and he wasn't likely to. Lately the man was
like a porcupine—there was no comfortable or safe way to
approach him. Though he felt justified, Cy knew he was going out on a limb.

"We've come a long way in IVF," he told Mrs. Moore,
"and we're still learning new techniques every day. There are
ways to adapt the process to your requirements that don't
involve expensive techniques."

"Like what?" she asked, her voice thick with tears.

"There are ways to help you get pregnant that are more
natural."

"Sure," she said. "That's what my husband and I did by
ourselves with no luck for seven years."

"No. More than that," he said.

"Do they work?" she asked. "Are they safe?"

"Absolutely."

She looked as if Cy were just trying to humor her.

"Let me tell you some things that we can do," he said.
"First, we can use your natural cycle. Normally, in the

clinic, we give you gonadotropin injections to induce superovulation—so you produce more eggs and therefore more embryos and you have a higher chance of getting pregnant. But these injections are a major cost of the cycle because they require frequent blood or urine tests to determine egg maturity. Plus, we have to be ready to do egg pickups at all hours of the day or night. But using your natural cycle minimizes the need to do the blood or urine tests, and allows us to time egg pickup to be during the day."

She wiped her eyes, considered. "But if I produce fewer eggs with the natural cycle, won't it take me longer to get pregnant?"

Cy nodded. "It might. But you could also afford to do many more cycles, so that would increase your chances."

She didn't seem convinced, but asked: "What other techniques are there?"

"Vaginal incubation," Cy said. "The eggs and sperm are placed in culture medium in a sterile vial which is hermetically sealed and then placed inside you where it is held in place with a diaphragm. This means that you would act like your own IVF incubator and keep your embryos at the right temperature. This method requires less handling of eggs and embryos and provides a fertilization rate comparable to that of conventional IVF—at much less expense."

She was quiet for a while, watching Cy—as if she hoped to read the future in my face, Cy thought.

"What would you recommend for me? How much would it cost?" she asked.

Cy had opened a Pandora's box. Now he wondered if it had been wise to discuss techniques Dr. Wyatt had not sanctioned. Lately, Dr. Wyatt had been even more short-tempered than usual. What would happen when he found out what Cy had told Mrs. Moore? Especially if Cy had been right and Dr. Wyatt was trying to ease Mrs. Moore out of the clinic. Cy needed some time to talk to Dr. Wyatt so this didn't backfire on Mrs. Moore.

"You need to relax," Cy said. He knew it was easier said than done, but stress could affect whether a woman became pregnant—or kept the pregnancy. "Could you spend some time with a sister or brother—some family member you enjoy being with—for a few days?" he asked.

She shook her head. "I don't have family," she said. She looked down at her stomach. "We were going to make one."

Something in Cy shifted, and he knew that if he had to, he would go outside the guidelines of the clinic to help her.

"Give me a few days to work it out," he said. "You're going to have your baby."

When Mrs. Moore left Cy's office, he realized what he had done. He had made a covenant with her. How was he going to keep it?

12

"Was your mother heavy, too?" Heather asked.

"Yes," Ham admitted.

Ham didn't elaborate, and there was an uncomfortable interval in the fertility support group, filled with tinny screeches and groans as the women shifted their bulks on metal folding chairs.

Finally Joan prodded: "And?"

"You know what it's like," Ham said. "Why do you want me to talk about it?"

"Because it will help," Marilyn said.

"Help what?" Ham asked. She wanted to ask: Help who?

"If you want to lose weight, you have to understand," Amy told her.

"Understand what?" Ham knew she was being stubborn and argumentative, but she couldn't help it. She was annoyed by these women. She looked around the circle, lit by fluorescent lights. Hopeful faces on top of shapeless forms. Their clothes draped them like dropcloths. They held their programs in their hands—there was no lap, just a ski slope of fabric from bust to knees.

Heather answered patiently, as if she were talking to someone slow. "If you don't understand why you're heavy, you'll never lose the weight."

"I know why I'm heavy, and I can lose the weight any time I want," Ham snapped.

The others just smiled; Ham thought they were looking at her as if she were an alcoholic or drug addict. As if she had no control over her own body. Ham was ready to snap at them again, but thought better of it. She had worked to get into this group; she had to follow some of their rules.

"I'm doing my best," she said defensively.

Joining this group had seemed like a good idea, but it had quickly become a weekly torture session. Like when her mother insisted she take swimming lessons. Everyone should know how to swim, she had said. You never know when you'll need it.

Ham hated the water. It terrified her to put her head under; she always felt as if she were drowning. It even gave her nightmares. No matter. She took every lesson, with her chest so tight she could hardly breathe, and the strap muscles in her throat so tense that they always ached.

And what did she have to show for it? If she ever fell overboard, she would flail frantically for a few seconds before she sank like a rock.

Ham felt the same way about this support group: totally out of her element—floundering around in emotions and old memories, analyzing everything. Ham was always afraid something would surface that would pull her under and not let her back up.

Ham pushed her right shoe off and rubbed the bare arch over the toe of her other shoe. Her soles always got itchy when she was under stress.

Heather was sitting right next to her. She reached over and patted Ham's hand encouragingly.

Ham had to say something. What was the least she could say that would get them off her back for another week? She looked around at the faces.

"I want to get rid of this weight," Ham began." It pulls me down. I know that. I want to be free of it." Her program started to slide down her dress. I used to have a lap, too, she thought. Still looking at her thighs, smoothing her dress over them, she said:

"My mother was heavy, for nearly as far back as I can remember. She always seemed to be weighed down by things. I used to talk with her all the time, help her in the house. I even made her clothes, because she would never buy nice things. She always wanted to wait until she was a smaller size. And she was never happy. Maybe the weight didn't have anything to do with it, but I always thought if she weren't so heavy she would have had a chance. I would have done anything to make her happy."

The small paisley print of her dress got vague and blurry and Ham realized with anger, embarrassment and surprise that there were tears in her eyes.

She lifted her head defensively, as if to challenge anyone to make something of her weakness—or worse, to analyze it. But no one was looking at her. All eyes were on the door, where a woman stood holding a small baby.

"Emma!" Heather called.

The heavy woman moved into the room, into the circle.

"This is our new baby," she said proudly.

"But she's beautiful!"

"When was she born?"

"Why didn't you tell us?"

"Was your pregnancy terribly hard?"

Ham watched Emma hold the infant. She was so effortless, so loving, so...The way it should be between a mother and her child, Ham thought.

Heather moved first, got up and gave Emma her chair. The others crowded around. Like a bunch of jumbo-sized fairy godmothers, Ham thought blackly. But she went over too.

The baby was sitting up, smiling at everyone.

"How old is she?"

"Six months," Emma said.

The baby smiled and gurgled.

"She's so happy."

"She looks so much like you."

"Is she a good eater?"

Everyone laughed.

"She's an angel," Emma said. "She sleeps through the night, eats perfectly, and has no colic. She's happy and perfect. We couldn't be happier...Or more grateful."

There was a short interval filled with murmurs of admiration and longing. Ham knew how much each one of these women wanted a baby. They would do anything to get pregnant. But their weight—and whatever demons from past or present it represented—was like a wall between them and a child of their own.

"We haven't seen you in so long, we didn't know if your last round of IVF's took," Heather said softly, as she played with a pink-socked foot.

"Thank God, it did," Emma said, smiling down at the infant.

Ham was so taken with what a Madonna and Child they made, that she stared at them until she thought she could memorize their features.

It just proves, Ham thought, that it doesn't matter who you are or how much money you have. Infertility could happen to anybody. Emma's husband was a bigwig with the CDC, but they had had to go through the same cycles as everyone else. Why they had left Dr. Wyatt's clinic mid-treatment, Ham didn't know. Apparently they had given up and decided to go somewhere else. Well, whoever they went to, the doctor had managed to give Emma her baby.

There was a rapping sound and everyone looked up at the glass panel in the door. It was the instructor of the yoga class—time for her turn.

A reluctance to leave was visible on every face, but the women filed out of the room. Last was Ham, who couldn't take her eyes from the baby over Emma's shoulder. There was something about the little one's face that captivated Ham. She reminded herself that she had joined this group for her own investigative reasons. She had never expected that she would end up—like all the other women in the group—wanting one of her own

13

She closed her hand over Cy's. A light shower of water fell on his hand, forming small trickles that ran from her fingertips to his wrist.

For a moment he didn't feel her touch. Cy's mind had drifted to the meeting he'd had with Ham. Her program was impressive: She seemed to know just what he was looking for. She had even come up with things he hadn't thought of.

Cy looked at the hand on top of his. Smooth, tanned skin, a light down of hair on the backs of her fingers. He raised his eyes to her face. Clear skin, but with the same light down above her upper lip. She curved her mouth to smile up at him. He wondered if she had the same downy hair on top of her toes.

"Sorry," she said. "I didn't mean to bump you." She chose another bunch of red leaf lettuce from the produce counter. "Not many men are big salad eaters."

"It's fast, not much cleanup," Cy said. He picked through the crisp bunches, dropped one in a plastic bag.

He glanced at her toes. Even from here he could see some fine tufts of hair on her big toes.

She followed his glance, gave him a questioning look.

Cy felt he had to say something. "I appreciate a well-turned ankle." That was pretty lame, but it was better than the truth: By now it was second nature for him to scan a woman for physical clues to her fertility. Any extra hair on the face, on the backs of the fingers and on the big toes often signalled higher testosterone levels. Higher levels led to more irregular periods, and often to a difficulty in getting pregnant...

"Well, they're in season," she said. She nodded around them. "Bare ankles everywhere. It could be overwhelming."

She smiled at him for a while, but when he said nothing more, she shrugged and pushed her basket down the aisle.

After she left, Cy realized she had given him an opening

for further conversation and he hadn't picked up on it. It surprised him that already he couldn't remember what she looked like.

What's going on with me? he wondered. Where is my head at?

Turning from the produce display, he bumped into a trim woman with three children.

"Dr. Cy!"

She should look embarrassed, he thought. "Hello, Mrs. Gensler."

He hadn't seen her for years, but he knew her at once. When she and her husband first came to the clinic, she had been fifty pounds overweight. They had been trying for five years to have a baby.

Lose weight, he had ended up telling her. Nothing else seems to be holding you back. Let's try that first. Then, if you still don't get pregnant, we can run more tests, try other ways.

He had tried to explain to her that the fat cells in a woman's body absorb and slowly release the female hormone estrogen. If a woman were obese, she had a lot of estrogen stored in her body that was slowly released—constantly, not in a cyclical fashion—and from places other than her ovaries. That estrogen from her fat cells would actually suppress her pituitary gland, and throw off all the processes related to her egg production.

But she had been angry with him, told him he didn't understand how hard it was to lose weight, that if he had never been heavy, he couldn't understand. Briefly, Cy had even wondered if she really did want to get pregnant, or was using her weight as an excuse.

The husband had been ambivalent about Cy's recommendations. On the one hand, he seemed glad that the fault for their infertility was not his. And Cy knew that the man wanted his wife to be slimmer. On the other hand, Cy's recommendation put the man's family prospects solely in his wife's hands, and the man clearly had little faith in her ability to lose weight.

The couple had left Cy's office and not come back. Dr.

Wyatt had berated Cy for two weeks about driving patients away. But Cy had been vindicated. Through the grapevine, he had learned that the wife had dug in and dropped forty pounds. She had gotten pregnant not just once, but three times in close succession.

The woman standing in front of him now was much lighter than she had been the last time he saw her. And she looked happy.

"I apologize." She smiled sheepishly, waving her hand at the three children. "You were right."

One of the kids ran down the aisle, emptying a box of cereal as he went, and Mrs. Gensler went after him.

A voice came from behind him: "Still always right, I see."

Cy knew the voice. He turned to face a reed-slender woman with clear, smooth skin and wide open eyes. He wanted to ask her what she was doing in a store that sold food, but decided not to go there.

"How are you, Diane?"

In answer she said: "Mrs. Gensler came to me after she saw you."

Cy hadn't known that, but it had a certain logic: His ex-patient getting a second opinion from his ex-wife.

"All she wanted to know was how I lose weight."

Cy couldn't help glancing at Diane's model-thin figure. He caught a fluttering of her eyebrows, decided she was trying to frown.

"I'm a dermatologist, not a weight-loss clinic," she said.

Cy's gaze dropped to Diane's hands. She carried two plastic bags, one with an avocado and the other with some almonds. He doubted she would eat either of them; one had too many calories, the other required chewing. They must be for a facial.

"How is work?" he asked her.

"Fine. And yours?"

"Growing all the time."

That had been about the extent of conversations between them toward the end of their marriage. Cy had to watch what he said because Diane was sensitive about how she made money. Botox was a big part of her practice. Cy knew she had a faithful following of women who got injections to paralyze certain facial muscles so they wouldn't wrinkle the skin. Diane was a great advertisement for the shots. Her enraged face was indistinguishable from her serene look.

"Do you need money?" Why did he ask her that?

In answer, she closed her eyes, inhaled, then let the air out and opened her eyes. Probably hoped I would disappear, Cy thought. For the first time, he could see real annoyance on her face.

"No, I don't need money."

When they had divorced, she had refused to take alimony. Cy had felt guilty then, and more guilty now, when his income was probably much more than hers.

"It's OK. You chose dermatology, I chose reproductive endocrinology," he said.

"Chose?" She nearly laughed at him. "I don't think so. I was there with you in medical school, remember? In class you were brilliant. At our first autopsy you were cool as a cucumber. But when we assisted at our first birth, you fell apart. I knew you were terrified. You acted as though the mother's and baby's survival depended on you alone."

She shook her head. "You didn't make a choice. You did the only thing you could. You wanted to do something important, but you didn't want to ever lose a patient. So you entered a field where your client is submicroscopic.

"Nobody ever dies on you, Cy. They just adopt.

"Here's a news flash for you," Diane said. "I wasn't your responsibility when we were married and I'm not now. You never understood that your concern didn't come across as caring. It always made me feel as if you had no faith in me, in what I could accomplish."

Cy saw her eyes glisten and figured he was hearing for the first time her real reason for divorcing him. Now he understood about the Botox: It wasn't just so she could look young— it was so her face wouldn't betray her emotions. Maybe if he'd understood that years ago, he could have done something to change things.

Diane brushed past him and disappeared around a corner. Cy stood, staring after her.

He realized Diane had been right on the money. Cy had never wanted to take responsibility for anyone's life. He had never even had a dog. Diane wasn't the only one who had accepted a form of paralysis.

So that's where my head is at, Cy thought.

The produce mister came on again, soaking his arm before he realized he was wet.

14

"She bit me!"

The large gold hoop earrings on the checkout girl swayed as she splayed her red-lacquered nails and stared wide-eyed at her finger.

A teenage girl straightened up from her shopping cart, wiping damp hair out of worried eyes. "What?"

Cy saw small pink-socked feet swing near the teenager's waist. The little girl sitting in the cart had her head bent over her animal crackers, so all Cy saw was wispy-fine blonde hair.

"I was reaching for the animal crackers and she bit me," the checkout girl said.

"Maybe you had your finger near her mouth when she had a cookie in it," the teen said pleadingly. "She wouldn't bite you. She doesn't bite."

"She bit me," the checkout girl insisted. She looked around her as if deciding who to call for help.

What was the checkout girl looking for? Cy wondered. Workmen's compensation, a free tetanus shot, a short work day? He knew he shouldn't get involved, but the teenager— probably a nanny or baby-sitter, she was so young and wasn't wearing a wedding ring—looked as if she needed help.

"I'm a doctor," Cy said. "Let me look at your finger."

Reluctantly, the checkout girl showed him a pink finger with no redness, no skin breaks, only some wet cookie crumbs. Cy turned her finger over, probed it gently.

"It looks OK," Cy told her. "I think she's too young to do much damage."

Cy watched as the teen did her own bagging, thanked him with her eyes, then quickly pushed her cart away and out the glass door. His attention came back to the counter when he heard a series of thumps.

"What are you doing?" Cy was angry. The checkout girl was dumping his carefully picked and bagged produce onto the counter.

"My nail," the checkout girl said.

Cy looked at her hands. One red talon was gone.

She rummaged through the fruit and vegetables on the counter as if they were so much garbage. Perfectly round flawless fruit rapidly got flattened sides.

Cy was steaming. He turned away from her, opened his mouth to tell her he didn't want damaged produce, but the words died as he faced the front of the store.

The teenager who had been in front of him was driving by. For the first time the little girl's face was visible, head-on in the car window. Though Cy wanted to run after her, his legs wouldn't move.

Cy was looking at Clea.

15

Dr. Wyatt never visited the mansion without feeling inadequate.

Each time, he reminded himself that he came from a distinguished family, grew up privileged, went to excellent schools, graduated from a top medical school, published scientific articles and books, was a world-renowned authority, and built an exceedingly successful and respected fertility clinic. But it didn't help. Each time the massive front door opened for him, he felt like a poor village boy, summoned to the great house.

It made him resent the inhabitants, as much as he was indebted to them.

The entrance hall was cavernous; he thought it could swallow his own house. Reminding himself not to let his jaw drop, he was led to an even larger room where the guests were already mingling. From a safe corner he surveyed the room and soon decided the dress code was clearly: Don't even try to upstage your hosts. It seemed that everyone was wearing black and white. The two colorful spots in the room were the host and hostess; at least it made it easy to find them.

Dr. Wyatt was offered a glass of wine and at the first taste was amazed at how good it was. All his attention was delightfully drawn into it after the first few sips, in spite of his insecurity and resentment. The wine was marvelous: such flavor, such a bouquet. He drank some more—it was wine for the gods. No surprise. Via the grapevine (he had made a pun; was the alcohol already going to his head?) he had heard that his hosts had bought a fabulous vineyard, and this was their wine. Entirely believable; they could buy a country. Between their legendary fortune and their legendary skill at making money, Dr. Wyatt was sure they could turn anything into a winning proposition.

He saw his hostess across the room—Mrs. Greene, the

woman who had made herself at home in his office earlier today—making her way to him in swaths of what shone like emerald silk shantung. Dr. Wyatt thought she must be happy. She only wore bright colors when she was happy. Jewelry, too. Regal earrings and necklace and bracelets and rings. Everything from her bearing to her dress said: Here I am queen.

"Dr. Wyatt. How delighted I am that you could come."

Dr. Wyatt knew perfectly well that an invitation from this couple was a command performance. You either appeared and played your assigned role, or you were written off. No one every declined an invitation. No one ever said no.

In spite of this, she made him feel she was delighted. He felt warm and smiled broadly, and he was sure it wasn't due to the wine.

"Thank you so much for inviting me," he said, and was surprised at how much he meant it. "You look beautiful," he said, and meant that, too. "Green is a wonderful color for you."

Was it the lighting or her makeup or did he see a faint blush in her cheeks? Surely she couldn't blush at will?

He lifted his wine glass. "This wine is wonderful," he said. "Captivating. Thank you for your generosity in sharing such lovely things."

She looked at him and sighed with a smile. "You are such a satisfying guest. It is a pleasure to make you happy."

She followed his gaze to the roomful of people. "They're not so different from you. People are more alike than you think. Everyone wants something, Dr. Wyatt. The only things that distinguish us are what we want and what we will do to get it."

At any other time his reaction would have been—though he would never have spoken it—that he didn't need advice or an analysis, and certainly not from her. But now? He was surprised that he was touched that she had taken an interest in him.

"You are a tense man," she said. "As if you are always preparing to defend yourself against something. But if you only react, you will always be powerless. To be a player, you must initiate." She searched his face. "The way you are now, you will never feel as if you have enough money."

As relaxed as he was, he started. It was as if she knew what he'd been thinking.

She nodded her head at the other people. "Do you think they are so much better than you? More intelligent? Harder working? I'm sure you'll agree with me that they are not. You think they differ because of opportunity or money. But if you had their money today, it wouldn't change what is inside you."

She put her hand on his forearm.

"You can be a player, Dr. Wyatt," she said. "Always be the one to make the first move."

They had known each other for years, but this was the first time she had ever said something personal like this to him. Dr. Wyatt wondered what she meant. All the things he had accomplished—hadn't he created what he wanted? He heard laughter, among it the unmistakable laugh of his host.

The hostess must have heard, too; her head lifted and Dr. Wyatt got a doglike image. But whether it was like a bloodhound when he catches a scent, or a lap dog who hears his master's voice, he couldn't decide.

"My husband particularly wanted you to meet someone tonight," she said. "Won't you come with me to him now."

By now Dr. Wyatt had drained his wineglass, and he had no objections to being led anywhere, even though he already knew what they wanted from him. Babies. All anyone wanted from him was babies. Though he had worked tirelessly to be the first person anyone thought of when they had problems making a baby, he still wished there were something else in him that people sought. For one brief moment, he understood how a woman feels when a man wants her only for sex.

A waiter came by to take his empty glass and to offer him a full one. His hostess encouraged him with a nod.

As he walked with her, Dr. Wyatt was surprised to note that the wine had lifted his mood without impairing his faculties. He could do his usual mental test (to let him know when he was reaching his limit) without any trouble, yet he was feeling on top of the world. They ought to bottle this, he thought. He chuckled.

She turned to him. "A joke?" she asked.

He was too happy to respond as he normally would: with uneasiness. "Not at all. A chuckle of happiness."

She took him by the elbow to her husband, to whom she nodded. "I'll leave you two merry men together," she said, smiling.

"Dr. Wyatt? How are you? You seem to be in great spirits tonight." Mr. Greene was a big man with gray hair who looked as if he could play Santa Claus.

"Thanks to your wonderful hospitality," Dr. Wyatt said. "And credit, too, to this wonderful wine. Wonderful wine." No matter that Dr. Wyatt was happy; he knew enough to stop short of asking his host if he was the owner of the vineyard.

The host held a glass of his wine as fondly as if he were dandling a grandchild on his knee. "I'm proud of this one, yes I am," he said softly. Then he pulled one of the men near him closer to Dr. Wyatt. "I'd like you to meet Mr. Sperling," he said. "He's with the World Health Organization."

The wine had apparently loosened Mr. Sperling's tongue as well, because in the next ten minutes he gave Dr. Wyatt a thorough summary of his and his wife's attempts to have a baby.

Dr. Wyatt was pleasantly surprised to note that this didn't disturb his buoyant mood at all. In fact, he wanted to help this man. "How long will you be in town?" he asked him.

"For the next six weeks," Mr. Sperling said.

Dr. Wyatt considered. That didn't give him much time, but he suddenly felt a great certainty that he would be able to help Mr. Sperling and his wife. He told him so, with great conviction. Dr. Wyatt was touched by the momentary misting in Mr. Sperling's eyes.

When a waiter told them that dinner would be announced in fifteen minutes, Dr. Wyatt realized he had had at least three glasses of wine, and should really visit the bathroom before he sat down for a long dinner. He gave Mr. Sperling his card and told him to call him personally.

Dr. Wyatt thought he remembered where one of the many bathrooms was, but it was so easy to make a wrong turn in the labyrinth of hallways. He was passing a partly open door when he heard the voice of his host, Mr. Greene. Dr. Wyatt knew eavesdropping was impolite—and could have unpleasant consequences if his host caught him—but he had the irresistible urge to peek in. He looked around, then leaned his head to the opening.

Mr. Greene sat at a round table in the center of the room, smoking a cigar. Seated across from him was another man, whom Dr. Wyatt was shocked to see was Brett Peterman, the president of the shopping channel. At first he thought he must be mistaken. Maybe it was the wine or the distance or his eyes. The man certainly wouldn't be here, so soon after losing his daughter and son-in-law in a car crash. Dr. Wyatt looked again; it was indeed Peterman. Dr. Wyatt had known both him and his wife; their daughter had been born thanks to their visits to his clinic. Dr. Wyatt shook his head, but couldn't pull himself away.

Just from the familiar way they sat together, and the faint feeling of envy it excited in him, Dr. Wyatt was sure that Peterman was a close friend of Greene's. No. More than that. Peterman acted as if he were an equal. Somehow that seemed out of place at this dinner—whose purpose seemed to be to showcase only two stars. And what were they discussing so earnestly?

Their heads were bent over the table, studying something in front of them. Every so often one would move something very slowly to another position, then consider the result. Finally Mr. Greene spoke.

"Would you like to draw or to choose?"

Peterman seemed to bristle. "Not choose, when you've put such limitations on how I can use a choice, that I could hardly make any profit on it. I'll have to draw, won't I?"

Peterman had what sounded to Dr. Wyatt like some kind

of British accent, though Dr. Wyatt had never heard—or no-ticed— it before. Maybe it was the wine, he thought. But he was having trouble understanding Peterman at this distance.

Mr. Greene shrugged. "It's a game and it has its rules. It wouldn't be nearly so entertaining if it were any easier. You know that as well as I do."

Mr. Greene spread out what looked to Dr. Wyatt like a deck of cards. The other man seemed to study what must be the backs of the cards. Dr. Wyatt wondered why he took so long a time. After all, it was only a game.

"Which card do you want?" Mr. Greene asked.

"I'd like your soddy card, that's what I'd like. But I'll have to choose one of these."

At last Peterman drew a card and slowly turned it over. "Skin man," he mused.

Dr. Wyatt was still sailing on his wine. He didn't recognize 'skin man' as a term belonging to any card game he knew.

Mr. Greene cocked his head to one side. "It has possibili-ties," he said.

The other man held up a hand, spread the fingers. "No suggestions, please," he said. "I'll work this out my own way. You didn't have any help with your CD..."

Mr. Greene coughed.

"...and what you did with that, who could have imagined?" The man shook his head. "I may not do as much with this," he lifted his card, "but I will make it serve." Now he was smil-ing.

"I'm quite sure you will," Mr. Greene said with a smile. He looked at his watch and said: "We'd better get back to the others."

Dr. Wyatt was frozen at his peephole, terrified they would discover him. But the host patted the other man on the back, and they strolled out through a door on the opposite side of the room.

No sooner had Dr. Wyatt's heart rate slowed down to a drum roll than he found his feet taking him into that room! What was wrong with him? Hadn't he learned his lesson?

It didn't matter; he strode in as if this were merely the next stop on a tour. He went up to the table at which the men had been seated. There was nothing there. Whatever card game they had been playing, they had taken the cards with them.

He wandered the room, marveling at the design, awed by its costliness. He ran his hands over furniture, fabrics, art objects. He admired the eccentric collection of paintings on the walls and stopped in front of a portrait of a man in what he guessed was mid-1800's dress.

The portly man sat on an elaborately carved wooden chair as if it were a throne. Bald on top with white hair on each side, a large handlebar mustache spanned his face, Beetle-brows hung over a fleshy nose and a stern but full mouth. His large hands gripped what looked like large knobs on the arms of his chair. When Dr. Wyatt came closer, he saw the outlines of continents on the globes clutched between the man's fingers. Long rows of text on the plaque below the painting lured Dr. Wyatt even closer:

"Once self-supported by intent, once embarked on the twin course of power and profit, the true player never yields. Neither public nor private influences produce the slightest effect on us, when we have once got our mission. Taxation may be the consequence of a mission; riots may be the consequence of a mission; wars may be the consequence of a mission; we go on with our work, irrespective of every human consideration which moves the world outside us. We are above reason; we are beyond ridicule; we see with nobody's eyes, we hear with nobody's ears, we feel with nobody's hearts, but our own. Glorious, glorious privilege! And how is it earned? Ah, my friends, you may spare yourselves the useless inquiry! We are the only people who can earn it—for we are the only people who are always right."

A zealot to be sure—from the look in his eyes to the way he sat in the painting. A curious, even disturbing piece for this room; Dr. Wyatt wondered why his host had chosen it.

As Dr. Wyatt finally turned his steps toward the door, he mused that he hadn't known his host was involved in CDs.

Not that he knew the man so well; he might be involved in anything. At first he thought CD referred to the kind one puts in a computer or a CD player. But now Dr. Wyatt considered that Mr. Greene might very well be involved in bank CDs—certificates of deposit. It made perfect sense. Still, what did either of those terms—skin man or CD—have to do with a card game?

He took one last look at the room and noticed there was writing around the circumference of the card table. Dr. Wyatt went back to the table and walked around it to read the inscription:

"Life is like a game of whist. We must play the hand we are dealt."

16

Though the woman seated on Dr. Wyatt's right had initially seemed very charming, she inexplicably became annoying before he even finished his appetizer.

Her voice, her gestures, her anecdotes, they all began to grate on him. What had made him think she was a pleasant dinner companion? He wished that he were seated next to anyone else.

He picked at his plate with a fork; her incessant talking was even making him lose his appetite. Though he knew that his hosts had arranged their guests for their own reasons— and his job was to be pleasant to those seated near him—he could not imagine what they thought the two of them had in common.

Dr. Wyatt turned to his left and saw a man with a dark beard.

"Dr. Wyatt," the man smiled. "I am Dr. Jagat Singh."

On any other occasion Dr. Wyatt might have been influenced by the man's looks and his name; but tonight he was glad for any distraction. Besides, the man was a doctor. "Hello, Doctor," he said. "May I ask your specialty?"

"I am a fertility specialist."

The competition bell rang in Dr. Wyatt's head, but when he thought about the thin woman on the other side of him— her mouth still open, but never filled—he decided to chance a small conversation with Dr. Singh.

"So am I," he answered.

Dr. Singh nodded, smiling. "I have heard of your clinic," he said. "I very much admire your work. I have read your papers in many journals."

Dr. Wyatt was flattered, but still had a feeling of unease. "Do you have your own offices, or are you affiliated with a hospital?"

"I have a clinic, but we are affiliated with a hospital. We

offer, in addition to the IVF that you do, both GIFT and ZIFT."

Years ago, Dr. Wyatt had decided to forego the facilities and expanded repertoire that a hospital operating room would afford, for the autonomy of his own private clinic. Gamete Intra Fallopian Transfer and Zygote Intra Fallopian Transfer required simple procedures. The first transferred eggs and sperm (gametes) directly into the woman's fallopian tubes; the latter transferred embryos (zygotes) into the fallopian tubes. Simple, but both procedures required an operating room.

Dr. Wyatt shifted uncomfortably in his seat. His unnamed discomfort seemed to have moved up a notch. Normally, he would never confide to anyone his feelings about his work or his clinic. So he was surprised to hear himself ask Dr. Singh: "Do you have trouble finding good people to work for you?"

Dr. Singh chuckled. "When I am having a good day, they are the most wonderful staff on earth. When I am having a bad day, there is no worse group of bunglers."

Was Dr. Singh making fun of him? Dr. Wyatt frowned; he was too important a man to allow himself to be insulted in a place like this. He would have turned away from the other doctor, but what alternatives did he have? He was between a rock and a hard place.

Dr. Singh had a question for him. "What do you think of the simpler techniques being developed by doctors who are trying to make Assisted Reproductive Technology available to everyone? In my own clinic, we are trying to offer our services for fees that just allow us to break even."

He had just met the man and already he was asking questions about money. What was he getting at? What did he know? Now Dr. Wyatt was feeling anxious. He looked around him, as if searching for the source.

Their hostess sailed by and smiled in general at her guests.

Dr. Singh nodded at the hostess, shrugged and said: "One is helpless if once he gets in the hands of a woman like that. She and her kind always get what they want. One either gives in to her and receives crumbs for his obedience, or one resists and is crushed for his stubbornness. It is all one."

Dr. Wyatt thought it was most assuredly not all one. Not to him, at least. And it was exactly opposite to what his hostess had just seemed to counsel him. But he didn't want to say anything that Dr. Singh could report back to her. God knew how the dark little man was going to misquote him anyway.

Dr. Singh dropped his smile and leaned forward. Dr. Wyatt mistrusted him even more. "The rich have their own club," Dr. Singh said. "If they are rich enough, it includes only them. If not so rich, it includes other rich people. They have no national allegiances; their loyalties lie only with themselves. Our hostess has no more interest in the well-being of you or me than she does in my dinner," he said. "But however this evening serves her purposes is no concern of mine. How I can use it to make connections that will help my patients, is."

"You seem to have an ambitious agenda," Dr. Wyatt said. He was beginning to actively dislike the man.

Dr. Singh smiled. "Please do not feel that I am intruding on your domain. I care only to learn how to provide the range and quality of services you provide, so that I can bring these benefits to the people of my own country."

Dr. Wyatt didn't believe a word the other man said. He was convinced that Dr. Singh wanted his hostess's patronage. Dr. Wyatt had given her too much to share her with anyone else.

"I feel I must strive to help my people, Doctor," Dr. Singh said. "No country has a monopoly on helping people to have healthy babies."

Dr. Wyatt was about to tell Dr. Singh exactly what he thought, when he found himself facing the forearm of a waiter who held a bottle of wine in his hand.

"Would you like another glass, sir?"

Dr. Wyatt nodded, realizing that his glass had been empty since the start of the meal. Dr. Wyatt took a sip, then another. His anxiety began to melt, a sense of well-being returned. His improved mood seemed to be tied to the wine, but he couldn't imagine that the effect would be so marked or so rapid. He had drunk enough alcohol in his life to know how it affected him, and this was out of the ordinary. He resolved not to finish his glass.

Another waiter bent his bottle over Dr. Singh's glass. Dr. Singh covered the glass with his hand.

Dr. Singh caught Dr. Wyatt watching him. "I do not drink," he explained. "It is a small thing to sacrifice," he added, with a wave of his hand.

Dr. Singh seemed determined to pursue his question. "Are you familiar with more simple methods used in ART?" he asked again.

Dr. Wyatt felt an unaccustomed surge of confidentiality. But when he realized what it was he was about to divulge, he became frightened.

Dr. Wyatt was glad he had stopped drinking the wine. Whatever effect it was having on him, he didn't like it. He glanced at his glass, expecting to find it three-fourths full.

It was empty.

17

There was something so disturbing about the noise in the neighbor's garage that Ham—freshly showered and dressed and ready for work—hurried heavily through the sweltering heat to investigate.

Through the open garage door of the house next to the one where she rented, she saw two young boys swinging what looked like rakes at something high above their heads.

Shouts and hot wafts of air buffeted Ham as she squeezed her way through the dirty and cluttered garage. Halfway in she saw the boys' quarry—a small bird, beating its wings frantically, trying to escape through the closed window above their heads.

Something in Ham snapped. She burst through the remaining obstacles, knocking over boxes and scattering tools, yelling and swinging her arms. "Stop it! Put those rakes down. Get out of here."

The boys were at first startled, then they began to laugh. But when she bore down on them, her hands reaching for them, they scattered.

Panting and dripping with sweat, Ham turned her face to look up at the small bird. He was still beating his wings in vain against the window pane. As Ham leaned closer, she saw something that caught at her heart: a tiny fogging of the window, made by the bird's terrified breaths.

Ham swung around to search the garage for something to capture the bird. Quickly she saw a small box and rejected it, decided she wanted something soft; a towel or blanket. Nothing usable was visible in the piles of junk.

Her swinging gaze stopped on her arms—she was wearing a light sweater, now covered with dust and grime. Ham tugged off the sweater as she looked for something to stand on. She almost missed the small folding ladder pinned behind garbage cans. By the time she'd dragged it over and set it up under the window, she was panting and drenched with sweat.

Ham cursed under her breath as she clung to the ladder, hoisting her weight step by step, her heart beating like a trip hammer. By the time she reached the top rung, she half-expected to find the bird's small heart had given out under the stress. But he was still flapping frantically.

"It's all right, little one," she whispered. "Just let me hold you. I don't want you to be trapped..." A sob clutched her throat and Ham swayed on the ladder.

With both hands, Ham lifted the sweater toward the bird, all the while fearing it might frighten him into flying away. But he only beat his wings harder, his desperation audible in the frantic thud of feathers against glass. Ham draped the sweater over his head and cupped it around him. He beat furiously against her hands and she agonized at each step that he would break a wing as she laboriously went back down the ladder.

Once on the garage floor, Ham trundled quickly outside and threw open her hands. The tightness in her chest uncoiled like a spring as the bird exploded out of her hands and tore away.

18

"What are you doing in my office?"

Dr. Wyatt had to push through the people crowding the room to confront a man who sat on his desk, turning over the pages of a small pad. The man took his time looking up, and then seemed to contemplate Dr. Wyatt as if deciding whether or not to answer him. The doctor started to burn as he saw that papers on his desk had been shoved aside to make room for the man's seat.

"I'm Detective Horn," the man said. "I'll get to you in a minute. I'm talking to these people."

His insolence infuriated the doctor.

"About what? By whose authority are you here?" Damned police are like storm troopers, riding roughshod over the rights of citizens. Hoodlums with badges. They weren't like this twenty-five years ago, he thought. Dr. Wyatt shouldered people aside to reach the detective; he was angry enough to grab him by the scruff of his neck and throw him out.

"Jane's dead, Dr. Wyatt." It was Aggie.

Dr. Wyatt got the news mid-stride; he was so stunned, it threw him off-balance. Arms caught him and steadied him. For a moment he forgot the detective. "That's impossible. She just left yesterday. How could this happen?"

"In Bermuda, in an accident," Aggie said.

His unflappable nurse was crying openly, tears running down her cheeks. Her face had crumpled along with her starched demeanor.

Unconsciously, Dr. Wyatt looked around the circle of faces, as if searching for some answer. But they all looked as stunned as he felt.

"What did she do here?" the detective asked.

"She was office manager," Aggie answered. "Ran the office."

Dr. Wyatt began to recover. What kind of detective is he?

he wondered. What kind of procedure is this? Calling every-one in together—no strategy, no discipline. He shouldn't be interviewing everyone together. He should talk to us one by one. And then it hit him.

"If it was an accident, why are you here?" he asked. "Why aren't you in Bermuda?"

Detective Horn kept writing something on his pad, as if by ignoring Dr. Wyatt's question it would go away.

"If you say she died in an accident, why are you here? Why aren't you there, where it happened?" Dr. Wyatt repeated.

Detective Horn didn't pick up his head when he answered. "It might have been more than that."

Dr. Wyatt heard rustling and murmuring as people shifted their positions.

Aggie gasped: "What do you mean?"

"It looks like she had an accident on a motorbike. Now some visitors die every year in motorbike accidents on Ber-muda, just like clockwork. But we have to check out the pos-sibility that someone might have had it in for her, someone she knew, someone from where she worked. Someone who knew where she was going." He looked at the people in the room.

Dr. Wyatt followed the detective's gaze. Everyone looked baffled by the detective's suggestion. "Jane was with me for a long time," he said. "Everyone liked her."

"We want to know if she had any enemies, if anyone might want to hurt her," the detective said.

"No." The word seemed to come from everyone, but most strongly from Aggie.

"So there was no person at the clinic or anyone among your patients who had an argument with her or had any rea-son to harm her?"

Dr. Wyatt saw heads shaking 'no.'

The detective closed his pad. "Well, that will be it for now. If I have any more questions, I'll be back. If any of you thinks of something, call me. I'll leave some of my cards."

Dr. Wyatt's anger was making headway against his shock

and grief. Damned police act as if they have some moral su-
periority, suggesting that someone in my clinic would have
hurt Jane. This detective wants to find justice for Jane? Who
was Jane to him? The damned law acts as if it has a greater
vested interest in victims than the people who were actually
close to them. This idiot detective probably 'solves' his cases
by throwing accusations out until one sticks on some poor
soul who doesn't have an alibi. Some justice.

"Some justice," Dr. Wyatt said aloud.

Detective Horn looked curiously at him as he left.

19

Betty hurried to her office, closed the door and agitatedly paced. This is too much of a coincidence, she told herself. I open an envelope addressed to Dr. Wyatt containing a cashier's check—made out to cash—for $50,000. I slip that envelope into a stack of mail on Jane's desk. Jane suddenly goes on a holiday—her first vacation in years—and is killed!

If Jane took the money, where was it? The detective didn't mention that any large sum of money was found on her body or in her room. Could the money have been stolen by someone after she died, or could her death have occurred during a robbery? For that matter, were there any signs of a robbery? The detective didn't say, and everyone in the clinic was probably like Betty—too upset this morning to even think to ask.

Don't jump to conclusions, Betty told herself. All you know for sure is that there was a cashier's check in the envelope, and that you put it on Jane's desk.

Betty was assuming that Jane took the check. Certainly, she had had opportunity. And anyone could have redeemed a cashier's check made out to cash. The whole clinic knew that Jane needed money. She hadn't made that much, and she had spent most of her savings taking care of her late mother. So she had had motive and opportunity, as that detective might say. But had Jane been the kind of person to steal a cashier's check? Wasn't anyone? If someone found a large some of money and knew he wouldn't get caught, how many people would keep it? How many would turn it in?

You're assuming Dr. Wyatt never got the envelope. It was possible that Jane had given it to Dr. Wyatt and explained that she hadn't opened it. But Betty didn't buy that. There would have been an explosion. Dr. Wyatt had made it clear from day one that no one was to open or sort his mail. He wanted every single piece addressed to him, junk mail and all. If he had discovered that someone opened an envelope of his—particularly one containing $50,000—he would have hit the roof. If he had believed that Jane hadn't opened it, he would have grilled the rest of the staff. Even if he had tried to handle it quietly, Aggie would have found out. And then the rest of the staff would have been told.

Betty stopped stock still. If Dr. Wyatt didn't know about the cashier's check, should she tell him about it? If Jane did take it, then only she and Jane knew about it. Betty cringed at the thought of telling Dr. Wyatt that she had opened his envelope, not told him, and left the opened envelope on Jane's desk. He would be furious, maybe even fire her.

With relief, Betty realized there was one other person who knew about the check—the person who sent it. Presumably he or she would contact Dr. Wyatt to confirm he had received it.

Betty realized she was wringing her hands. What purpose would it serve at this point to tell Dr. Wyatt about the check? She hadn't done anything wrong, hadn't taken anything from anyone. She had accidentally opened an envelope, then put it back in the mail pile. What had happened after that wasn't her responsibility.

If Jane did take the check, maybe telling the police would help them to find out why she died. The thought gnawed at Betty. But so did another thought. Maybe revealing her knowledge of the check would put her in the middle of something more serious than a theft. The more Betty thought about it, the more sure she was that something more than an opportunistic murder had occurred.

Betty suddenly remembered something. When she had opened the envelope and seen the check, she had turned the envelope over to check the addressee. She had been so upset to realize she'd opened Dr. Wyatt's mail, that the return address on the envelope—seen only peripherally—had slipped to the back of her mind. Now she remembered. The return address hadn't been a person. It had been *Amazing Sweepstakes*.

Betty didn't think the person who had sent the envelope

worked at Amazing Sweepstakes—if it even existed. She did think it was possible that the person had used a return address that made the envelope look like junk mail so that no one who handled it would suspect it contained something valuable.

Why would Dr. Wyatt receive an envelope disguised as junk mail, containing an untraceable sum of money? she asked herself. Why is it any of your business? came the reply. The best course of action was to keep her own nose clean and just do her job.

Betty shook her head, forced herself to stop pacing. She was going over the edge with this. She was a scientist by training; all this speculation wasn't rational. And, more importantly, it wasn't productive. It wasn't going to bring Jane back. And it had nothing to do with Betty.

Her intercom buzzed, and Betty composed herself for her next patient. But all through the appointment, she couldn't stop wondering why someone would pay a fertility doctor in a way that couldn't be traced. She couldn't shake the feeling that the whole situation *was* her business; that it had a lot to do with her. What if Dr. Wyatt was trying to hide his income and wasn't paying his taxes?

Betty didn't know it she felt better or worse for having named her fear. If Dr. Wyatt was doing something wrong, wouldn't that endanger the clinic—and her?

20

Cy opened the incubator containing the embryos. It was Day 3 after he had performed in vitro fertilization—IVF—and the embryos were ready to be biopsied.

Even the death of a staff member couldn't stop the gears of the clinic. The requirements of the embryos took precedence over anything else. Two days ago, Cy had collected eggs and sperm from a young couple. Once the sperm had been introduced to the eggs in a culture media, the process was on a precise internal timetable. Fertilization of the eggs took place in the culture dish, outside the woman's body, and the fertilized eggs began to divide.

By day 3, the fertilized eggs had become 8-celled embryos. Cy's task was to remove one cell, or blastomere, from each of the embryos. These blastomeres would be sent to the DNA lab for a special analysis called Preimplantation Genetic Diagnosis, or PGD.

Dr. Wyatt had ordered the test, and Cy understood the rationale behind his decision. PGD was indicated when there was a likelihood that a couple's embryos would be affected by certain chromosomal conditions. These conditions could prevent implantation of embryos in the woman's uterus, lead to pregnancy loss or result in the birth of a child with physical problems and/or mental retardation. PGD had first been performed in 1989, but still wasn't a widely used test. Dr. Wyatt ordered the tests with a frequency greater than that of other fertility centers. Cy wasn't sure why that troubled him.

As Cy sat at the bench in the lab, an image of the little girl he'd seen last night at the grocery store came into his mind. She couldn't be Clea, but maybe she could be related to her, like a daughter. He admitted to himself that she might not actually look as much like Clea as he'd thought last night. After all, he'd only seen her after she was in the car, driving away. If only he hadn't been so slow to react last night. If he had thought and moved faster, he might at least have gotten the license number of the car she was in. Cy exhaled so deeply that his shoulders sagged.

Using microscopic guidance, Cy's gloved hands held the first 8-celled embryo in place on a micromanipulator with a holding pipette. He breathed softly and evenly behind his mask. When the orientation between the embryo and the laser was right, he used the laser to cut a precise opening through the zona or shell of the embryo.

Cy then introduced the embryo biopsy pipette through the opening and applied gentle suction to dislodge a single cell, or blastomere, from the embryo. He returned the biopsied embryo—undamaged by the loss of the single cell—to the incubator for further culture. One after another, with patience and dexterity, he repeated the procedure with each of the embryos he took out of the incubator.

Finally, he prepared the blastomeres to be sent to the DNA lab for analysis. When the results came back—typically within one day—several of the unaffected embryos would be transferred back to the woman on day 4 or even 5.

When Cy was finished, he peeled off his gloves and took off his cap and mask. He wiped the sweat from his face and sighed with relief. No matter how many times he performed this procedure, it never became mechanical or routine. He was acutely aware of how precious these tiny entities were. A couple's hopes to bear their own children might lie in a dozen such embryos. The decline in a couple's fertility with time; the emotional and financial toll each IVF cycle took—not to mention the unpredictable nature of pregnancy—made each embryo important.

Cy pushed away from the lab bench, walked past the liquid nitrogen tanks that held frozen embryos. When many extra eggs or embryos were obtained for an IVF cycle, obviously they could not all be placed back into the woman. It would create too great a risk of multiple births. In order not to waste these 'extras' after the required three to five embryos had been replaced in the woman's uterus, embryo freezing had been developed. Though freezing an egg would kill it, Cy and his colleagues regularly froze—and later thawed—sperm and embryos.

Cy knew the procedure; he had done it himself on a number of occasions. Embryos were put into a solution that pulled water out osmotically. The embryos were then aspirated into a tiny plastic freezing straw and the ends were hermetically sealed. The straw was very carefully labeled and placed into a programmed 'freezing machine.' The straw was then immediately plunged into the liquid nitrogen storage container.

It was not a perfect process; not all embryos survived the freezing and thawing process. But the process was a way of maximizing the embryo's chance of eventually becoming a baby.

Cy noticed that the log book was open. He flipped through a few pages before he closed it. He recognized a number of the donors' names. Some of their embryos had been frozen for more than five years. Sometimes a couple never came back for them—they either got pregnant or gave up.

Thinking about how precious life was made him think again of Jane. Jane had been a quiet, competent, cheerful presence in the office and he had accepted her at that. But how much more there must have been to her, that probably none of them knew.

As Cy wrote up his notes in the patient's file, he realized what probably bothered him about PGD. Certain genetic defects are known to only affect males, others only females. In these cases, while the exact gene defect may not be known, the DNA of the biopsied blastomeres can be examined to determine the sex of each embryo. Then, only the embryos of the unaffected sex would be transferred back to the mother's uterus. It troubled Cy that this test might one day be used solely for gender selection—to ensure that a couple had a child of the sex they preferred.

****

Cy checked his appointment book. He had a consultation with Dr. Wyatt in fifteen minutes. Enough time to get a cup of coffee.

When he stepped into the small kitchen, he found Ham at the sink. It was the first time he could remember seeing her in the room—she usually sat at her desk. When he passed her to pour a cup of coffee, she turned away from him, but not before he saw the tear-tracks on her cheeks. Had Jane's death hit her that hard? He hadn't known Ham was that close to her.

He wanted to say something but didn't want to trigger more tears. "Water?" he asked.

Ham nodded.

He filled a cup and handed it to her. "I don't know if I've told you how much we appreciate your work," he said. "How did you get so good so young?"

Ham wiped her cheeks and turned toward him. "My father was in the military and we were always moving around, new towns, new schools," she said. "I had to find something that I could pretty much learn on my own. Computer programming turned out to be a lucky choice."

"You seem to be a natural with a computer," Cy told her. "I've noticed how you hit the keys, watch the screen. You remind me of a concert pianist I saw years ago; you have that same effortless quality." He watched her face for a reaction; got a polite smile.

"What about you?" Ham asked.

Cy had two immediate images. One was Diane telling him in the grocery store that he had chosen this profession because he wanted to do something important, but didn't want to lose any patients. The second image was of a little boy's pajamas with spaceships on them. Years ago he had wanted to be an astronaut. Of course, little boys want to be firemen and grow up to be investment bankers. But he wondered why he had decided to do what he did.

"I didn't mean to pry," Ham said.

"You're not. I was just thinking," Cy said. "I guess I chose the fertility field because I can make a difference in people's lives."

Ham nodded.

"Although it would give me a lot more satisfaction if I had been able to help a little girl a long time ago," Cy added.

Cy looked at his watch; he had to get going. "Well, the sacrifice you made for your father looks as if it worked out all right in the end."

Ham seemed stung by his comment. What did I say? Cy wondered. "I just meant that moving around for his military career ended up making you a great programmer."

"Sure," Ham said. "It's just hard to see it that way when you're growing up."

On the way to Dr. Wyatt's office, Cy had the feeling that what he had said had been interpreted in a different way by Ham. And that he had hurt her. He never meant to do that.

21

The dusky-skinned woman held a basket of large, perfect, red tomatoes on her lap. "We brought them for you," she said. She was beaming.

Dr. Wyatt accepted the gift as if it were truffles.

"Your first of the summer," he said, smiling broadly. "They look beautiful. Thank you for remembering how much I enjoy them."

Mr. and Mrs. Ortiz exchanged satisfied glances.

How quickly he can put people at ease, Cy thought. It's a gift. Cy had been introduced to the couple, then quickly forgotten.

And how quickly he could bind people to him, Cy marveled. This couple had met Dr. Wyatt when they came to him three years ago, desperate to have a child. They had tried for years on their own. Then they had gone to a local clinic, where the doctor had taken another two years to do nothing but discourage them. Someone had told them about Dr. Wyatt, and he had literally welcomed them with open arms.

"How is Tomas?" Dr. Wyatt asked.

The mother beamed, Cy noted, but the father—he looked as if he would burst with pride.

"He is this big," the man said, holding his palm parallel to the floor. "Such a strong boy, so smart. And such a good heart."

The mother nodded. "And he loves playing with the other children. He is so happy to go in the morning. Thank you for helping us to take him there; the people are so good to him."

Cy remembered; they both worked. The little boy was in a fine day care center that Dr. Wyatt had gotten him into.

"So, everything sounds wonderful, wonderful," Dr. Wyatt said. "I'm so glad that you stopped by to visit me." He put both palms on the desk, as if he were going to stand up.

What's going on? Cy wondered. They had an appointment

with Dr. Wyatt. Then Cy noticed that the couple hadn't budged. They were smiling with Dr. Wyatt as if they shared a secret. And Dr. Wyatt had what—a twinkle in his eye? Cy couldn't believe it.

The woman spoke first. "We would like to give him a little sister," she said.

"Or another fine boy for a brother," her husband added.

Dr. Wyatt leaned back in his chair, nodding, considering. "Yes," he agreed. "A sister or a brother. Or maybe even both."

22

"Ham! What is this?" Dr. Wyatt had been running back and forth all day in the clinic, wearing out a path between the lab and his office. Now he stopped to nudge the object he'd nearly tripped over, using the toe of a polished black wingtip.

Ham got up and waddled over. "It's a centipede."

"A what?" he asked. What is it with all these stupid names? First she has to call herself Ham; now she's calling an electronic device an insect.

"You use it when you have to connect a computer to more peripherals than the computer has ports," she explained.

"Fine, fine," Dr. Wyatt said. He watched her bend over to retrieve the object, as a handful of cellophane-wrapped candies ran out of her pocket. Does she ever stop eating? If she didn't irritate him so much, he would help her pick everything up. She looked like a mattress trying to bend itself in half.

"You were going to simplify that routine that helps me track all the appointments in the office," he told her. It was important to stay on top of things, especially since he had lost Jane. Where was he going to find a replacement for her? Interviewing people was the last thing he wanted to do. But it was too important to leave to Aggie.

When she lifted her head, he saw that her face was red. Is it embarrassment or something more serious? Good grief, don't get sick. Since Jane's death he had begun expecting the worst at every turn.

"Are you all right?" he asked. "Your face is flushed."

"I'm fine," Ham said. "I can have the changes ready by the end of the day."

But she wobbled a little as she spoke and Dr. Wyatt instinctively reached to steady her. Ham recoiled from him, backing up against a desk. He thought she was overreacting, though by now he figured she was as uncomfortable with him as he was with her. Maybe she sensed his disapproval of her. He thought that perennially fat people were just plain undisciplined. After all, Ham had no children, no other responsibilities. Why didn't she lose weight?

"Is your support group helping?" he asked.

Ham frowned, shrugged.

Does she think I'm being intrusive? Dr. Wyatt thought. Too bad. She had told him that she wanted to lose weight so she could eventually have children. He had helped her to get into the support group, but she had to make some effort. Otherwise, she would just waste the time of the other women, maybe even demoralize them. And those women really did want children.

Ham waddled back to her desk.

Dr. Wyatt stood watching her, thinking. Centipede, my foot. It's a hub that takes 7 USB connectors. Nothing wrong with that, except it isn't compatible with anything in this office. What is she up to?

23

Aggie was ushering out the last patient of the day when a pregnant woman in dark glasses pushed past her.

Ham heard Aggie's cry of surprise and looked up to see the dark-haired woman cross to Dr. Wyatt's office and disappear in a swirl of pale blue designer chiffon behind his closed door.

Aggie posted herself at her desk and was unnaturally quiet, apparently trying to hear what was going on in Dr. Wyatt's office. Ham didn't think Aggie would hear anything; between the acoustic ceiling tiles and the padded fabric walls, Dr. Wyatt's office was nearly soundproof.

Ham felt the stacks of papers on her desk for a hidden candy bar. No luck. She opened drawer after drawer and came up empty. Hauling herself up, she headed out of the office, down the corridor and to the back exit door.

Noisily, Ham threw open the back door of the clinic and blinked in the glaring sunlight. She waddled through stifling heat across to her car, passing a big black Mercedes parked near the back door. Ham caught a glimpse of the driver; he had all the windows closed and the motor running. His sun visor was down and he was wearing dark glasses.

Struggling to unlock and open the door of her car, Ham bent over to pull a bag of candy bars from under the front seat. She tore open the bag and rummaged around to reach a bar. Ripping the wrapper with frenzied movements, she stuffed the half-melted chocolate in her mouth, and leaned against her car with a sigh of bliss. Looking under her lashes, she saw the man in the Mercedes shake his head and look away.

With the bag of candy under her arm, she waddled back inside. By the time she got to her desk, Aggie was there.

"She walked right past me!" Aggie whispered, but indignation made her voice loud enough to carry across the office. "Who is she? I know his patients and I've never seen her here."

Suddenly her face had a look that was half-hopeful, half-frightened. "What if Dr. Wyatt doesn't know her either? Or if she's threatening him? Maybe I should check on him."

Without waiting for a reply—which Ham knew she never wanted—Aggie headed to Dr. Wyatt's door and put a tentative hand on the knob. It will be locked, Aggie, Ham thought. And it was.

Aggie just had time to get away from the door before it opened and the pregnant woman came out, all dark glasses and chiffon, and left the way she had come.

"What was that all about?" Aggie demanded. For once she looked at Ham.

Ham shrugged. "Beats me." But Ham had managed to glean two things during the woman's visit. One, the number on the license plate of the car the woman arrived in. Two, that she was less pregnant when she left than when she came in.

24

"Why didn't you clean Dr. Wyatt's office?" Aggie's broad shoulders blocked the cleaning woman's way.

Betty Winter was picking up her messages at the front desk. She recognized Aggie's 'don't mess with me' stance and didn't want to watch Aggie question the small, dark-haired woman. She hurried to get her things together and leave the office.

"I hear angry voice. I stay out."

Well, that sounds about right, Betty thought, picking up her purse and her briefcase. Dr. Wyatt was angry a good portion of the time he spent at the clinic. The only people he wasn't angry at were his patients.

"You mean someone was arguing with Dr. Wyatt?" Aggie asked.

Betty could hear the incredulity in Aggie's voice. The woman idolized that imperious...Betty was sure Aggie couldn't imagine anyone even questioning the man.

"I hear just one voice."

Betty smiled wryly. Dr. Wyatt was just as comfortable dressing people down on the phone as in person. She was surprised that the cleaning woman had heard him. When Dr. Wyatt was in his office, he kept his door closed, and the room was virtually soundproof.

"Why didn't you wait until he finished his call and then go in?"

Though she thought that was a reasonable question, Betty didn't want to hear the rest of the interrogation. She paused at her office door, making sure she wasn't forgetting something.

"He is so angry," the cleaning woman said. "I don't understand. I hear '$50,000. Sweepstakes. $50,000. Sweepstakes.' But he is shouting, angry. I don't want to go near him. Then he comes out. His face is white."

Betty froze, her hand on the doorframe. Oh, my God, Jane did take the cashier's check.

She had been dreading this for days. Though Betty had prayed that the envelope had been delivered to Dr. Wyatt, Jane must have taken the cashier's check. Oh, Jane, damn you, she thought. What have you created?

On the way to her car, Betty tortured herself by imagining different actions she could have taken to avoid this outcome. What if she hadn't opened the envelope; what if she hadn't looked inside; what if she had given it to Dr. Wyatt; what if she'd taped the envelope shut. What if, what if. Thinking about it just made her miserable. The fact was that she had opened a piece of Dr. Wyatt's mail and hadn't told him. She had left on Jane's desk an open envelope containing a cashier's check—how irresponsible that had been—that Jane promptly stole.

How long would it take Dr. Wyatt to connect the missing check to Jane's sudden vacation and her death? If he figured out that Jane took the money, would he assume she'd acted on her own, or that she'd had accomplices? Betty was sickeningly sure that Dr. Wyatt would interrogate each person in the office. She started to sweat, and not because the day was still muggy. Dr. Wyatt managed to shake Betty's poise every time she spoke with him. He had a way of making her feel guilty, as if she were always doing something wrong. How would she act when she really did have something to hide?

25

A single, glistening red talon slid from the folds of the curly leaf lettuce as Cy shook the dripping bunch over his kitchen counter. The long red oval hit the white Corian surface with a click, and then rocked itself to a stop.

Cy immediately recognized the nail as having been on the fingertip of the checkout girl at the grocery store two days ago. All his fruit—manhandled by her as she searched for her nail—had had to be thrown out the next day. That connection, combined with its presence in his dinner, made the red nail as unwelcome as a roach.

Cy swept the nail and the lettuce onto a paper plate, opened a cabinet door under the sink, and was about to shove the whole mess into a garbage can, when a thought made him stop and hold the plate hovering in midair.

That red nail had been in the mouth of the little girl he would have sworn was Clea.

He was sure of it. He had seen the checkout girl's 'bitten' finger; there had been wet cookie crumbs on it. The child must have grasped the finger when it came near her box of animal crackers, and put it in her mouth. The artificial red nail would have come loose when the checkout girl retrieved her finger, most likely scraping against the child's gums or the inside of her cheek along the way. Then the nail had fallen in the lettuce bag while the girl was totalling Cy's order.

Cy's nostrils flared and his heart beat faster as he realized the implication: The red nail almost surely contained cells from the little girl's mouth. Cy could have a DNA test done on those cells. He could compare them to Clea's DNA. Though he didn't recall seeing the license plate, under hypnosis he might be able to...

A sudden jolt of disgust made Cy jerk the paper plate closer to the garbage can. Was he crazy? A little knowledge really was a dangerous thing. He knew too much about DNA testing, had too easy access to it. That gave his preoccupation with Clea a shove into high gear. It took him closer to doing something crazy,

Cy closed his eyes and saw an image of Clea—the little hand reaching out to him, the small pink-socked foot leaving bloodprints in her crib. And he saw a pink hairbrush, Clea's hairbrush, the one he had used to brush her hair the night of the fire, the only thing of hers that he still had. That hairbrush must still contain her hairs. Some of those hairs must have follicles. If they did, they should contain her DNA.

Now Cy's hands were shaking, his heart was beating so hard. And his head was throbbing, with the beginning of a major headache.

He felt like a junkie holding his drug over the toilet, knowing he should flush it down, be rid of it. But like a junkie he told himself that all he wanted was one more high. For Cy, his high was hope.

Cy had had twenty years to become addicted. Every feeling of guilt or regret, every remembered image of Clea, every memory of her voice, had helped to hook Cy on the hope that she had not died, that he could find her and redeem himself.

Redeem himself? Cy shook his head. It still amazed him that his feelings could run so independently of his mind. He was intelligent; he knew he had no reason to feel guilty. But reason never seemed to win a battle against guilt. Guilt told him that Clea's survival had hinged on one thing: Cy returning to her room that night to get her. If he had come back, everything would have been different.

Cy told himself the chances that Clea was alive were probably slim to nonexistent. And he didn't look forward to the story he would have to give—along with the samples of hair and cheek cells—to the DNA testing lab. But Cy took the red nail off the paper plate and put it carefully into an envelope.

A part of Cy asked when it was time to give up. His twenty-year search for Clea reminded him of when he was a small boy with poison ivy. You wanted to scratch something that itched you so furiously, but in the end it just prolonged the misery.

By now his head was throbbing painfully. He was in the kitchen looking for aspirin when he heard a knock on his front door. When he opened it, he saw his ex-wife standing there.

"Hi," Diane said with what Cy thought was an effort to smile. "I decided to take you up on your offer."

26

It was the first time she'd touched him in years, since well before their divorce. Her fingertips were cool, and she moved them expertly.

She watched him intently as she asked: "Can you feel the difference between my right hand and my left hand?"

Cy was afraid he wouldn't be able to tell, and he didn't want to humor her—she was looking for an honest response. Surprisingly, he could feel the difference.

"You developed this yourself?" he asked.

He raised his hand to touch his left cheek. The skin felt smooth and supple—much better than his right cheek, to which Diane had applied one of the most expensive and famous creams on the market.

Cy and Diane sat side by side on the sofa, Diane's slim figure barely denting the seat cushion. On the coffee table in front of them were jars and bottles of skin care products, and two cups of tea.

Diane picked up her jar of cream and smiled. "With the help of a friend of mine who's a chemist," she said. "I started with what I've found to be the most effective ingredients."

She handed Cy some literature on her products; Cy recognized antioxidants among the contents.

"Then I varied the amount of each ingredient to find the best combination," she said. "After that we had to ensure that the product was stable and that we could make large quantities economically."

Diane sighed. "A long time and many wrong turns. But we came up with a winner. I believe this cream is above and beyond the others."

Cy imagined her industriously grinding almonds and squashing avocados in her kitchen. Diane had always been a self-starter, a go-getter. Trite expressions, but the truth was that Cy had always admired her. Even in the rough patches.

"I'd guess that a lot of dermatologists would like to develop their own line of skin care products," he said. "But there must be a tiny percentage who would see it through as far as you have."

Diane opened and shut her mouth, as if she were deciding whether to say something. "The chemist thought we were going to have trouble with the eye cream the day I saw you at the grocery store. It turned out to be OK, but all that day I was in a black mood. I'm sorry."

Cy shook his head slowly. "I've thought about what you said. About my not wanting to even chance losing a patient. You're right."

"No," Diane said. "I had no right to say that."

"Why not? Who knows me better?" Cy asked. He thought about the false nail he had found tonight. He wanted to tell Diane about it. He wanted to talk to someone about the weight of guilt he'd been carrying in his chest all these years.

"It had nothing to do with you," Diane said. "This project has taken a toll on me, and I took it out on you." Somehow she managed to look contrite for a moment before she burst out: "But I'm so proud of it!"

Cy saw a light in her eyes that he hadn't seen for years. He decided not to mention Clea, and the throbbing in his head got worse.

Whether it was the effect of the cream, or her pride in her accomplishment, Diane looked as if she had a glow. Cy told her.

"I've been using the products on myself for months, and my patients are begging me to share them," Diane said. "The whole regimen will be ready soon—a cleanser, a day cream, a night cream and an eye cream. And I have other products in the works."

"Do you mean you tested them on yourself?" Cy was surprised. He knew that lipid-soluble substances were generally readily absorbed by the skin. "I thought you tested on small animals, like rabbits."

"No animal testing," Diane said. "I wouldn't allow that. Besides, testing face creams is a lot less risky than what Borel did." She looked sideways at Cy, with a dare in her eyes.

A slow grin spread over Cy's face. It was their old game of obscure scientific references. It had helped keep them sane in medical school. He tried to remember. "Borel was a drug researcher, right? He tested some antibiotic on himself."

"An immunosuppressant," she corrected. "Cyclosporine."

"He couldn't get the company he worked for interested in testing it, so he took it himself," Cy remembered.

"Lucky he did," Diane said. "Transplant patients rely on it."

She had her happy face on, the one she was wearing when Cy first saw her. But Cy was still concerned. He chose his words carefully: "What made you decide to do all the testing on yourself?" he asked.

"Easy," she said. "Control. When you go through others, you're always limited—both by their knowledge of what they're looking for, and their vocabulary for describing what they experience. I know best what I'm looking for and what it means."

Cy picked up his tea cup and raised it to Diane. "Not every experimenter has the courage of his convictions," he said. "One day women all over the world will be grateful to you for your sacrifice." After Cy said it, he was worried she might think he was being sarcastic.

Diane laughed. "I like the 'women all over the world' part. I hope you're right."

Cy hadn't seen her this animated and relaxed in a long time, not for years. She was her old self, the bright, eager young woman he had loved. He felt a surge of affection for her.

"Have you approached any of the big cosmetics companies?" he asked.

Diane shook her head. "No. I don't want to go that route. If they give me financial backing, they'll have the final say about everything. They could change the composition of my formulas, how they're manufactured, packaged, and sold. I would end up having no say in my own product. I'm happy to start small, and let the reputation of my product spread by word of mouth."

"So you want to do this yourself?" he asked.

"I put together a business plan and had my accountant look it over," Diane said. "And I told some of my patients. I'm grateful that they believe in me—a number of them offered to invest, or to give me advice or the benefit of their connections. Bottom line is that I've been able to raise all but $50,000." She paused. "Can you loan me part of that?"

Cy nodded and realized how much he wanted to do something good for her. Something with no strings attached.

"I'd like to give you a check for the whole $50,000, no loan," he said.

For a moment Diane just looked at him, and Cy thought he might have offended her. But then she threw her arms around his neck and hugged him.

It felt good to be generous, but Cy's head still throbbed.

27

"Cy, tell me you're kidding."

The Ph.D.'s eyes said Cy was crazy. Pinching the small paper envelopes between rubber-gloved fingers, the man held them at arm's length.

"What are these? You think we're some kind of crime scene investigators? That we rummage through people's garbage so we can prove murder? This isn't a scandal sheet operation, either. We do regular science here."

Cy realized he had seriously ruffled the man's feathers. It wasn't even a matter of money. The lab had a big enough backlog that its director could find reasons not to do the work, even if Cy presented him with pristine cheek swabs or purple-capped vials of blood.

Cy was reluctant to tell him about Clea, even more reluctant to explain the red fingernail. But he was desperate to have the two samples tested. If it took baring his soul to get the DNA in the two samples compared, so be it.

Cy swallowed whatever pride he had left. "It's personal," he said. "I was adopted by a family who had a little girl. Twenty years ago there was a fire in our house. I got out, but the little girl disappeared. The only way I've been able to live with it is to believe that Clea somehow survived. The other day I saw a small girl who looked just like her. One of the envelopes contains Clea's hair; the other envelope has a fingernail with cheek cells from the small girl."

"Surely you don't think the child was Clea," the director began.

"No, of course not. But her mother might be," Cy said. It sounded so farfetched that Cy couldn't press his case any more.

The director didn't say anything, just frowned at him for a long time. Cy wondered if he was going to have to explain where the hair came from, or how he had gotten a fingernail with cheek cells. Cy was sure the man was going to tell him to get out and never come back.

But then the man slowly nodded. "Guilt has a hell of a half-life, doesn't it?" he said.

The director brought the samples to the counter, put them carefully on a tray. He crossed the arms of his starched white lab coat, tucked his gloved hands under his arms.

"The hair is twenty years old," he said to himself. "That shouldn't matter, as long as there are hair follicles. The cheek cells should be more straightforward, assuming there isn't any contamination from other DNA on the fingernail. A thirteen loci STR should compare the two."

Cy did some mental calculations to figure out how long he would have to wait for the results. Since he just wanted to compare the two DNA samples, it wouldn't be practical or necessary for the director to analyze the entire chromosome.

A human genome had about a billion base pairs, but more than 99.9% of human genomes were identical. It was the inherited variations in DNA sequence that made individuals unique. And DNA sequences with the greatest variation were most useful in DNA analysis. STR's were short sequences (2 to 5 base pairs; this lab used 4) of non-coding DNA that were repeated numerous times, head to tail. Thus the name: Short Tandem Repeat. The variations in STR's were due to the different number of times these sequences were repeated in different individuals.

The STR test looked at thirteen of these STR locations on the chromosome. When the director had the results for each sample ready for Cy, they would be in this form: the code for the locus; the number of repetitions at that locus on each chromosome (one contribution from each parent); and the expected frequency of those repetitions in a representative population sample.

The director looked up at Cy. "It's going to take me a couple of days. I know STR profiles can be obtained with very small amounts of DNA. But I may still have to use PCR before I run the gels. I want to be careful, since we can't get any more samples."

PCR was a method for amplifying small amounts of DNA so they could be tested. When the director mentioned PCR, Cy suddenly realized how precious those strands of Clea's hair were, and what it meant to ask for this test. The few blonde hairs were the last link he had to her. But they had to be destroyed so he could get the information he wanted. Suddenly, irrationally, he didn't want to part with them.

The director said: "I'll let you know when I have something."

Now Cy thought about Dr. Wyatt; he didn't want him to know what he was doing here. Cy opened his mouth to ask the director to keep this confidential.

The man must have anticipated him; he smiled. "Don't worry. I'm not going to advertise that I'm as crazy as you are."

Cy made himself just say thank you and leave.

28

Dr. Wyatt hated to confide in Aggie, let alone ask for her help. But he had no alternative.

When Aggie arrived, Dr. Wyatt told her that what he had to say must be kept in the strictest confidence. As soon as the words were out of his mouth, he wondered if he was making a mistake. Aggie seemed so eager—she was holding her breath and her eyes were shining with curiosity.

Since he knew Aggie would try to squeeze every last bit of information from him, he decided he might as well cut to the chase. "I have reason to believe that Jane stole money from my office, and I need to find out if anyone else was involved in the theft."

Dr. Wyatt watched a tumble of emotions cross Aggie's face. Then tears brimmed in her eyes. I wasn't expecting this, he thought. Who knew she was this close to Jane?

"I can't believe she took any money," Aggie said, dabbing her eyes. "Jane wasn't like that. It just doesn't seem fair to accuse her when she's dead." Aggie's eyes brimmed anew.

The slight rebuke was the closest Aggie had ever come to criticizing him. However, it was unusual enough to stop Dr. Wyatt mid-purpose and make him wonder why her allegiance to Jane should be greater than her allegiance to him.

"My money disappears and Jane goes off on a sudden vacation," he said, indignant. "It's more than coincidence."

"She needed to get away," Aggie said. "And the police didn't mention anything about money being found on her."

"Exactly," Dr. Wyatt said. "If she was killed by robbers, you wouldn't expect them to leave any money behind, would you?"

"And you'd also expect that she'd be found without money if she started out without money." Aggie looked defiant. She was so different from what Dr. Wyatt had expected that he was silenced again.

Detective Horn had called Dr. Wyatt to say that the police in Bermuda were classifying Jane's death as a homicide. Horn had specifically asked again if anyone in the clinic knew why someone would kill Jane. Dr. Wyatt had been silent. Now he waited for Aggie to ask him why he hadn't mentioned the theft to the detective when he was here the other day. Surely a large sum of money was motive for murder.

But she didn't.

"What makes you think that whoever took your money had any help?" Aggie asked.

Dr. Wyatt was taken aback, both by the way the question was phrased and by Aggie's tone of voice. She wasn't even willing to consider Jane's theft a possibility.

"I don't," he finally said. "I just want to make sure that no one else was involved."

Before he spoke with her, he had expected her to leap at his authorization to dig into the comings and goings of the office staff. It was something she already did on her own. But she seemed reluctant, almost sullen.

"Why didn't you mention this to the detective?" she asked.

There it was. "No publicity, Aggie," he said. "That's the last thing we need. If she took the money and the police find out, we'll be the losers, although we're the victims in this crime."

"The victims? Jane was murdered," Aggie said. "If the police knew that she was carrying a large sum of money, that would be motive. Don't you think that might help them solve the crime?"

"Why should we be punished for Jane's crime?" The indignation nearly burst out of Dr. Wyatt. "She brought this on herself. She made a decision to take my money and go on a vacation with it."

Dr. Wyatt didn't like the shadow he saw flit across Aggie's face. He felt sure he shouldn't ask her the next question, but this was why he'd sent for her in the first place.

"Can you do some investigating, very discreet, to find out if anyone else had anything to do with the theft?" he asked.

Her mouth twisted and he thought she was going to say some-thing angry. But all she said was: "Of course, Doctor." Aggie's tone was cold. She got up without being dismissed and left the office.

Dr. Wyatt watched the closed door for a long moment. He was sorry he'd said anything to Aggie, and felt an uneasy sureness that he would be even sorrier. But he hadn't had a choice. This was something he could in no way afford to let pass.

Several times during their conversation he had been taken aback when Aggie's reactions were not what he would have predicted. Now he knew what it was that bothered him most. Aggie hadn't seemed to be surprised that money had been stolen. Only that he had accused Jane of taking it.

Did he really think that Aggie would steal from him? Though he dismissed the idea as absurd, a small worry niggled at him that he had perhaps just sent the thief to interrogate the rest of the office.

29

Ham was grateful that she saw the hand descending a split second before it grasped her wrist. Otherwise she would have been startled, and Dr. Betty Winter would think she'd flinched at her touch.

"Come with me," Dr. Winter whispered. Then, as Ham got up immediately to follow her, she added: "Take your purse. We'll go to lunch."

Shoving her file drawer closed, Ham winced at the sound of candy wrappers crackling—how many Butterfingers had she crushed to satisfy Dr. Winter's urgency? Ham didn't get it—day in and day out Dr. Winter looked at her as if she had the Black Plague, and now she wanted lunch? Whatever it was about, Ham promised herself she was going to eat. She was starving. Aggie's little inquisition this morning had kept her from her snack.

As Dr. Winter strode swiftly away, Ham waddled behind her. Slim figure, nice clothes, Ham thought. But enough with the red outfits. Nobody who comes here needs to see a power color to know who's in charge.

They weren't even to the exit door when Ham's breathing became labored and her lower back started to ache. This weight is killing me, she thought. It hangs back and drags down every muscle and tendon I own. How much longer can I put up with it?

Pushing the metal bar to open the fire door, Dr. Winter pointed toward the parking lot. "You take your own car and meet me at Seagulls. OK?"

The 'OK' accompanied the first direct look at Ham. Ham saw immediately that the word meant 'Do you understand?' and not 'Is that all right with you?'

"Sure," Ham said.

The humidity and heat hit Ham hard. She felt as if she

were pulling air into her lungs through a wet sponge. Her back was soaked and her thighs were chafed by the time she reached her Honda.

Ham squeezed behind the steering wheel, feeling the hot plastic seat steaming her in her own sweat.

"Damn," she said as she turned the ignition key. Curiosity, even apprehension had met Dr. Winter's command. Now Ham was just annoyed.

****

Dr. Winter had ordered food just to have something to fidget with, Ham decided. The iced tea and the ham and swiss on rye just slid back and forth on the plastic table top as Dr. Winter prodded them with a manicured nail. Ham tried to keep her eyes on Dr. Winter's face, and her mind on what she was saying, but the moving food was like running a mouse in front of a hungry cat.

Just the sight of the neon yellow lemon wedge perched on the glass rim made Ham's mouth pucker. And the little rivulets of condensation ran down the glass in synch with Ham's own salivation. When Dr. Winter absently patted her sandwich, Ham was captivated by the recovering depressions in the rye bread. How soft, how fresh. She could imagine her teeth cleaving the thick, pink ham and yielding swiss.

"The office manager, did you know her well?" Dr. Winter's question jarred Ham out of her reverie.

For a moment, Ham forgot her hunger. The hush, the urgency, the sweating to get here—just to have Winter ask her about Jane? Why couldn't she ask Ham these questions at the office? And why didn't Winter refer to Jane by name?

"Why?" Ham was annoyed.

Dr. Winter glanced around her, as if to ensure she wasn't overheard. "I gather that Dr. Wyatt thinks Jane might have taken some money."

Ham wondered what she was getting at. "Yes. Aggie said he thinks that Jane's trip and her death are too coincidental."

Dr. Winter asked: "Did he say how he thought she knew

about the money?"

Ham's annoyance could no longer compete with her hunger. Her attention went back to Dr. Winter's sandwich.

"All the mail came across her desk," Ham said. "Maybe she accidentally opened something. Maybe she systematically opened mail."

Ham was immediately sorry she'd said that. Just because she was hungry and uncomfortable, she shouldn't cast aspersions on Jane's character. She had liked Jane. When Ham finally looked up, she caught Dr. Winter studying her face. She thinks I had something to do with it, Ham thought. She was steamed.

Ham was going to say something, but she was distracted by her growling stomach. She couldn't help darting another glance at the sandwich. Where was her food? She looked up to see disdain in Dr. Winter's face. She's probably never hungry, Ham thought. And she probably thinks I always am. Bitch.

Their harried waitress came by with a tray for someone else's table, and shouted as she ran past: "We ran out of shrimp. What else do you want? I'll be back."

Tears jumped to Ham's eyes, she was so hungry. And so angry she could have thrown something. Now there would be another long wait, and her heart had been set on shrimp. Amazed and embarrassed that she could be moved so strongly by food, Ham glanced at Dr. Winter. The woman's tight face showed nothing but disapproval of Ham's lack of self-control. Clearly, lunch was a pretext. Ham's sole purpose was to be pumped for information.

Ham's tears dried fast. What did Winter think? That she had been in league with Jane to steal money? Ham was hungry, insulted, and angry. She decided that Betty Winter needed a taste of her own medicine. Let her know how it felt to be used and made a fool of.

Ham leaned across the table, lowered her voice. "You think I may have been Jane's accomplice?"

Dr. Winter shook her head, but her eyes told Ham that was exactly what she was getting at.

Ham spoke slowly. "A conspiracy," she said. "Sure. This is how it worked: Jane would tell me to come to a particular restaurant, where to sit, what to order." She tapped the table softly. "There would be a message written with invisible ink, right here."

Dr. Winter frowned as Ham plucked the lemon wedge from her glass.

"To get the message, I'd have to make it visible," Ham said. She squeezed the lemon wedge as she moved her hand in a zig zag pattern. "But there would be nonsense words in the message, so I needed a template to read it. That's where the cheese came in." She opened Dr. Winter's sandwich, took the cheese slice and dropped it on the table. "I would read the message in the holes."

Dr. Winter's face said she didn't know whether to be frightened or angry.

"Then, of course, I'd have to get rid of the template." Ham peeled up the cheese and ate it in two quick bites.

Ham had intended for it to stop there, but hunger overruled her. She snatched the rest of Dr. Winter's sandwich and wolfed it down.

Dr. Winter stared wordlessly at her, threw a twenty dollar bill on the table and left.

The waitress swung by the table and clattered a plate of fried shrimp and french fries in front of her. "I was wrong. There was one more order left. Enjoy."

****

Ham chewed on her lower lip as she drove back to the clinic. Her shrimp platter had sunk to the pit of her stomach and stayed there. She hadn't felt good about her scene with Dr. Winter. As much as the woman got under her skin, Ham didn't like to be unkind. She had been on the receiving end too often to want to do it to anyone else.

Ham's spurt of unkindness, however, was not the reason for her indigestion. It was caused by the item that Dr. Winter had unknowingly flung onto the table along with a twenty dollar bill as she went off in a huff.

It took Ham one look to be sorry she had it. She was completely sure that Dr. Winter didn't want anyone else to see it, least of all Ham.

****

Ham leaned over to get a candy bar from her file drawer and felt a sharp jab in her breast. She flooded with fear, certain she was having a heart attack. How many times had she been warned not to lug around so much weight? If she were unable to use her body, what would she do? Ham shuddered at the thought of being at the mercy of some incompetent doctor...

With relief she realized the jab came from what she had tucked in her bra. Guilty about taking what Dr. Winter had left behind on the table at lunch, Ham had worried that the woman would confront her as soon as she walked into the clinic. Ham had stuffed the item into her bra and immediately buried herself in her work. So far, Dr. Winter had said nothing.

Ham pulled out a partly crushed Butterfinger bar and tore off a corner of the wrapper. Shaking some shards of the candy into her palm, she wondered why Dr. Winter would keep something like that in her purse. In her mind's eye Ham saw a very different Dr. Winter than the highly skilled, confident and polished woman who nearly always wore something red.

Ham felt torn about returning the item. Would Dr. Winter be grateful to have it back—or resentful that Ham knew something personal about her? Ham chewed her way through the question and through an entire Butterfinger bar before she made her decision.

30

"This check isn't for $50,000," Diane said.

"No," Cy agreed. From the tone of her voice, he wondered: had he miscalculated?

"Is this like a final payment?" she asked. "Take this and I don't want to hear from you again?"

"No. Why do you say that?" Was she angry with him?

"I thought we might be friends again," she said. "Real friends. But this..." She waved the check.

"I just wanted to celebrate your achievement." It sounded embarrassingly corny.

Diane looked at him. "$100,000 is more than celebrating."

Cy's generosity hadn't been calculated. It had been impulsive. "We missed years of celebrating and supporting each other. I can't change that, but I want to give this to you now. Please take it."

"So this isn't a 'get lost' check?"

Cy finally figured it out: Diane wasn't angry; she was teasing him. It hadn't happened in so many years that he was out of practice. "No," he said, relieved.

"This isn't guilt or pity. You really just want to contribute to the cause?"

"Yes."

"And you won't regret it? There isn't something special you're saving for?"

"No."

"I'd rather not take it than have the lines of communication closed again."

Cy was touched. "I don't want them closed, either."

"Because I'd really rather have the communication *and* the money."

For the first time in a long while, Diane gave him a real grin.

"You know, there's something else to celebrate," she said.

Cy couldn't guess what. Diane had been in an unusual mood since she came to the clinic.

She looked like a kid with a secret, ready to burst.

"You know the shopping channel?"

Cy nodded.

"They want to sell my skin care line!"

Cy burst out laughing, he was so happy for her. "When?"

"Tomorrow. Can you believe it?" She shook her head. "It's all happened so fast. One of my patients knows someone at the shopping channel and told them about me. And they want to do it right away. Something about needing something new in skin care to run against their competition."

She took a deep breath. "I've been so high I haven't come down enough to be scared. They said I just have to talk about my products and look good. Some of my patients are going to call in testimonials."

Diane looked so genuinely happy that Cy impulsively reached for her.

They hugged—just as Aggie stuck her unannounced head in the door to tell him his next appointment was here.

31

Dr. Betty Winter was still angry when she got back to her office. That Ham had made fun of her. She'd turned to her for help, she'd confided her suspicions, and Ham had made fun of her. And taken her food. Suddenly, Dr. Winter's breath stopped as a memory of her childhood surfaced, clear and unsettling.

She had been six. She was certain of the age—when she started school was the first time she could count on eating something every day. And two of the little girls in her class, with carefully curled hair and ironed dresses, had been playing at lunch. Not eating, playing.

One of them had knocked Betty's sandwich out of her hands, and Betty had gotten down on her knees and eaten it, right off the ground. The two little girls had pointed at her and laughed, and though it had killed her to let them make fun of her, Betty wouldn't have put that sandwich down at gunpoint.

Betty closed her eyes and felt a tear slip down her cheek. Would it ever go away? How much of who she was and how she thought, was because of what that child had gone through? Was it so ingrained that she would never be able to make an objective decision? Were her suspicions about Jane's death real? Or was she just punishing herself for the cowardly act of putting the opened envelope on Jane's desk?

A knock at her door startled Betty out of her thoughts. "Come in."

Ham pushed the door open and squeezed herself through. Before Betty could build up a head of steam—After what she'd done to Betty at lunch, she had the gall to come here?—Ham had closed the door and advanced on Betty's desk. She put her palm down on the desk and then lifted it.

A large, colored card lay underneath.

Ham spoke rapidly, as if she wanted to get rid of something. "You left this behind when you paid for lunch today. I didn't want you to miss it and worry about where it was. Thank you for lunch. I'm sorry if I acted cranky or odd. I was so hungry."

Betty stared at the card. She recognized it at once. Belatedly, she berated herself for taking them in her purse. She knew there was always the chance, however remote, that she would lose one or all of them. Her luck, she had to lose one of them for Ham to find.

Betty's discomfort worked itself into the beginnings of anger. She would have answered sharply if she hadn't seen Ham's face. The young woman was sweating profusely. Rivulets were running from her temples down her cheeks. Betty's gaze dropped compassionately to the tent Ham was wearing. She must be sweltering, Betty thought. It was a stifling day and there was not enough relief inside; Dr. Wyatt kept the offices a bit too warm for everyone's taste but his own. Betty had once been heavy; she had a good idea of how uncomfortable Ham must feel.

Ham had turned as soon as she delivered the card, and was waddling back to the door before Betty spoke. "Wait."

Ham stopped, rotated slowly and faced Betty.

"Thank you for bringing it back." Betty had let the word 'it' hang in the air, as if inviting comment. Maybe Ham didn't know what 'it' was.

"It's a Tarot card," Ham said. "The Hanged Man. One of the twenty-two Major Arcana."

So she did know something. Betty felt deflated, wondering what Ham would do with the information that a senior doctor at the fertility clinic carried Tarot cards. Betty felt like someone waiting to hear about a ransom demand.

Finally Ham said: "My mother used to read the cards. She said they were good. That they gave her a way to connect with her own inner knowledge, to help her find her way." Ham shook her head. "I hope they gave her comfort, because she never seemed to find a way out..." Ham stopped, as if she'd said too much.

Betty watched as another rivulet began to run down Ham's cheek, finally realized this one was made by tears. Betty was on a knife edge, wondering what to do next. She glanced at the small clock on her desk. Calculated there was an hour before her next appointment. Made a decision.

"Sit down." She motioned Ham to the chair in front of her desk. "You want to know what I do with these." Betty didn't wait for Ham to agree or disagree. "I'll show you."

Betty took her purse out of her desk drawer, opened it and unzipped an inner compartment. Gently she lifted out a silk scarf-wrapped package.

With great care she unwrapped the brilliant red silk. Inside was a large deck of cards with a blue and white diagonal plaid pattern on the backs. Expertly, Betty riffled through the deck, satisfying herself that no other card was missing.

It was funny. They let doctors practice who drank or used drugs. They let them practice after they had hurt or killed people through negligence or incompetence. People would go back to them, put their fate in their hands.

Betty looked down at the worn card deck in her palms. But who would go to a black woman doctor who consulted the Tarot? There wouldn't be small girls snickering. There would be adults laughing, picturing her in a turban and a loud-colored dress. There would be large-scale shunning by her colleagues. There would be wholesale walking away by her patients. She winced. There might even be a dead chicken on her doorstep.

She picked up The Hanged Man card and put it on top of the deck. She lifted the deck and began shuffling it.

The familiar weight and feel of the cards calmed Betty. There was a rhythm and an energy in the cards. She always felt it. As she shuffled, her mind focused on her intent—to be open and clear so she would read well for Ham. She shuffled the deck three times, then nodded at Ham. "Your turn," she said. "Shuffle the deck three times, and think of a question you want answered. Then put the deck down."

Betty's worry began to ebb. She felt the calm yet heightened senses that came as she began a reading. She was getting impressions even as Ham began to handle the cards. Her intuition had told her to offer this reading. Now it told her the reading would be good for both of them.

She cleared her desk to make room for a spread.

32

Ham eased herself into her chair and clenched her eyes shut. Why had she returned the Tarot card? Why had she given her a question for the reading? Dr. Winter had told her the answer to her question was yes. But then she had frowned at the cards until Ham had made an excuse to leave. What had Betty Winter seen in the cards that she hadn't told Ham? Did she know something about Ham that Ham didn't know?

Ham shook her head, rubbed her eyes—dry and gritty as if they had sand in them—then opened them to see a pair of pointy-toed shoes between the heels of her hands.

Ham blinked and looked up to see who was attached to the shoes. It was a willowy woman with blonde hair who looked at Ham as if she were the prize pig at a county fair. Ham had heard enough about Diane to recognize her immediately. Ham quickly turned her attention back to her computer, not daring to pick up the candy bar sitting seductively in a torn wrapper on her desk.

Moments after Diane was gone, the furious rustle of nylons told Ham that Aggie was descending on her. Aggie stopped near Ham's desk, but stared over Ham's head at Dr. Cy's closed door, and visibly fumed.

"Well, that is just beyond the pale," Aggie said.

Ham didn't really want to hear it, but she had to be pleasant. She stopped typing, but left her fingers on the keys in a fruitless hint that she was working.

"His ex-wife is here, in his office, with the door closed," Aggie added.

"He always meets with people with his door closed," Ham said. So why was her anxiety starting to rise?

"After all these years..." Aggie muttered.

Ham's fingers started to feel like little frozen sausage links on the keyboard.

"I just glanced in his office, and I saw him *hug* her."

Ham's stomach was getting cold. She braced for bad news.

"I'll bet my bottom dollar I know why she's here."

Ham hated herself; she knew she was looking pleadingly at Aggie for the answer.

"She wants a baby."

Ham's chest felt tight; she had trouble breathing and began wheezing.

Without once looking at Ham, Aggie turned on her heels and bustled back to her desk.

Ham realized she was hyperventilating. She pulled open her desk drawer, fished out the well-worn brown paper bag, and fitted it over her mouth. She didn't care that she looked like a horse with its head in a feedbag. Breathing into the bag helped.

"You OK?"

Startled, Ham jerked her brown paper muzzle to find Dr. Cy at her elbow. She spluttered something into the bag, making it vibrate and sound like a cow. What was there to say to him? She was paid to work on the computer, period. Dr. Wyatt had made that clear to her any number of times. Besides, she might lose her job if she overstepped her bounds. Ham couldn't chance that. She had to keep her job here. Don't say anything, she told herself. *Be a professional.*

Ham crumpled the paper bag in her fists. "How can you treat your ex-wife?" she demanded. "Isn't that inappropriate? Unprofessional?"

Cy looked surprised.

Ham closed her eyes. Why did I say that? What right did I have? She felt her cheeks get hot with embarrassment as she braced for his reply.

"Whatever goes on in my office is private, not open to discussion or explanation."

Ham heard no anger or sarcasm in his voice. She opened her eyes to find no discernible emotion in his face. She turned cold inside. He must intend to just fire her. Or worse, not to speak to her again.

"It's not my business," Ham muttered, staring at the floor.

"I'm so sorry. I shouldn't have said anything. It wasn't professional of me."

"Well, it's too late for that," Dr. Cy said.

Oh, God, she thought. She looked up to find he had an amused look on his face.

"Forget about it," he said.

He began to walk away, but came back, this time with a curious look. "What do you think bothers you about it?"

Bothers me? she thought. It has nothing to do with me. It's just not right. Ham shrugged. "I don't know what got into me," she said.

Cy nodded toward the paper bag she still held. "I think you popped it," he said. "You may want to patch it before you put it back in your drawer."

Ham's face got hot as she threw the bag in her wastebasket.

"By the way," he said as he walked away, "Aggie is misinformed."

This time Ham didn't reach for a candy bar.

33

Betty found Cy in his office, up to his elbows in scientific journals. She hated to interrupt him in the little time he had available to stay current with research in assisted reproductive technology.

"Can you help me?" she asked. "I've got a patient in my office who is close to hysteria. She was working with Jane to finance her IVF cycles, and now that Jane is gone, she thinks everything is going to fall apart. To compound things, she had her embryo transfer twelve days ago. We're so close to knowing if it's implanted—just two days more to testing—and I don't want her anxiety to jeopardize this..."

Betty didn't have to finish. She and Cy both knew that even if the embryos implanted, there was a chance for miscarriage after an IVF, just as in an unassisted conception. But an IVF cycle had additional strains—the physical and emotional stress intrinsic to the process, plus the financial burden. It was no wonder that some women—and their husbands—cracked.

Cy nodded. "Absolutely. I can clear things for the next hour and a half. What do you want me to do?"

"Will you spend some time calming and reassuring her? Normally I would do it, but she came in without an appointment. And I've just harvested eggs from another of my patients, and her husband's sperm sample is ready."

Cy stood up. "I'll be happy to talk with her. I'll go get her and bring her in here."

"Thanks," Betty relaxed. It was like Cy to do whatever he could to make a patient feel comfortable. He never stood on ceremony. She knew the woman would be in good hands with him. Relieved, she headed for the lab.

****

Gloved and masked, Betty prepared to work quickly. The husband had given a sample about three hours before the

IVF procedure. This had given Betty time to 'wash' the sperm—separate the sperm from the semen—by mixing the semen with culture media and centrifuging it.

Now she removed from the incubator the first of the test tubes containing the wife's follicular fluid and eggs, and took it to the laboratory work table. She immediately emptied the contents into a petri dish, and scanned the contents of the dish under the microscope to find the egg. Using microscopic control, she picked up the egg with a small pipette and placed it in a very small microdroplet of culture media, on the bottom of a culture dish. She added fluid containing about three thousand sperm to the microdroplet, and laid purified mineral oil over the droplet. This procedure helped to ensure that the eggs and sperm would be kept in a stable environment as they developed into embryos.

Skillfully and quickly, Betty prepared all the eggs and sperm using the oil overlay and microdroplet technique. Then she returned them to the carbon dioxide incubator.

As Betty unmasked and stripped off her gloves, out of habit she went over in her mind what would happen in the incubator in the next two to three days. The conditions in the incubator and the culture media were designed to mimic the conditions in the fallopian tubes, so the embryos would grow successfully in vitro. The incubator was kept at a controlled temperature that was the same as a woman's body. The culture medium, which had to be very pure, contained such ingredients as proteins, salts, buffer and antibiotics to allow optimal growth of the embryo.

About 18 hours after insemination, Betty would check to see how many of the eggs had fertilized. Abnormally fertilized embryos or those which had failed to fertilize, would be discarded.

The successfully fertilized embryos were left in culture, where they continued to divide, and their quality would be graded after another 24 hours. Good quality embryos divided rapidly and produced cells of equal size, with clear cytoplasm, and few fragments. After 48 to 72 hours, when the embryos consisted of two to eight cells each, Betty would place some of them in the woman's uterus in a procedure known as embryo transfer.

Betty always visualized the entire process taking place successfully, as a kind of litany for the woman's pregnancy. For good measure, before she left the lab, she said a small prayer for the tiny potential beings in the incubator.

34

"This is going to work out," Cy told the distraught woman. "I want you to know that. Now let's just sit down and give it a chance." He seated her across from him at his desk, brought her a glass of water and a box of tissues.

Mrs. Baker sat hunched over in the chair, weeping and trembling. Cy was acquainted with her background and the strain she was under. She could have been the sister of the woman Cy had seen two days earlier. Both were having trouble paying for the services of the clinic. Both would benefit from an adaptation of the procedures that didn't involve expensive techniques.

Cy got her to calm down by taking a series of deep breaths.

****

By the time the appointment was over, Cy was sitting behind his desk, holding his head in his hands. A headache raged inside his skull.

He had seen too many women who had been treated for years by doctors who didn't know what they were doing. Then, by the time they finally reached a clinic like Dr. Wyatt's, they were on the downslope of their reproductive lives. They were producing fewer eggs and fewer good quality eggs than they needed to have a good chance to get pregnant.

Mrs. Baker was a perfect example. If she didn't get pregnant in this cycle, how many more would it make sense for her to endure?

If she couldn't produce her own viable eggs, there were two alternatives—donor eggs or adoption. Cy had looked in Mrs. Baker's eyes while he spoke with her. He was convinced that she had a deep desire to bear a child. How would she feel about a baby that was genetically related only to her husband—assuming they could get her someone else's eggs—or not related to either of them?

Diane had told Cy that his patients never died, they just adopted—as if that decision were simple and his involvement only professional. But the path that led a woman to adopt rather than having one of her own was a long and painful one—and one that Cy traveled with her.

If Cy had to guess, he would say that Mrs. Baker would choose bearing a child, no matter whose it was. She would want that connection, to have carried the baby and given it life.

How much Cy wanted to make that possible for her.

35

"What did you say to her?"

Betty strode into Cy's office without any preamble and waited at his desk for an answer. Cy soon thought he knew what must have happened. He had counseled Betty's patient, discussing fertility techniques that weren't sanctioned by Dr. Wyatt. The woman must have said something that got back to Dr. Wyatt. Dr. Wyatt had exploded at Betty, and now she was in here. Cy's stomach tensed in anticipation of Betty's next words.

"Dr. Wyatt says you're brilliant."

Cy had gotten so used to Dr. Wyatt blowing up at him for no reason, that he was nearly as traumatized when he was being praised. He was also suspicious. "What actually does he think I did?"

"Recommended simple treatments that would make assisted reproductive technology more accessible to more people."

OK so far, Cy thought. "It's not something that he's ever done," Cy said.

"He knows that. He thinks it's way overdue."

"But he isn't the one who thought of it." Cy felt guilty as soon as he'd said it. "What I meant is that he established this clinic. He's led the way. He's..."

Betty held up her hand. "I understand. Student teaching the Master. I believe it's covered in the I Ching by the general upheaval symbol."

Cy had to smile. "Sorry I had my revelation while I was talking with your patient. She's not the first who's needed this kind of help. I guess it finally just got to me."

Betty shook her head. "I'm on your side. I actually think we might have better success with these methods than the statistics show. We'll be getting these women more involved in the process, giving them more control over what's happening with their bodies. I know some of them feel as if they're programmed by the drugs they have to take, and as if they practically live at the clinic."

Cy still didn't believe his recommendations would be accepted so easily. Especially since he had not approached Dr. Wyatt directly, but had effectively 'shamed' him into it. "So what's the catch?" he asked her.

"He wants you to take over the women who are the best candidates for this form of treatment." Betty grimaced. "No good deed goes unpunished."

Cy felt as if someone had unloaded a dump truck on him. Dr. Wyatt had just added about twenty to thirty women to Cy's already burdened schedule. But he hadn't given Cy the go-ahead to use the simpler treatments. Cy doubted that he ever would. Dr. Wyatt knew exactly what he was doing. He had very neatly inundated Cy as a way of telling him to butt out. Period.

36

"There are three male embryos," Cy told the couple.

He had already given Mr. and Mrs. Binn this information, as soon as results of the PGD had been available. After he had removed one cell from each of their embryos, he had sent the cells to the DNA lab for analysis. It turned out that the three best quality embryos were all male.

But Cy repeated this information, along with a review of each step of the implantation process he was about to perform. He wanted to be sure that the couple was informed and comfortable, so he told them again exactly what was going to happen and what they could expect.

Cy knew that when people went through such an emotion-intensive experience, they tended to be overwhelmed. Often, they didn't take in information the first or even the second time they heard it. The husband was proving a perfect example—apparently the implications had just hit him.

The man who had said all along that he only cared that the baby was healthy, now opened his eyes wide. Cy thought he looked like someone who has found out there is a Santa Claus.

"You mean I could have a boy?" Mr. Binn asked.

Cy smiled and said yes.

The husband blinked and looked around the room. "You mean I could have three boys?"

Cy didn't want to be pessimistic, but he had to be cautious. "If all three embryos implant and successfully reach term, yes," he said.

Cy exchanged a smile with the wife. She nodded that she was ready.

The man held his wife's hand as Cy explained that he had aspirated the embryos (in about 1/100th teaspoon of fluid) into a small catheter using a tiny syringe on the end.

Cy told the couple what he was doing as he carefully threaded the catheter through the wife's cervix and into her uterus. He was keenly aware of how fragile were the embryos, and that they would not easily 'lodge' in the area where they were injected. Cy made his movements delicate and careful so that the embryos stayed where they were supposed to stay and weren't accidentally yanked back as he withdrew his catheter.

After the embryos were inserted, Cy waited before slowly and carefully pulling out the catheter. He remembered a study that dramatized the necessity of this care. Researchers had calculated the force and speed at which embryos would leave a catheter if the procedure weren't done properly: the embryos could hit the uterine wall at six hundred miles per hour.

Cy glanced at the couple; they both seemed to have tolerated the procedure well. The husband had blossomed at the prospect of having a boy. He looked at his wife with a kind of awe, as if she held his future. Well, she does, Cy thought. All through the procedure, the man had held her hand and wiped her brow.

The husband stayed with her afterwards, for two hours as she rested, and Cy thought he walked her out of the clinic only because he couldn't carry her.

After the procedure, as Cy was putting instruments away in the clinic's lab, his thoughts returned to Dr. Wyatt and his assignment to Cy of the women who would most benefit from simpler and more natural ART methods. As Cy had predicted, Dr. Wyatt still hadn't given him clearance to use the simple methods on these patients. Cy didn't know how he was going to help these women, yet not run afoul of the clinic's policies. The stress of the added workload and the 'rock and a hard place' restrictions had been taking a toll on him.

Cy rubbed tired eyes and wondered what he had been thinking. Dr. Wyatt had his reputation and that of the clinic to think of. What would happen to his success rate when more natural methods were used? Without drugs to ensure a large number of mature eggs, a woman would produce only one egg per cycle, and that one egg might not be of good quality. Cy felt that Dr. Wyatt would see the simpler method as a way of handicapping him in his race to have the most successful clinic.

Cy felt slightly ashamed of his thoughts. Dr. Wyatt had been working for more than twenty-five years to help couples have children.

From the beginning, there had been no government research support for assisted reproductive technology. Everything had been done with private funding. Far from helping, the government had even put stumbling blocks in the way. For example, Cy knew that one of the catheters most popularly used with the highest pregnancy rate for IVF was the 'Tom Cat'—so called because it had been originally designed for removing bladder stones from tomcats. Yet this catheter was not legally sanctioned by the government or approved for use in humans. That meant that IVF was an illegal use of the catheter. Doctors in the United States had had to get overseas physicians to buy the catheter and ship them over here, because they couldn't legally buy them in this country.

Suddenly, Cy wondered if Dr. Wyatt intended for him to fail these women. Maybe he was setting Cy up to be the one who ended up turning these women away from the clinic. Cy could not shake himself of this thought, nor of the stomach-churning anxiety it brought him.

On his way out of the lab, Cy stopped beside the liquid nitrogen tanks which contained frozen embryos. The log book was open. Cy was closing it when he wondered how far back the entries went. He flipped through the pages, noticing the donors, the dates, and the comments. He was surprised that so many comments were some version of: 'Parents have passed the age when the wife wants to carry a child.'

What will happen to all of those embryos? he wondered.

37

Dr. Wyatt had picked up a local paper for its coverage of a talk he'd given at a recent conference. But as he neared the end of the piece, something in a nearby column caught his eye.

It was a follow-up article about an accident that had taken place several days before. He thought he recognized it as the crash that had killed Brett Peterman's daughter and son-in-law. Dr. Wyatt remembered having heard about the accident on the news: A car had skidded off the Merritt Parkway and burst into flames. By the time fire trucks had arrived, the car was an inferno. Despite firemen's efforts, virtually nothing had remained but a blackened shell.

The accident had a curious twist to it.

'Police said that two people had been in the car. To date, forensics has found evidence of only one individual. When the police were questioned, a detective associated with the case who asked to remain anonymous said: 'When temperatures this high are involved, a lot of evidence is destroyed. We have to work with what we can find.'

The last lines of the article confirmed Dr. Wyatt's memory:

'One of the victims was the daughter of Brett Peterman, president of a shopping channel company. The other was her husband. The Peterman family is in seclusion.'

Seclusion? He had just seen Peterman at the Greenes' mansion, playing cards with Mr. Greene. Dr. Wyatt dropped his hands to his lap, closed his eyes. He had been able to help the Petermans have a little girl—the young woman in the article. They had seemed like wonderful people and had recommended many patients to him. What a tragedy to happen to them.

Dr. Wyatt pondered: What do you say to a couple who have lost a grown daughter, just as she was about to start her own family? There was no way to replace a child; but if a couple was young, they could try again to have a baby. At the Petermans' ages, starting over wasn't even a possibility. The wife, in fact, had been near the upper age limit twenty odd years ago when they first came to him.

He looked at his watch. He had an appointment tonight, and she didn't like to be kept waiting.

38

Betty held the flame to the wick of the eighth candle. When it caught, she let out her breath in a relieved sigh, shuddering the match flame in her hand. Somehow it was always important that she light all eight on the first try.

Betty stood in front of the choir of red glass cylinders and let the small flickering lights inside comfort her. She drew a long-stemmed red rose from her bag, laid it in front of the candles.

Eight candles, one for each month that she had carried him. She whispered a prayer as she tucked a folded bill into the metal clasp around each light.

It wasn't true, what people said. They told you that your feelings would wane with time. But she loved him now even more than she had before.

The basso of a heavy door swinging open sounded from the other end of the church. Who is here in the middle of the day? She always tried to come when she would be alone. The draft from the door stirred the air and lifted the scent of hot beeswax to her nostrils. Tears sprang to her eyes—that scent meant funeral mass to her.

A mixture of shuffling and staccato footsteps started and soon stopped. People are coming in for something, she thought. It's not the time for a mass; maybe a group is going to pray the rosary. Now that they had interrupted her ritual, she didn't want to stay. She took one last look at the lights, then walked along the side wall toward the back of the church.

She was halfway there before she saw the people, arranged in semicircles just inside the double doors of the church. The group was in dress clothes, many of them bright colors, their attention focused on something in the center of their circle. Betty caught a glimpse of a stone font. Now she knew why they were here—a baptism.

Betty stopped, trapped. Though she blinked back tears at the prospect of watching a baptism, she didn't want to plow her way through the group to reach the doors. A quick glance around the church told her that the only other exit was across the sanctuary and through the sacristy. She wasn't going that way.

Backing herself against the stone wall, she hid behind a niche holding a statue of the Virgin Mary. She forced herself to focus on the decorations and statues inside the church, and not listen to the muffled words of the priest, or strain her ears listening for the baby's cry.

On the long wall of the church across from her she saw the stations of the cross—small bas reliefs depicting in fourteen scenes, the scourging, suffering, and crucifixion of Christ. Mentally she began to go over each station and what it represented. Light shifted in the church as clouds moved outside. Bright afternoon sunshine hit the windows on her side of the church, and one narrow shaft crossed the church to burst over one of the stations. Even in the glare she could make out which one it was: The seventh station, Jesus falls for the second time.

Betty could no longer restrain herself. She peered around the niche at the group at the baptismal font. Across from the priest a young woman held the infant; a young man stood next to her. They were not the mother and father, Betty knew, but the godmother and godfather, individuals who swore the baby's allegiance to the Church for him, and promised to protect him.

Who had protected her baby? Tears ran down Betty's cheeks. No one. Not after he...Betty clenched her jaws; the old pain and anger flared.

A *doctor,* she thought. He was a doctor, at the top of his agency, sworn to 'first, do no harm.' But he had killed her child. How could she believe that he had any qualms about killing others?

The baby cried. Betty's tears stopped and her gaze was riveted on the space above the baptismal font. The little person was waving his arms and legs in the white christening gown, and crying as the priest poured water on his forehead. So small.

The ceremony was drawing to a close. Another young couple—these must be the parents, she thought—moved from the shadows to take the baby. Betty was watching their arms, how they gathered up the child with such tenderness. The parents were thanking the priest before Betty noticed their faces. She knew these people.

She couldn't remember their names, but she was sure they had come to the clinic for help in having a child. Betty furrowed her forehead, trying to remember them. It had been several years ago, there had been some secrecy involved in their appointments, something about needing to keep everything private.

She remembered more. Both of them had had problems; the husband with the number and viability of his sperm, the wife with the quality of her eggs. They had tried everything— Dr. Wyatt had made it clear that money wasn't an object— but nothing had worked. The couple had been so disappointed.

That made Betty wonder if the baby had been adopted. Betty looked again at the wife, noted more closely her face, her dress, how she stood. Betty couldn't be sure, but her guess was that the wife had given birth to the baby. Where had they gone to have this success? Betty knew that Dr. Wyatt prided himself on having the best methods and the best track record.

All of a sudden it came to her who these people were, and she was surprised that she hadn't recognized them before. The attorney and his wife were very public figures.

The baptismal party left the church, Betty following them at a distance until she reached her car. The image of the baby was still in her mind. She had received no justice or closure when she lost her child. Her husband's power had managed to put him out of reach of any kind of accountability. But Betty had never forgotten. She had introduced red in every shade into her life, as a reminder of the small life she had lost.

Betty saw her face reflected in her car window, and realized that grief wasn't the only emotion she kept alive. Though she knew it was wrong, a small part of her still wanted to avenge her child's death.

39

Ham's wastebasket, once again overflowing with water bottles and candy wrappers, confirmed it. These marathon data entry sessions were a kind of torture

Ham had had to ply herself with chocolate bars, wash them down with bottled water, and make frequent trips to the ladies room just to keep herself from going nuts.

She felt as if she'd entered every detail of every visit of every patient the clinic had ever had. Of course she hadn't (not yet, at least); the clinic had been in business for more than twenty-five years. Ham had started with the records of current patients and worked backwards; she would stop when Dr. Wyatt told her to. Though she felt as if she'd entered everything contained in the patients' files, the clinic was just interested in the kinds of information that helped determine how effective their methods were (every clinic compiled success rates for pregnancy), and where problems might lie.

Ham calculated that the real killer of this task had been the tension. Her challenge hadn't just been to enter an enormous amount of data, but to stay vigilant. Since she was doing all of the input herself, she had double-checked everything as she went along. What good was her clever new program if the information was questionable? Garbage In, Garbage Out.

By the end of three days of this kind of effort, her eyes were grainy from staring at a computer screen. Her neck and hands were cramped. And despite the breaks she had taken to get up, move around and stretch, her bottom felt as if she had been sitting on a rock the whole time.

Now she was sorry that she had come up with such an ingenious program. Dr. Wyatt had unexpectedly approved it with few changes—and then ordered her to implement it immediately.

I'm not getting paid enough to do this, she thought, turning off her computer. Not in money or in information. She had never expected to have to sift through so much to get the answers she was sure lay in the clinic. It was like trying to extract gold from seawater.

And she was certain that Dr. Wyatt was pushing her so hard because he didn't like her. He sets impossible goals because he can't make me write: 'I am a fat, undisciplined slob' 1000 times on a blackboard.

Dr. Wyatt acted as if he thought—because Ham was heavy—that she had no feelings, that she didn't know what it was to love.

An image of four furry feet flashed in her mind. Running ahead of her, eating up the sidewalk. Bouncing with an energy and a joy that never became jaded.

It was long ago, long before she had this bulk, when she could fit in a twin bed with him curled up at her side. How contentedly he sank down beside her with a sigh each night. She slept with her hand on his chest, feeling his heart beat against her fingers.

When she lost him, she couldn't sleep in that bed without him. She never let her mother know that she slept on the floor every night.

Ham didn't hear the footsteps until they reached her candy wrappers, littering the zone of light cast by her computer on the dark office's floor. Startled, she swiveled her unwieldy bulk to face the intruder. When she saw who it was, the jolt tumbled her glasses down her front and onto the floor.

"Working late," Dr. Wyatt said. He stood with his face in shadow, outside her computer's light, but Ham could still see that he was wearing evening clothes. He had left earlier this afternoon. What had made him come back to the office?

Too late to change what's on the computer screen, Ham thought. Her heart was already pounding. She stretched a hand toward her glasses, but with her stomach in the middle, she came up short.

Dr. Wyatt swept up her glasses and slapped them into her palm. Ham didn't need light to pick up the disdain in his gesture. He tossed a file on her desk. "I reviewed it and made some notes," he said. "I came back to leave it for you to work on."

Ham fumbled her glasses back on her nose, glanced at the file. It looked like the one she'd given him this morning. *Damn.* She'd hoped it would provoke a response from him, but she hadn't dreamed it would make him come back tonight. She avoided looking at the screen, as if that would keep his attention away, too.

"Isn't that accounting data?" he asked.

Ham's heart sank. She knew what was coming. "Yes," she said.

"What are you doing with patients' billing information?" he demanded. "Didn't I make it clear that you were to work on the computer programming alone and leave the input of billing data to others?"

"Jane used to do it," Ham said. "Aggie asked me to help until you got someone else." That was true; she didn't refuse Aggie's requests. But this time Ham had welcomed the extra work because it gave her access to the flow of money in the clinic. Ham still didn't know exactly what she was looking for, but she sensed she was getting closer.

Dr. Wyatt stepped toward Ham, so that his face was illumined by the light from her computer screen. He looked ghastly, and he was now close enough for her to smell him. He reeked of the medicated soap he constantly used on his hands. Ham sensed menace in his movements and suddenly wished she hadn't taken off her shoes. She felt vulnerable without them. *Do I think I'm going to have to run?*

"Aggie doesn't run the office," he said. "If I don't tell you to do it, don't do it."

It was all Ham could do, not to cringe. There was something in his voice that made her think Dr. Wyatt was just barely holding himself back from striking her.

Dr. Wyatt backed up a step. "Turn that off," he ordered.

"Do your own job or don't work here." He waited while she obeyed him.

Ham had been afraid, but now her whole body burned with anger and humiliation. She was staying late, not getting paid, and he was upbraiding her as if she were chattel. Her toes groped for her shoes under her desk; she shoved her swollen feet into them. By the time she got to her feet, she was sweating profusely.

Dr. Wyatt indicated the exit with a curt nod. He waited for Ham to go first, following her and making her feel like a shoplifter being escorted out by security. The candy bars she'd been eating churned angrily in Ham's stomach.

Ham found herself outside the back door of the clinic, waddling to her car. She didn't have the nerve to look around and see where Dr. Wyatt went. Her cheeks still burned with embarrassment and anger. She had never been so humiliated in her life.

Dr. Wyatt had been impatient, demanding, and critical of his staff—but until now, never demeaning. What else didn't she know about him? He treats me like so much loose change, Ham thought, raging inside. How can he do this to people?

As she trudged across the parking lot in the heat, for the first time since she had joined the weight-control group, she was actually looking forward to the company of those women tonight.

****

Ham settled into one of the metal folding chairs, arranged in a circle under the buzzing fluorescent lights. She even managed to smile at the two new members. At each meeting, one member would share an insight as to why she thought she was overweight and what she planned to do about it. The others would then jump in with their advice. Since Ham had shared at the last meeting, she would be off the hook for a while.

Tonight it was Heather's turn, and Ham was ready to sit back and observe the group. But once Heather began talking, Ham was surprised at how uncomfortable she felt. Heather was one of the founding members of the group; she usually kept the group's discussions on track and their emotions in check. But tonight she could hardly hold back her own tears.

"I've got a vicious circle going in my life," she told them. "I guess it's my own fault. Dr. Wyatt told me at the outset that I'd have a better chance of getting pregnant if I lost weight first. But I didn't want to lose time."

That phrase 'lose time' looked as if it struck a chord with all the women. Ham could see heads nodding. She realized with surprise that she was one of them.

"So I opted to go through IVF cycles at the same time I was dieting." Heather looked down at her lap, as if to apologize for it not being any smaller.

"I don't know what happened. They said I was producing good eggs; Harry was making good sperm. We even had viable embryos. Then, nothing."

Heather's face crumpled and turned red. Though she didn't sob out loud, everyone seemed to feel her distress. Ham shot worried glances around the circle. If Heather lost it, who would keep things together? The women were all walking on emotional tightropes to begin with. The drugs they took made it harder to keep their balance. All it might take to demoralize them was for the group's leader to say she couldn't go on any longer.

Ham wanted to reach out to Heather, but she felt helpless. Since she was the only one in the group not in an IVF cycle, she instinctively knew she had no right to offer sympathy, let alone make any comments. The others would feel that Ham was intruding.

As first one and then another woman offered encouragement or sympathy to Heather, Ham found herself watching Heather's face. She had never really studied her before. Now she seemed to remind Ham of someone. By the end of the evening Ham realized who it was. Emma, the woman who had brought her baby girl to their last meeting. Though Heather and Emma didn't look identical, or even like sisters, there were similarities—in facial features, eye color, height, body build, even hair color.

As Ham trudged out in the still muggy evening air to her car, she thought that it just confirmed what she already believed—there were no one-of-a-kinds. Everyone had experienced someone telling them: 'I have a friend (or sister, brother, teacher, doctor) who looks just like you.'

40

Betty hugged herself and stared at the single red rose in the small vase on her mantel. Her mind was back in the church, in front of the bank of glowing lights. Slowly she let herself sink into her memories and sorrow.

She started when the phone rang.

"Betty? It's Cy. I'm not waking you up, am I?"

She stifled a bitter laugh. "Not yet. Is everything all right?"

"Sure. I just wanted to tell you that Diane is on TV tonight."

"Diane? Is she being interviewed? What channel?" Betty picked up the remote control and turned the television on.

"The shopping channel."

"I know it." She knew the channel by heart and flipped to it.

"I forgot to tell you that the skin care line she developed has been picked up by them. They're doing the first show on her products tonight."

There was a shopping commercial on when Betty got to the channel. "That's fast, isn't it? I always thought there was a big lag time between when they found new items and when they managed to schedule them. They must really love her products."

"You sound like you know more about this than I do," Cy said.

Betty dropped into a chair. "I ought to. At the end of the day I don't have the energy to go out and shop. I have a couple of favorite websites I order from. I use the shopping channel for a lot of things, including skin care. They offer products I would never know about otherwise."

"She's on the air now," Cy said.

While Betty listened to Cy and watched Diane chat with the channel's hostess, she realized that her depression had vaporized. She was surprised again what a balm for the spirits the familiar and the mundane could be.

"I'm watching her," Betty said. The camera did a close-up of Diane. "She looks terrific and her skin is beautiful." She listened as Diane described the merits of her products; and assumed Cy was doing the same on the other end of the line.

"No wonder they wanted her," Betty said. "She knows what she's talking about and you believe what she says. And just looking at her, you want to have her products. I'm so glad you told me, Cy. She's worked hard for this."

"I know. I feel the same way."

Betty was feeling better. "You know, I'm going to order her products," she told Cy. "I'm sure they'll be just as good as she says they are."

"I'm glad I thought to call you. See you tomorrow."

When Cy hung up, Betty dialed the shopping channel's number. She followed the automated ordering procedure, which she knew by heart. She entered her phone number and then her zip code as she watched Diane's presentation on the television. The recorded voice offered the set of Diane's skin products just as Diane was demonstrating them onscreen. Betty decided to take advantage of express shipping—she wanted to start using them right away—and the autoship option. With autoship, the skin products would be shipped to her every ninety days. Betty thought that was a great idea. All she had to do was go to her mailbox.

After she had OK'd the use of the credit card that the shopping channel kept on file for her, and had gotten a confirmation of her order, Betty hung up. She watched the rest of Diane's presentation and smiled as she watched. She had never seen Diane so happy and animated.

Happy is a good thing, Betty thought. Take some of your own medicine, doctor.

41

"You didn't really expect there to be any match, did you, Cy?"

Cy was standing at the nurse's station, when he got the call he'd been expecting—from the director of the DNA testing center. The man told him there was no match between the DNA in Clea's hair and the DNA in the cheek cells from the little girl in the grocery store.

Cy had known he would probably be disappointed. Had known in his heart he had seen Clea's face on the child because he had wanted to so badly. But he hadn't been prepared for it to hurt so much. When he saw the avid look Aggie was giving him, he realized his disappointment must show on his face. Be a professional, he thought. The director went out of his way to help you.

"Thanks for getting back to me so quickly," Cy told him. "I really appreciate the trouble you went to."

Aggie was now openly eavesdropping, so Cy turned away from her.

The director had been almost curt while delivering the information, and Cy wondered if he had damaged their professional relationship by asking him for this favor. Or maybe he just hadn't adequately expressed his appreciation.

"Maybe I haven't expressed..." Cy began, but the director interrupted.

"I don't suppose there's any reason not to mention this," he said.

There was a long pause while Cy wondered: mention what?

"It doesn't mean anything, but at least you'll know that there couldn't possibly be any mistake in the tests we did."

Cy was mystified.

"Your clinic sent us samples from the parents of this child— the one whose cheek cells we tested—a couple of years ago."

Cy had run into one of the clinic's test tube babies? It

wasn't impossible for him to believe; Dr. Wyatt had been doing in vitro fertilizations for the past twenty-five years. There
were a lot of people he was responsible for bringing into the
world.

Then Cy started thinking what else the man's information
implied.

"But how could you compare the two tests?" he asked.
"Weren't they two different tests, looking for different things?
When we send you samples from the clinic—either from the
embryo or from the parents—you check specific DNA sites
that are correlated with certain diseases. When I brought you
the samples the other day, I just wanted you to compare them.
The STR test looks at non-coding areas of the DNA. It would
have been totally different from the test you performed on the
parents' DNA samples."

"You're half right, Cy," the director said. "We did screen
the parents' DNA. But your clinic also asked us to do an STR."

Cy didn't understand that at all. "Why?"

"They don't give us reasons, just jobs," the director answered. "You know that. Maybe they're doing some kind of
statistical correlation between STR profiles and different kinds
of genetic problems. STR results are fairly quick, they're reliable and easy to store digitally—they practically beg researchers to find ways to use them. Besides, if you think you'll ever
need to identify a patient, you do the test when you have the
chance."

That made some sense to Cy. Dr. Wyatt was an infinitely
thorough man, a researcher who had written several books
and gave frequent talks about his work. Then Cy thought to
ask the question he should have asked first.

"What made you compare them—the two samples I brought
you—to your database?" Cy asked.

"Why not? It's the only thing I had to compare them to. It
was just a shot in the dark, but in this case it paid off."

Cy couldn't argue with that. You worked with what you
had, used the things that were at hand.

"Look," the director said. "You know there are no names at-tached to the samples we got a couple of years ago, but I do have the date that your clinic sent them. I know this isn't what you were looking for, but it's all I have to give you. Do you want it?"

Cy had no interest in pursuing the ancestry of the cheek cells any further, but he didn't want to be ungrateful. He searched the counter for a notepad. Aggie pushed one toward him and he wrote down the date. When he hung up with the lab director, he tore off the top page, stuffed it in his pocket, and headed to his office.

42

As if it were standard operating procedure, Aggie pulled the notepad toward her and squinted at the indentations on its surface.

She selected a pencil with a long, sharp point. Turning it on its side, she rubbed the lead over the surface of the paper. When the message Cy had just written down appeared, she smiled.

Even from her desk Ham could see what Aggie was brazenly doing. Aggie didn't hesitate to inform herself about anything that took place in the clinic. Whether Aggie did it out of curiosity or some misplaced loyalty to Dr. Wyatt, Ham didn't know and didn't care—as long as Aggie left her alone.

Ham turned her attention back to her computer, stared at the glowing screen. She felt as if her world were circumscribed by this faintly humming box. For all the information she put into it, all her clever work on programs—at the end of the day it often seemed as if all she had to show for it was eyestrain and a sore neck.

Ham sighed. Her most recent accomplishment was a picture gallery of clients and their babies. It had taken little effort to convince Dr. Wyatt and Cy that it was a good thing to have. People loved babies, loved happy families. What better advertising for a fertility center than a gallery of satisfied customers?

Ham's heart jumped when she heard someone clear her throat behind her. It was Aggie.

"I want to check some records," Aggie said.

Aggie never opened a conversation with 'hello' or 'please.' Ham put a smile on her face. "Right away," she said.

Ham helped Aggie with whatever she wanted, no questions asked. In tacit return, Aggie didn't pry into Ham's work. Ham sweated enough from her bulk. If she thought she had to worry about Aggie sticking her nose in whenever Ham was at the computer, she would live in a state of anxious perspiration.

"I want to know whose samples were sent to the DNA testing center on a particular date," Aggie said.

Ham nodded. So that was who Dr. Cy had been talking to. The clinic sent out samples for DNA testing on a regular basis. Why was Aggie interested in one particular sample date?

Ham opened the file, typed in the type of test she wanted. Then the program offered her a choice of fields. Ham selected 'date.'

Aggie had been watching the screen; now she pushed a piece of paper toward Ham. A date was on it, in Aggie's handwriting. At least she had the decency to rewrite it, Ham thought. She entered the date.

On the screen appeared: NO ENTRIES FOR THIS DATE.

Aggie frowned at the computer as if it had offended her. "What does that mean?"

"Maybe the testing lab made a mistake," Ham said. "No samples were sent on that date."

Aggie didn't look as if she were going to leave it alone. But her phone rang and she bustled off.

Ham let out her breath. The real reason there was nothing for that date was because she hadn't finished entering information from the files of women who had been patients at that time. Ham had started with current patient data and worked backwards. Ham could have told that to Aggie; could have said she was close to entering information from that date; could have told Aggie she would alert her when she got to it. But Ham resented Aggie's spying—particularly on Dr. Cy—and Ham had deliberately misled her.

She hoped Aggie never found out.

43

"What in God's name were you thinking?"

Dr. Wyatt's face was red with blotches of white. Cy had never seen him so angry. As worried as he was about his own predicament, he was more concerned that Dr. Wyatt not have a stroke.

"I don't understand why you're so upset." Cy said it in a calm, low voice, hoping to cool Dr. Wyatt's hot temper.

Dr. Wyatt was nearly spluttering. "These samples going to the DNA lab. How in God's name could you do this to me?"

Cy's mind immediately raced to the director of the DNA lab. Had he said something to Dr. Wyatt after all?

Cy was mortified by the prospect of explaining the two samples he had taken to the DNA lab. For the first time in his life, he considered lying to Dr. Wyatt. He was ashamed that the only reason he wasn't going to, was because he couldn't think up a good story fast enough. The only plausible ones he could think of, would put him in worse trouble than he was already.

If Cy made up a story about taking a sample from the clinic, how could he justify it? Cy knew Dr. Wyatt kept an iron-tight grip on all of the genetic material. It would be a slap in his face to suggest that any eggs or sperm were not well-identified or stored.

For the second time, Cy prepared to explain why he'd wanted the two DNA samples compared. This time was worse than the first. The lab director could just have refused to help him. The way Dr. Wyatt looked today, Cy thought he could lose his job.

"...and your bill at the DNA lab is out of sight!"

Cy's head snapped up. What had he missed hearing?

"Do you hear me?"

Once again Dr. Wyatt had caught Cy unawares. And once again he was blaming Cy for procedures that he himself had put in place. Dr. Wyatt insisted that DNA testing be done on every patient who came to the clinic. He also regularly ordered preimplantation genetic diagnoses of cells from embryos, more than other clinics did. Cy knew Dr. Wyatt was a stickler for perfection. That was hard enough to live up to. But when you also had to play a recurring role as a scapegoat...

Cy was relieved and angry at the same time. He bit his tongue and asked Dr. Wyatt: "What do you want me to do differently?"

Dr. Wyatt frowned as if the question was almost infuriating in its obviousness. "Spend less money! I'm not made of money!"

Cy's head was spinning as he left Dr. Wyatt's office. His mentor had always had a knack for keeping him on his toes. At the beginning of his career, Cy had attributed this behavior to Dr. Wyatt's interest in preparing him to be a good doctor. Emergencies happened and a doctor had to be able to meet them with a clear head and a steady hand. That was one of the reasons they pushed interns so hard—if they could function well under the dual loads of too much work and too little sleep, they would probably be fine in the normal stress of their practices.

But over the years Dr. Wyatt's testing had turned into an almost methodical practice of keeping Cy off balance. Dr. Wyatt pushed his buttons, hit him from every side, until Cy didn't know what was coming at him next. At this point in his career, Cy couldn't fathom Dr. Wyatt's purpose in treating him this way. Nor could he figure out why a brilliant man like Dr. Wyatt made a practice of ordering expensive tests, then blew up when the bills came in. How could he not understand the consequences of his own orders?

But what Cy really didn't understand was why Aggie hadn't told Dr. Wyatt about this morning's call from the DNA lab. She told him everything else. For once she wasn't sticking her nose in. Why not?

44

Betty walked into Cy's office with her face drawn. "I couldn't help hearing his voice when you were with him. Is everything all right?"

Cy had no reservations about sharing his conversation with Dr. Wyatt. There was nothing behind Betty's question but real concern. "He was angry about our bill at the DNA lab," Cy said. "I didn't remind him that samples are sent over because of his clinic procedures."

"How much longer can you take his abuse?"

It was the first time Betty had called it what it was. Cy had the feeling she was asking herself the same question.

"I don't know. I used to think I could live with it. Now I'm not so sure. I owe him a lot, but he seems to be getting worse." Cy had never been so frank.

"I gather that he's under a lot of stress," Betty said. "More than usual. Has he said anything to you?"

It was the first time that Cy thought Betty was fishing. "Out with it," he said. "Tell me what you know and what you really want to know. And I'll do the same."

Betty hesitated, then looked behind her at Cy's door, as if she wished she could lock it. She lowered her voice to a near whisper. "A couple of days ago, I accidentally opened an envelope addressed to Dr. Wyatt. Before I realized it was his, I saw a cashier's check—made out to cash—for $50,000 inside. The return address was Amazing Sweepstakes."

Betty paused, let out a breath. "I put it on Jane's desk, in a stack of mail. That day Jane left for vacation, on the spur of the moment. She hadn't scheduled it, but Dr. Wyatt let her go. The next day, a detective turns up here to tell us that she's dead. Then the other day, a cleaning woman said Dr. Wyatt was on a phone call in his office, screaming something about $50,000 and a sweepstakes."

The news stunned Cy, but he'd asked for it—he had told Betty to be honest. His first instinct was to focus on what Betty had said, and try to summarize what he thought her reactions were. "You're concerned not just about the money he was sent, but that it seems it may have been taken by Jane and figured in her death."

"Exactly."

Cy thought Betty suddenly looked younger, as if five years worth of stress had gone out of her face. "This has been weighing on you, hasn't it?" he asked. He well knew the feeling.

She nodded. "I tell myself that it's not my business, but what if it is and I don't do anything?"

Cy searched her face. "What do you mean—do anything?"

"Don't you think it's unusual that the head of a fertility clinic gets a cashier's check in an envelope from something called Amazing Sweepstakes? For $50,000? Why not a regular check? Why not deliver it in person? Why make it in a form that makes the sender and the receiver completely untraceable?"

Cy shook his head; it was too much too soon for him to have an answer. Betty had had time to think about it. "What do you make of it?" he asked.

"Money laundering?" she suggested.

Cy didn't laugh. "If a lot of money is flowing through here," he said slowly, "why is Dr. Wyatt always worried about the clinic's expenses?"

"I don't know," she said. "Maybe he's spending money somewhere else in addition to the clinic."

Cy was tired and stressed, but he couldn't help the slow smile that crossed his face. "Like the race track?"

"Or fast cars?" Betty said.

Cy was surprised that it felt good to cross the boundaries surrounding Dr. Wyatt. For too long he had held the older man sacrosanct. He had grown up accepting that Dr. Wyatt could never be questioned, contradicted, or disobeyed. Now a $50,000 cashier's check was telling him there were limits.

It was the anonymity of such a large sum that bothered Cy and made him remember Betty's comment. "You said that maybe you should do something about it," he said. "What did you mean?"

"Try to find out who the money came from and what it was for."

They looked at each other. Cy was pretty sure that they would agree they were discussing a hopeless task. "If the point is to make the money untraceable, what would we look for? It was just luck that you happened to open that envelope and saw what was inside. After any money got to him, it would disappear."

For the second time Cy surprised himself; this time because he so easily accepted the premise that Dr. Wyatt was doing something illegal. He reminded himself that just because you don't like the way someone behaves toward you, doesn't make him a criminal.

"What are you thinking?" Betty asked.

"I owe a great deal to Dr. Wyatt," Cy said. "He raised me, saw me through school and medical school, took me into his practice. Yet here I am, ready to believe there may be something negative—even criminal—about his activities."

"So why are you open to the possibility?" she asked.

"Until now, I haven't admitted to myself how many inconsistencies there are in Dr. Wyatt's behavior," he said. "I'd always dismissed my suspicions as disloyal, or due to envy. Now I see these things—the secrecy, the unexplainable anger, the extensive testing—as symptomatic of a troubled man."

"Troubled how?" Betty looked worried. "You don't think he would do anything to hurt a patient?"

"Of course not." Cy was sure about that. His patients' welfare had always been Dr. Wyatt's first concern.

"It sounds as if we're back where we started," Betty said. "Except we're more understanding of him than we were before."

Cy nodded. "Dr. Wyatt has that effect on people. Just when you think you're ready to blow up at him, he turns it around so you feel guilty that you're upsetting him."

"There must be some way to get a handle on the finances of the clinic," Betty said.

Cy saw that Betty wasn't satisfied with just getting her worries off her chest. She wanted to know if they were justified, and if so, to take action.

"God forbid, he's doing something he shouldn't," Betty added. "But if he is and we should have known about it, we could be liable too."

"The billing records may be of some help," Cy said. "I know that Ham has been entering that data on Aggie's orders, since Jane died." He thought some more. "But even if I can see some of those records, and I'm not sure I can, what will they tell us? Any off-the-books money isn't going to show up there."

Betty shivered. "If things keep happening like they've been happening, we may not have to look for evidence. It will come looking for us."

45

Ham was jerked awake by her head falling on her chest. She had never before fallen asleep at work and she was instantly mortified. Her heart thumped fast as she upbraided herself. It was beyond unprofessional behavior; it was unattractive. But then, she thought, just about anything fat people do is unattractive. She said a silent prayer of gratitude that at least she hadn't fallen off her chair. They would never stop talking about it; and if they'd had to help her off the floor...

She shot glances around her; fortunately, no one was nearby. Even Aggie hadn't seen her. Ham lifted her hands to the keyboard and found a Hershey's Kiss stuck to her palm. Her eating was getting out of hand. Shaking her head sadly, she wiped her hands using the roll of paper towels she kept in her desk drawer. She needed to have her hands cleaned regularly, the way she had years ago when she was a small, messy child.

Ham squinted at her computer screen; her nap hadn't helped—her eyes were still tired and dry. She was out of eye drops, so she made herself yawn several times until her eyes watered. After stretching her neck, she went back to entering patient data.

Ten minutes later she was nearly nodding off again. Concerned about the accuracy of the data she'd just entered, she reviewed it carefully. Something rang her alarm bell—at first she thought she might have entered the same data for two clients—until she saw the test dates. This patient's and her husband's DNA samples had been sent to the DNA lab on the date Aggie retrieved from Dr. Cy's notepad.

If for no other reason than to wake herself up, Ham opened the client's file and read through it. It was for a Mr. and Mrs. Hutching. Ham went through the entire file: tests, treatments, drugs, even payments. Everything was normal. Nothing was unusual. As far as she could see, there was nothing here to make Dr. Cy interested in them.

Ham continued entering client information, although she feared she was going to fall off her chair from exhaustion or boredom.

46

Although Betty had thought several times about Rose since their first meeting—hoping she would call, hoping she was safe and that her husband hadn't hurt her again—she was still startled to hear the young woman's voice on the other end of the line.

"Dr. Winter? I need to talk to you. I won't take much of your time, but I have to see you in person. Can you meet me at the Fairfield Library today, at one?"

She had said it in one breath and with such urgency in her voice, that Betty had simply looked at her schedule, made sure she was free, and said 'yes.'

****

Betty was startled to hear her name spoken by the woman who slunk quickly past her.

Shabby and unkempt, the waiflike figure and her clothes looked unwashed. The face fleetingly turned to Betty was haggard, with dark shadows under her eyes.. Betty recognized Rose only by her voice.

The retreating figure was so different from the well-groomed young woman who had sat in her office just days ago, that Betty stood rooted to the sidewalk, staring after her. What had happened to make her look and move like a hunted creature? And why had Rose just changed their meeting place to the town green?

Betty was about to call out to Rose, but something told her not to. What was going on?

Her silk blouse began to cling to a damp back, and Betty regretted that they wouldn't be meeting in an air-conditioned space. But if Rose's appearance was any indication of what was to come, the discomfort of sweating would be the least of her worries.

As she walked toward the intersection, on her way to the green, Betty felt the hot sun burning her scalp. Whenever it got this hot, she remembered that weekend in college, just before she graduated. She had finished all her exams and gone with friends to the beach to celebrate. She hated suntan oil and hadn't used any. Betty had ended up just short of sun poisoning, with a reddish, puffy body that couldn't stand the touch of clothes for three days. She had stayed in her room while her roommate brought her food and sprayed her entire body with sunburn spray. Thank God she had been able to attend graduation.

Where was the suntan oil for this situation? Betty hoped she wasn't going to be burned by offering to help Rose. While waiting for a light to cross Old Post Road, she was newly conscious of people near her: Two young women with bags from the nearby lingerie store, giggling over their purchases. A man in a suit, smelling of onions and finishing a bag of potato chips. When the light changed, Betty hurried across the street, down the sidewalk past the short strip of stores and onto the tree-shaded Sherman green.

At the center of the green was Betty's destination—a large, white, elevated pavilion. To reach it, Betty had to thread her way through young mothers and children sitting on blankets on the grass. As she glanced at happily waving little feet and hands, she felt that familiar twinge of loss and regret.

At the top of the steps to the pavilion, she paused to mop her forehead with a tissue, then crossed to the far side. Leaning against the rail, she looked over the green, appreciating Rose's choice. It was public enough to have people on all sides, yet it provided an elevated vantage point and enough distance to prevent anyone from eavesdropping. Where was Rose? She should have gotten here first.

A voice close behind her made Betty spin, both startled and provoked.

Misery was written all over Rose's face. She looked even more vulnerable than she had in the clinic. "Oh, Rose, I'm sorry," Betty said. "You just scared me."

"You said I should call if I needed help," Rose said. But her face and body said something else. Betty knew when someone was ready to run. Say something to keep her here long enough to try to help her, she told herself.

"Rose, I understand. I can help you."

Betty had meant it, she had helped others, but it sounded pat. Rose looked crushed, as if she'd already been brushed off. Her gaze swept Betty, as if taking in every expensive detail of her outfit.

"No, you can't even imagine," Rose whispered. She backed away, shaking her head, and Betty saw ugly bruises the length of her neck.

There was no chance Betty was going to let the girl go back to that. "You think I don't know what an abusive husband is like," Betty said. "I do."

Rose turned, trudged toward the stairs.

Betty didn't want to use it, but she was desperate. "I lost a baby," she said.

47

Rose walked back slowly, reluctantly.

"It was after I lost the baby," Betty said.

Old grief sabotaged Betty, tightened her throat. Second thoughts about baring her soul to an almost-stranger made her hesitate. But Betty shook them off; she had made a decision.

"I needed some comfort from him, especially that morning, but when Trowe woke up, he was cold and remote. He kept sighing and starting to say something, as if he didn't know how to begin. I'd seen him do that so many times. Something had occupied him all night, tortured his thoughts, robbed him of sleep. That something usually turned out to be my fault.

"I should have known better, but I wanted him to hold me, to talk to me, so I asked him what was troubling him. Finally he asked, 'Why did you have to go out?'

"He was talking about the night I went out with a girl-friend to dinner. Afterwards, on our way back to the car, we heard a commotion. Then we heard feet running. A man ran right into me and knocked me down. I went to the hospital, but I lost the baby the next day."

Betty looked down to where her sweaty hands were tearing a tissue to shreds. "I could have screamed at Trowe. It was so unfair, so crazy for him to say that. I'd been careful since before I got pregnant. What I ate, the exercise I got, even the kinds of things I thought and said. I cut down my working hours early in my pregnancy, went to my doctor regularly, followed everything he told me to do."

Betty stopped to swallow.

"What Trowe said." Betty stopped again. She glanced at Rose, who was watching her closely. "I didn't know where it came from. He knew how careful I'd been, how much I wanted that baby. What had he expected me to do differently? Going out to dinner wasn't careless. He knew all of that, yet not only did he give me no comfort, he acted as if losing the baby was my fault.

"When I told him that, he said I'd misunderstood him, that he hadn't meant anything. That was typical of him, too. He'd back off after he made a jab. Talking with him was like boxing with a shadow."

Before, Betty had been perspiring heavily. Now she began to shiver. "By then I didn't want to be anywhere near him. I packed up and went to my sister's. He never came for me."

Betty looked at Rose. "Trowe had a knack for making me doubt myself and feel guilty. I started thinking maybe he was right, that maybe I had subconsciously not wanted the baby, and had somehow attracted that accident. I knew that wasn't true, but I couldn't shake the doubt."

Betty wasn't going to reveal the worst part about the whole thing; what she had already shared was bad enough. But something made her tell it. "Later I found out Trowe was the man who ran into me."

Rose's dark-rimmed eyes searched Betty's face. She nodded. "I believe you."

At first, Betty was too shocked to register any emotion. Then, feeling as if she'd been made a fool of, she inhaled, ready to blast Rose.

Rose must have seen it coming. "I had to know if I could trust you," she said. "Somebody is trying to kill me. I had to make sure it had nothing to do with you."

48

Betty still didn't know whether to be insulted or stunned. She had suspected abuse, but not attempted murder.

"He hits me sometimes," Rose told her. "Usually it's when he's had a bad day at work. I always thought I could handle him. That I knew what not to say, how to stay out of his way. I never thought he really meant to hurt me.

"But last week, right after our appointment with you, I was out for a walk in our neighborhood, and I came home a different way than I usually do. I cut through the neighbor's yard, tripped over a tree root and fell flat on my face. I heard voices but I didn't pay attention to them. Until I heard someone say: 'Rose dies.'

"There was a hedge between me and the road. I could see a car parked at the curb. There were two men in the front seat, and the driver's window was open. I stayed down and listened. I thought I was being paranoid and I must have heard wrong. But I heard one of them say: 'So it has to look like an accident.'"

Rose's dirty face was wide open with bewilderment.

"I thought—my husband wants me dead. But why? We were trying to have a baby. It just didn't make sense. But who else would want to kill me? And why?"

Rose was wringing her hands and pacing. Betty had to keep moving to stay with her so she could see her face.

"I didn't know what to do. I couldn't go to my husband. Even if he wasn't the one trying to kill me, what would he do to me if I told him a story like that? He's insanely jealous. He'd probably accuse me of having some kind of affair. I had to find out if I was right. So I stayed on the ground for maybe an hour. They never got out of the car. Finally one of them said: 'It's getting too busy. We can't take a chance somebody sees us.' And they left."

Rose stopped, her lips trembling, and Betty thought that was the end of her story. No wonder she looked so forlorn. Where had she been for two days? But there was more to Rose and her story.

"I took a chance, went into the house long enough to get a few things and some money. I didn't know where to go. I couldn't chance going to friends, or even staying at a motel. There wasn't that much cash in the house, and I didn't know who could trace me from credit cards. And I didn't know who was looking for me or what resources they might have."

Rose looked at Betty as if she were invoking a covenant. "Then I remembered you said I should call you, even if I didn't make another appointment."

Betty shook her head, speechless. There was a lot more to Rose than a suffering young wife. "Rose, that took courage and clear thinking. I don't know if I would have had the presence of mind to do what you did."

For the first time, light broke in Rose's face. Despite the dirt, she was almost radiant, like a child who had been praised. Betty was sure that praise was a new experience for Rose. Anger rose when she thought what life must have been like with Rose's husband.

Betty wasn't sure how to broach it. "So you've been sleeping...?"

"Outside." The light was gone.

"Rose, we're going to get you someplace safe. So you have a second chance."

****

Betty kicked off her high heels and peeled off her clothes in relief. A red Chanel-style suit, silk blouse, bra, briefs, and pantyhose went into an uncharacteristic pile on her floor. She couldn't wait for a tub to fill; she stepped into the shower.

Oh, how good it felt. She let the water pummel her sore muscles for a long time before she picked up the soap. Along with perspiration and makeup, Betty washed away all the tensions of her meeting with Rose. The responsibility she felt for the young woman was now taken over by people she trusted. Betty knew Rose was in good hands. And Rose—that young woman had such potential. Betty had been impressed with her intelligence, resourcefulness, and presence of mind. She was sure that Rose would be all right.

****

Wrapped in a soft robe, Betty headed to the kitchen for a nice glass of wine, a salad, and some soothing music. When she passed the living room, something dark, contrasting against the all-cream room, caught her eye.

Men's pants legs, stretched out in one of her chairs.

49

Something had been wrong with the air conditioning system all day. It wasn't cooling the air sufficiently, or removing the moisture. It had been barely tolerable earlier in the day, but now everyone noticed. Staff and patients alike seemed to be in dark moods, but Ham was truly suffering.

Dr. Wyatt had reprimanded Aggie in front of a patient, something he had never done before. Aggie had glared at him—a first for her—but got on the phone and reached a repairman who promised to come out immediately.

Ham thought that her section of the clinic had to be the hottest. She had pulled out her small desk fan for some relief, but Dr. Wyatt told her to 'put that garbage away.' She had turned to chocolate for comfort, but it wasn't helping. She didn't dare cool herself by drinking water, because it sent her to the bathroom, and even that short trip left her dripping with sweat.

Dr. Wyatt had seemed more than angry all day. Ham thought there was an element of anxiety or even fear in him. He had been running back and forth between the lab and his office, and slamming the door behind him. Ham had had trouble concentrating on her work; every time he passed her desk, she flinched. He seemed so tense, as if he might explode at any moment.

****

Dr. Wyatt burst out of the lab, making a beeline for his office. As he passed Ham's desk, the toe of his wingtip caught on the carpeting and he fell flat on his face. There was absolute silence in the clinic, as if everyone were holding his breath.

Ham was frightened, sure she had never seen his face so red. As Dr. Wyatt slowly got to his knees, Ham saw him clutch at his chest. Automatically she reached out to help him, but he pushed her hand away, revealing a wet patch on his pocket. Dr. Wyatt closed his eyes, and his face grayed. Ham swung her head around, looking for one of the other doctors, to ask for help. When Ham turned back to Dr. Wyatt, he was glaring at her.

Her very bad luck.

Dr. Wyatt jabbed a finger at the floor near Ham's desk, where a few candy wrappers lay. "I slipped on those wrappers!" He was red again, so red Ham thought his head would burst.

Though her instinct warned her to say nothing, she murmured: "They weren't anywhere near you."

"Don't you tell me where they were." Dr. Wyatt got on all fours, tripped on his lab coat, fell down again. He became angrier and redder, if possible.

"Get out!" he spat through gritted teeth. "Get out."

Ham backed away from him, bumped up against her desk. The heat, the frustration, the undeserved anger pushed her over the edge. Ham had had it.

"I'll get out," she said "You try to do the work by yourself." She groped behind her for her purse; she didn't want to turn her back on Dr. Wyatt, even here, even for a moment.

She clutched her purse to her chest as she edged to the exit, giving him wide berth.

50

"I lost the baby."

Cy had heard that sobbed not once, but three times this week. Three of the women whom Dr. Wyatt had turned over to him, had lost the implanted embryos.

Cy had accepted these patients from Dr. Wyatt with the understanding that Cy would be able to use more simple methods of assisted reproductive technology. But Dr. Wyatt had frustrated Cy at every turn. He had insisted that his own procedures be followed. Cy had ended up being forced to do what he had suspected was Dr. Wyatt's plan all along: to tell these women the clinic could no longer help them.

The woman he was going to see tomorrow had not produced any viable eggs, despite the drugs she was taking. Cy did not want to tell her there was nothing more he could do for her. And he was furious with Dr. Wyatt for having lied to him and put him in this position.

Cy started out pacing in his office and talking to himself, somehow ended up in the lab, next to the liquid nitrogen tanks containing the frozen embryos. Almost as if he were preparing for a test, Cy found his mind reviewing what he knew about embryo freezing and thawing procedures.

Unlike eggs, embryos could be frozen and preserved indefinitely—stored in liquid nitrogen tanks—until they were placed in a woman's uterus at some point in the future.

Embryo freezing had been developed to deal with the extra embryos obtained for an IVF cycle. Although a woman might produce up to thirty eggs in a cycle—by stimulating her ovaries with drugs—no more than three to five of the embryos produced would be placed in her uterus. Implanting more than this number would run the risk of producing quadruplets, quintuplets or even higher birth numbers.

Cy opened the log book for the frozen embryos, flipped through until he found the section with the earliest entries.

Lowering the temperature to -273°C does not poison any metabolic process. It just stops everything. Freezing normally kills cells because over 70% of a cell is water, and when water freezes it crystallizes and expands. The expansion damages the inside of a cell.

But this damage could be avoided in two ways. One, before freezing, remove as much water from the cell as possible. Two, introduce a 'cryoprotectant'—an antifreeze-like solution—into the cell to prevent the formation of ice crystals. It is the permeability of the embryo membrane that allows embryos to be frozen and stay alive.

Cy ran his finger down the list. Stopped on a line where the embryos' donors were listed as deceased.

The method for freezing embryos was relatively simple. The embryos were placed in a solution containing propanediol (the antifreeze) and sucrose (a sugar that stayed outside the cell and pulled water out osmotically). The embryos in the solution were then aspirated into a tiny plastic freezing straw, whose ends were hermetically sealed. The sealed straw was very carefully labeled.

The straw was then placed into a programmed 'freezing machine,' whose temperature was slowly reduced at a tightly controlled rate. Once it was just above freezing, crystal formation was induced. Then the temperature was slowly reduced to about -30°C or -40°C. At this point, the straw was immediately plunged into the liquid nitrogen storage container.

Cy noted the code in the log which identified the location in the liquid nitrogen tank of the straw containing the 'orphan' embryos.

Thawing the embryos required a similar, gradual process. The embryos would die from 'osmotic shock'—swelling and bursting—if they were just placed into the body's normal osmotic environment. Thawing involved placing the embryos in successively more dilute solutions of sucrose to gradually get all the propanediol out and put small amounts of water back into the cell.

Cy reread the procedure for opening the liquid nitrogen tank.

"Dr. Cy!"

Cy ran toward the voice, found the prostrate form of Dr. Wyatt in the office area. "Dr. Wyatt? Are you all right?"

"Get out of here, you idiots!"

Dr. Wyatt swung an arm at Cy, pulled himself to his feet and ran to his office.

"What happened?" Cy asked Aggie. He expected her to be worried, or at least solicitous, but her face was indifferent. Aggie only gave him a shrug.

She doesn't know? Cy thought. What's going on here?

"Where's Ham?" Cy asked Aggie.

Aggie pointed to the parking lot.

51

Cy walked quickly out of the clinic, then ran after Ham's re-treating figure in the parking lot. "Ham! Wait."

She heard him call her, but she just waddled faster under a cooking-hot sun. Even with a headstart, she couldn't out-distance him. He reached her before she got to her car.

"Wait," he said. He walked around her so they were face to face. "Don't go. You know how Dr. Wyatt is. No one can talk back to him. I've known him for years—I grew up with him—and I've never argued with him."

"That's your problem."

Ham was still steaming mad. She could feel sweat pour-ing down her back and between her breasts. Rivulets trickled down her forehead and into her eyes.

"It's your problem if you give up your job just because he blew up at you. He'll get over it. You're doing a great job here and I know you've enjoyed at least part of the work."

He paused and Ham noticed the sweat beading above Cy's lip. For a moment she considered that she might have acted rashly.

"Maybe you could spend a little less time eating in the office."

Ham felt as if he had slapped her across the face. Of all the unexpected, undeserved things to say to her, that had to be the worst. He had no idea why she ate. No idea at all. She let go of any last remnants of caution and lashed into him.

"And maybe you could spend less time sending unautho-rized samples to the DNA lab so I wouldn't have to follow your trail for Aggie."

Shock froze Cy's face. "What do you know about the samples I sent?"

Ham's anger still had considerable momentum.

"As much as Aggie told me. She was eavesdropping on your call; you know that. She keeps tabs on everybody. After you finished talking, she rubbed a pencil over the notepad you wrote the date on. She knew where the call came from, so she had me look up all the samples sent to the DNA lab on that date."

Now Cy looked gray. "What did you tell her?"

Ham was on the verge of telling him to go to hell, to ask Aggie for the answer. But she relented because of the gray face. "The computer said there were no samples sent on that day."

Cy frowned. "But..."

"It was because I hadn't gotten that far back in the patients' files. But I didn't tell her that. And I didn't tell her what I found when I got to that date."

"Thanks," Cy said. He looked shaken.

"Sure. You're welcome. Why didn't you just go through regular channels if you wanted to retest that couple? Or if you wanted to do it off the record, why did you have the DNA lab call you at the office?" She was disgusted at how he'd bungled it.

Cy looked as if he were struggling with something. Then he shrugged, as if he'd given up. "Because it wasn't a couple that I was having tested. The sample was from a child."

Ham had been turning angrily away from Cy. The shock made her totter, then fall against her car. Her hands began to tremble until the keys they held jingled. Her voice was a choked whisper. "So that's what he was doing."

"What is it, Ham? What's wrong?" Dr. Cy reached for her, but she managed to push him away.

Her throat felt as if someone were squeezing it. "From a child? The Hutchings didn't have a baby. I remember their file. They went through several IVF cycles but they didn't get pregnant."

It was unspeakable, but Ham had to say the words. "He stole their embryo and gave it to someone else."

52

Shock made Betty's heart beat so violently she thought it would explode in her chest. What kept her legs from buckling must have been anger, because within seconds she had grabbed a marble candlestick and pulled her arm back to swing it. Somewhere in the anger and adrenaline was a flicker of gratitude: She knew she could count on herself to defend her life.

"Get out of this house before I call the police." She said it to the back of the chair, through teeth clenched tight so they wouldn't chatter.

The man in the chair stretched, turned his head to look at her. "You lost weight," he observed. Trowe sat there, long and elegant.

Betty was furious that he had frightened her, furious that he had broken into her home. And fury made her face flame at his gall. "Get out of here, Trowe."

He uncrossed his legs, motioned her to sit. "We have to talk."

"There's nothing I have to say to you."

He sniffed several times.

Betty curled her mouth with disdain. "Get your cocaine nose out of my life before I forget I took a vow to save lives, not end them."

"It's not what you think. It's a cold." Trowe was on his feet, defending himself. "I wasn't using drugs that night and I'm not now. You know I never did."

Betty lowered the candlestick, more because it was getting heavy than because she still wouldn't love to hit him.

"You always did rewrite history," she said. "Your stories always changed to suit you, make you look good or blameless. Whose fault is your life now, Trowe? You've got—if you're still at the CDC—a good job, a career. What did you foul up now and who has to pay for it?"

"I wasn't using drugs." He was angry now and Betty again readied herself to swing the candlestick. "I was running away from something I saw."

"No one is running after you now. What's your excuse for breaking into my home?"

Trowe looked as if he was going to tell her another story, and Betty felt her face pull into a mask of disgust. It must have brought him up short; Trowe closed his mouth.

"They're making children take the drugs," he finally said. "It's killing them."

So he did want something from her. What was it this time? Absolution? Comfort? Advice? Whatever he wanted, he had come to the wrong place.

"You knew that when you went there. Don't look to me for sympathy—or anything else."

"It's not what the studies showed..." he began.

So he was going to take that tack, Betty thought. He was going to hide behind the so-called scientific studies used to justify this horror.

"Oh, b..." Betty bit her tongue. She wasn't going to be driven to profanity by him. "Then you wanted to be taken in by them," she said. "To get a big job in a big place with big money. You're not stupid, Trowe, and it isn't hard to figure out. Your *pandemic* isn't even a disease. It's a syndrome."

"Only fringe groups parrot that," he said. But he didn't sound convinced.

"You're a scientist, Trowe. To prove that a germ causes a disease, the germ has to satisfy all three of Koch's postulates. Remember? First the germ must be found growing abundantly in every patient and every diseased tissue."

"This is the third millenium," Trowe said. "Koch has been taken too literally and too seriously for too long."

"Second, the germ must be isolated and grown in the laboratory."

"In the last century we've made progress in technology far beyond Koch's fantasies," Trowe said.

"Third, the purified germ must cause the disease again in another host," Betty finished.

"Koch's postulates are far from absolute in the real world," Trowe said. "They belong in the classroom, and maybe not even there anymore."

Betty couldn't believe that this was a man whose science had been touted by the *Times*. "Technology is continually outdated, Trowe. But logic is permanent."

Trowe waved a hand as if he were dismissing her.

"If you don't want Koch's postulates, then with what rigorous scientific rules do you propose to replace them?" she asked. "You need to have some scientific standards."

"What background do you have, to understand the science?" he asked, but he didn't look at her when he said it.

"I have a brain and I understand the concept of cause and effect. Tell me what evidence there is for the existence of AIDS."

"That microbe has caused a disease the likes of which this world has never seen," Trowe said. "It makes the Black Plague look like a skinned knee."

"That isn't an answer. It's a quote from someone's P.R. speech. You can't prove a disease exists simply by making a declaration of it in a press conference. You have to have proof."

"Millions of people are dying," Trowe said.

Betty nodded. "Millions of people are dying," she agreed. "They're dying from diseases that were unrelated to your pandemic until someone conveniently swept them under its tent. They're dying from the use of illegal drugs that destroy the immune system. And they're dying from the use of legal drugs that their own manufacturers label as poisons—drugs that were never intended to be used the way you're using them."

"We're trying to save lives."

"You're trying to save lives? How? By patenting a test for an innocuous microbe, and pocketing the royalties? By convincing people all over the world that the presence of this microbe is sufficient justification for taking drugs that destroy them? By forcing people to give these drugs to their children?" Betty's stomach turned. "Who is it helping beside the people who are making money from it?"

From the expression on Trowe's face, Betty thought he might just as well be a big animated black nutcracker. "It's scientifically established protocol," he said.

"Is that what they call it?" Betty's voice dropped to a whisper. "You should think about what they're doing. For God's sake, Trowe, of all people you should understand. You're black."

He looked at her as if she were trying to pull him into the deep end of a pool.

"If a pandemic is declared to exist in a press conference— not proven in scientific journals, by scientists—what happens next? If proof isn't required in science, how long before it isn't required in law?" Betty asked.

"Now you sound like some of the radicals at the ACLU. Carrying something to crazy extremes."

Betty didn't remind him that, if it weren't for organizations like the ACLU, he might never have gone to college. "How long before the courts can say: 'Doctor, we don't have any of your so-called proof that you killed a man. But we don't need it. Proof is an outdated concept. We have other, more sophisticated methods that tell us that you did it. No, we can't explain them to you. We don't have to. We're the law.'"

Betty felt a chill just talking about it. It wasn't so long ago that they were saying things like that to blacks.

Trowe had had a disdainful look on his face, but Betty now saw a wavering look in his eyes.

"If we throw away logic, we allow anyone with power to do anything he wants to us," she said. "Anytime he wants. Science is the last bastion of truth. I've always believed that. Don't let them tell you it's all right to dispense with the truth. Not even once."

"You're talking about two different situations." But his voice wasn't convincing.

Betty shook her head. "You can't have it both ways. You can't keep a dangerous concept in a box, let it out when it suits you. It's like a real disease. It finds its way in everywhere."

"It's just as well you got out of the public health business," Trowe told her. "You would ruin everything."

"No. I would just prevent people from being ground up and spit out by individuals like you. You and your ilk are the worst because you know the truth, yet you hide it for your own profit."

Trowe stalked toward the door. "I came here to help you," he said. "But you don't need anyone's help, Betty."

Tears jumped to her eyes, but anger steadied her voice and her face. "I needed a husband who didn't kill my baby. I needed a husband who didn't try to blame it on me so he could drive me away."

He didn't turn around. "You would never have forgiven me."

Betty said nothing. For once, he was probably right.

Trowe paused at the door, turned his head to her. "I wanted to tell you how they manage to get so many people to tow the party line. But you're so smart, you'll figure it out."

Betty assumed this was just another of Trowe's stories, so she ignored it. "One last question," she said. "What happens when they decide they have one more black man than they need for their conspiracy?"

Trowe slammed himself out the front door. Betty still didn't know how he'd gotten in.

53

Cy stood in the sweltering heat of the parking lot after Ham left, paralyzed by two terrible revelations. He had been on the brink of a pit. Had Dr. Wyatt fallen into it?

What else was I doing at the liquid nitrogen tank, if not to take an embryo?

It was no relief for Cy that he hadn't even touched the tank, let alone stolen an embryo. The thought, the intention had been bad enough. Nor was his guilt lessened by the fact that he had only wanted to help a woman desperate to have a baby. Or that Dr. Wyatt had put every stumbling block he could in Cy's way. No reason could justify stealing a potential human life. God only knew what had motivated Dr. Wyatt to take the Hutching embryo. It briefly occurred to Cy that tormented guilt might explain Dr. Wyatt's short temper and aberrant behavior.

A thunderclap of a thought hit Cy. An alternate explanation for the existence of the little girl in the grocery store had occurred to him. Why had it taken him so long to think of it? Was his mind getting slow or was he jumping to too many conclusions? He retraced his steps, running back into the clinic and hurrying to his office.

This time Aggie was right behind him. "You're not leaving, are you? What about Dr. Wyatt?"

Even in his hurry, Cy didn't miss Aggie's tone. She seemed much more concerned about what Dr. Wyatt might do than what might happen to him. Cy didn't answer her at once; he was busy calling up patient files on his computer, searching for a name and an address.

"Dr. Wyatt is just fine, Aggie. He just tripped. He doesn't need me. I have to go out."

"But..."

Cy glanced at her face. She really did seem to be reluctant to be left here alone with Dr. Wyatt. When had that happened?

"He'll be fine."

Cy wrote down the information he wanted and raced out of the clinic to his car.

Both he and Ham had jumped to the same awful conclusion. Now Cy realized there were other explanations for the child's existence. For one, the Hutchings might have gone to another doctor, or even several other doctors. They might even have gotten pregnant by themselves, with no help from the medical profession.

Cy pulled out of the parking lot, headed down the Post Road toward Bridgeport.

Cy knew there was no love lost between Dr. Wyatt and Ham. But Ham's reaction to the revelation had been intense, almost personal. Why? Was there some complaint she had had against Dr. Wyatt even before she came to work at the clinic? It crossed Cy's mind that Ham might have a sister or close friend who had had an embryo stolen.

Stolen? Cy was still assuming that Dr. Wyatt had taken the Hutching embryo. He revised his guess. Maybe Ham had a sister or close friend who had come to the clinic, failed to get pregnant, and now held a grudge against Dr. Wyatt.

Cy drove a little more slowly as he considered this alternative and its implications. Ham was smart. Even if she'd jumped to a conclusion, she would still check it out. The only way she could be sure was to visit the Hutchings. If they had never had a child, then Dr. Wyatt was guilty.

Cy increased his pressure on the accelerator.

****

As Cy drove through Black Rock he pulled out the street address of the Hutchings. Cy hoped that he could at least undo any of Ham's damage. He was afraid that he was already too late to prevent it. He wondered how Ham's visit would look to the Hutchings. Their last visit to the clinic had been two years ago. Now someone from the clinic was visiting them, asking questions that stirred up old wounds. For what purpose? At best, it might seem like some aggressive marketing attempt. And what if they called Dr. Wyatt, to question him or to complain? Cy asked himself the same question over and over. What was driving Ham to do this?

Finally he asked himself the question he didn't want to answer: What if Ham was right?

****

Cy had had trouble finding the address. When he pulled onto the Hutchings' street, he was sure he'd arrived long after Ham had left. He parked his car and hurried up the steps to the front door. At the door, he glanced up and down the street. He was surprised to see Ham walking away from him, about a hundred yards distant.

Anger made him pause and almost decide to do whatever damage control he could now, then talk to Ham later. He didn't trust himself not to blow up at her. But he decided that it made more sense to find out what she had said and what she had learned, before he went in. It might help him to smooth things over with the couple.

Cy hurried down the steps and after Ham. He lost sight of her behind some trees and shrubs for a few moments, and when he saw her again, there was a man walking quickly behind her.

Nothing was good about the way the man looked and the way he was walking. Cy's heart raced as he jumped down onto the sidewalk and ran, yelling. Ham began to turn. Cy saw the man grab Ham, swing her around to face him. Cy screamed "Stop!" but the man acted as if he hadn't heard him.

Now standing in front of Ham, the man pulled his arm back. A slight glint told Cy that what he held was a blade. With a fast cutting motion, he drew several large X's across Ham's midsection. Cy ran helplessly, watching in horror as Ham crumpled to the sidewalk. The man sprinted away.

"No!" Cy screamed.

There was a jog in the sidewalk and a lot of overgrown bushes; Cy tripped and fell flat out. The shock jarred and stunned him. He dragged himself to his feet and stumbled around the bushes to the scene of the attack, where he almost collapsed again, out of shock.

There was nothing there.

He jerked his head left and right, expecting to see a bleeding Ham dragging herself away. But there was nothing. It was as if nothing had happened.

Cy stumbled to the spot where he had seen Ham fall just seconds ago. Dropping to his knees, he stared dumbly at the sidewalk, looking for but not wanting to find some trace of her. He ran his hands over the concrete, as if they could feel what his eyes couldn't see.

He felt something and gathered his fingertips to pick it up. He lifted his hand and rubbed his thumb against his fingertips. Nothing wet, no blood.

Only shreds of what looked like foam rubber.

What was going on? He'd shouted to Ham, seen her midriff slashed, run to help her—but found nothing but an empty sidewalk. Why hadn't she waited for him? Where had she gone? Cy got to his feet and made several 360° turns, searching for Ham or any trace of her. Nothing.

He wasn't getting anywhere here, so he ran back to the Hutchings' house and bounded up their stairs. When he knocked at the front door, a face came to the window. The man looked surprised, but clearly recognized Cy.

Mr. Hutching opened the door and invited Cy in. Inside was Mrs. Hutching, playing with a little girl on the floor of the living room. She rolled a tennis ball across the floor to the child, and the child rolled it back to her.

Cy watched the little girl until he was convinced of two things: she was real, and she was the same child Cy had seen at the grocery store.

54

Nothing. Not one entry.

Betty shook her head and looked around her home office as if her furniture would share her surprise. She had entered the name 'Amazing Sweepstakes' in the window of her search engine and waited. She'd expected to get lots of results—including a website and mentions in many other locations. But there was nothing. How could that be?

Amazing Sweepstakes didn't exist.

Why was she surprised? After all, her first reaction to the name had been one of skepticism, that it had just been a front. But she'd managed to discount her impressions since then, and today had expected to find that the sweepstakes existed somewhere.

Betty tried several other search engines but they all came up empty. She felt chilled rather than gratified at having her suspicions confirmed: The person who had sent Dr. Wyatt a cashier's check through the mail hadn't wanted to be tracked. So he had used an untraceable source of money and a nonexistent organization.

Flexing her long fingers over the keys, Betty considered what to do next. A building sense of unease made her feel she had to do something. Both old and new upsets were to blame: The anniversary of the loss of her unborn son. An unsettling encounter with her ex-husband, Trowe. Jane's death following the disappearance of the cashier's check sent to Dr. Wyatt. Getting Rose to a safe place, far from the abuse of a husband who might be trying to kill her.

Keeping things at the boiling point was Dr. Wyatt, who set everyone on edge.

Betty hated to feel helpless. She had chosen a career in medicine nearly as much for the security it offered as for the opportunity it gave her to help others. She saw Dr. Wyatt's connection with large, untraceable sums of money as a serious threat to her hard-won security.

Now she was determined to know more about Amazing Sweepstakes.

Betty knew where to start. She had an old friend in New York City who would help her without a lot of fuss.

As the phone rang, Betty thought through what she knew, what she needed to ask. Though she couldn't remember the post office box number on the envelope, she did remember that it was in New York City. And she was sure that to get a box in the city, you had to fulfill certain requirements. Betty was hopeful that there would be some kind of a trail leading from the box to the person who sent Dr. Wyatt a $50,000 cashier's check.

"Barbara? It's Betty. If you have a few minutes to talk right now, I need your help." Without giving Barbara specifics, Betty briefly explained that she was looking for the person who was behind Amazing Sweepstakes.

"So you think he's just using the company name as camouflage, so people will assume there's nothing valuable in the envelopes he sends?"

"You summed that up perfectly," Betty said. "Doesn't the post office have certain requirements for someone to get a box?"

"Sure does," Barbara said. "And even more requirements for the box to be used by a business. Whoever applied for the box had to bring a proof of address, and a letter on company stationery that authorized that person to open a box in the name of the company. They also had to bring a raised seal of the company, a business certificate, or a tax ID number from the IRS."

"I should be able to find out who runs the company from any of those," Betty said.

"Are you sure all you remember is the name and that it was somewhere in New York City?"

"Yes." Suddenly Betty wondered what she was asking for.

It seemed like looking for a needle in a haystack.

"That might take a while to check," Barbara said slowly. "The information about a box is entered in a computer at each of the post office branches. Someone at another branch can get that information if he has the zip code. Since you don't remember the zip, I'll have to check all of them."

It took the wind out of Betty's sails. She didn't know how many branches there were, but there had to be a lot. "I didn't realize how much work that would be," she said. "I can't ask you to do it. It's a job in itself. It's..."

"Don't start telling me what is or isn't too much work. There are forty-four zip codes in the city. That's not an impossible number. Besides, if someone is using the mail to do something illegal..."

"I can't prove that—yet," Betty said quickly. "It just looks that way." There seemed to be less and less justification for what she planned to do.

Betty heard a long sigh on the other end of the phone.

"But it bothers you enough to call me on a Saturday and ask for my help."

"Yes."

"That's good enough for me. I don't think I can even get to the records until Monday. But I'm going to do my best to find out for you."

"Thank you." Betty had one more question, though at this point, she almost didn't want to ask. "Is it legal for you to get me this information?"

Barbara was ready with an answer; she must have been asked this question many times before.

"Sure. All post office box applicants provide information on PS Form 1093. The US Postal Service is authorized by 39 U.S.C. 403 and 404 to collect the information on that form. And we can disclose that information to anyone, if the box is used for doing business with the public."

Betty could hear the smile in Barbara's voice as she said: "I guess a sweepstakes qualifies. Even if it is a sham."

55

"Dr. Cy."

Cy's mind had been somewhere all day. He looked up at the woman sitting across his desk. She was twisting her wedding band nervously on her finger.

"Is something wrong?" she asked.

Cy shook his head, smiled. "No. Everything's great. We're on track. Just where we want to be."

If only the rest of his life were on track. He had gone to see the Hutchings and found out that they did have a child. And Cy had seen her: It was the little girl he had seen in the grocery store. Of course. It was the most logical and simple explanation. So Dr. Wyatt hadn't stolen their embryo and given it to someone else. Cy winced inside to think that he could even have considered that a possibility.

Now if Ham hadn't been attacked, if Cy hadn't discovered that she had been wearing a fat suit, if she hadn't deceived them all, he might feel better.

When his patient left, Cy pulled his desk drawer open and pulled out an envelope. Inside were some shreds of foam rubber. He had brought them back, as if to prove that he really had seen Ham collapse on the sidewalk. Though there had been no reason to doubt that Ham had visited the Hutchings, Cy had asked them when he went back to see the couple. They confirmed Ham had been there before him, and that they had told her the same thing they'd told him. They had had a beautiful little girl, without the help of the clinic. Simple and wonderful.

Shreds of foam rubber. Not blood. He kept away from the obvious, not wanting to jump to conclusions as Ham had.

Except that Cy knew he was right about Ham.

She hadn't come to the clinic because she needed the job, but to do some kind of an investigation. And she had disguised herself in order to do it. Cy thought his wild guess about Ham was probably right: She knew someone who had come to the clinic and failed to get pregnant—and couldn't handle the failure. So she had cooked up some kind of conspiracy with Dr. Wyatt at the center. Ham had gotten the job at the clinic so she could find evidence. And after two years, all she had come up with was the mistaken suspicion that Dr. Wyatt had stolen the Hutchings' embryo.

It explained a lot about Ham. The way she kept to herself. Her interest in computers—where she would have access to all aspects of the clinic's business. The long hours she put in. Her willingness to do extra work.

And her fat disguise.

Cy didn't think there was any other explanation for it. There was no way that an overweight woman could sustain the slashing that Ham had gotten, and live. Not to mention walk away and not leave any blood trail. Just shreds of foam rubber.

Cy wondered what Ham was going to do, now that she knew her suspicions about Dr. Wyatt were unfounded. She had lost her job at the clinic, had her disguise blown—and had nearly been killed because she had been in the wrong place at the wrong time. Cy was surprised that he felt a stab of loss—as if he were remembering a loved one who had died—when he realized he would never see Ham again.

Cy pushed away from his desk, started pacing his floor. Why should he miss her at all? Yes, she had been an unusually gifted young woman. But he had gone out on a limb to hire her, and she had used the clinic and him for her own purposes.

It was funny. What bothered him most about Ham was that she hadn't confided in him. Though he couldn't have expected her to. She had probably seen him the way most other people did—as a loyal disciple of Dr. Wyatt.

That reminded Cy of something he'd been trying to push out of his mind—his near brush with embryo theft. It had been a wake-up call to dial down the intensity with which he did everything. For Cy, everything needed to have a certain outcome—what *he* thought should happen. He shuddered when he thought how close he had come to doing something terrible and irreversible because he couldn't stand for things to happen otherwise. He had somehow decided it was so important for him to help his patient have a baby that he had contemplated stealing an embryo to make it happen. Forget that the donors of the embryo were deceased. The embryo hadn't been his to take. The decision hadn't been his to make.

The pressures of the clinic weren't going to diminish. Cy told himself he would have to tread carefully.

56

He emerged from the Egyptian temple and crossed to the water. It was evening and the moon was reflected next to his face on the gently undulating surface. He stood staring at the water, letting the wavering images hypnotize him.

Another face materialized next to his in the water. "Champagne or white wine?" it asked.

Dr. Wyatt accepted another glass of champagne and turned reluctantly to study the other guests—hundreds of select invitees were milling about. The hall of the Temple of Dendur was cavernous; the glass vaulted space contained the temple, a large rectangular pool of water, and an enormous expanse of stone floor to accommodate the museum's daily visitors, as well as parties like the benefit tonight.

He recognized many of the wealthy and powerful individuals in the room from their pictures. Although Dr. Wyatt spent a good part of his life peering through a microscope, at events like these, he felt like the object of scrutiny. To him there were two kinds of people: those who ran the show and those who played small parts in it. Those who were patrons and those who were catchers of crumbs. Dr. Wyatt still felt like a catcher of crumbs. Despite his success, despite all the people who applauded his skill, who came to him with prayers in their hearts and money in their hands, he never felt as if he'd crossed the line from the have-nots to the haves.

Still, the sea of people intrigued him. He was fascinated whenever humans displayed behavior different from other animals. In nature, it was generally the male of the species that was colorful and eye-catching. But at formal events like this one, all the males wore some variation of a black tuxedo. The females wore jewels and glistening fabrics and strutted and preened, proudly baring as much as possible of their fashionably thin bodies.

"What do you find amusing?"

The face at his shoulder was a woman's. Though her individual features were attractive enough, there was such hardness in her face that Dr. Wyatt thought it was money and influence that made her desirable.

He shared his observations about formal dressing.

"It keeps them busy," the woman said. "If they used that energy to compete with me in business, I wouldn't be able to make a cent."

The woman, who ran a matching service for people who wanted to buy donor eggs, suppressed a yawn. "It's not the company. I've been traveling so much overseas I never seem to get over jet lag."

"Then why do you travel so much?" he asked her.

"Business."

He was surprised. "Surely there are enough clients in this city." How much money did she need? There were probably enough clients in this room for several businesses like hers.

"I go where the need is greatest," she said with mock seriousness.

An older woman strode imperiously toward him. It was Mrs. Greene, his rich patroness. She had hosted the dinner party at her mansion a few days ago. Tonight, instead of green silk, she was wearing black. She ignored the first woman and said: "Dr. Wyatt. Dance with me."

On the dance floor, Dr. Wyatt was unusually graceful. He thought it was odd that most people were more surprised by his dancing ability than by his manual dexterity as a doctor. He moved skillfully among the other couples and the lady in his arms appreciated it.

"You never cease to surprise me, Dr. Wyatt," she said. "Nor have you ever disappointed me. Until now."

He must have tensed his body, and she must have sensed his fear.

"I know you want to please me," she said.

She whispered to him, her lips grazing his ear, as they

danced. It took all the control he could muster not to shrink from her touch or push away the mouth that so insistently and relentlessly poured words into his brain.

He had dropped all pretense of leading. She paraded him all over the dance floor, then dropped him on the other side of the room,. "Dr. Wyatt wants to dance with you," she said to someone.

Dr. Wyatt was reeling from what he had been told. He turned his head to see Diane. Practice alone made him smile.

He couldn't think right now about what Mrs. Greene wanted. He felt panicky and trapped by her and he didn't want to lose control, not here. He took Diane in his arms and moved slowly along the side of the room. As if he were learning to dance, he had to tell his feet what to do. As if by doing something normal he could restore some order to his life.

"You look beautiful," he told her. Even now he couldn't help thinking what a waste it had been that she and Cy divorced. They would have made such beautiful and intelligent children.

She smiled. "Thank you, Dr. Wyatt. How are you?"

He shrugged slightly. "Wondering a little what I'm doing here." He had never before said anything unguarded. But what had just happened had never happened before.

Diane seemed inclined to be unguarded as well. "But the kinds of connections you make at these events are just irreplaceable. Where else would I have the opportunity to meet so many of these people?"

"You're too modest. You have a fine practice." He was resentful toward these powers that had brought Diane and him and the others together tonight. They didn't create everything. Diane had built her own practice. He had built his clinic.

Diane kept smiling; she seemed to be bursting with her own news. "Do you know the shopping channel? They've started promoting my skin care line. It's selling out. Isn't that wonderful? Millions of women all over the country saw my products. And so many ordered them. I did the first show two days ago and they want me to do a show every day next week."

Dr. Wyatt felt a chill. He couldn't help wondering what the ulterior motive had been behind the deal. Though he was sure that Diane's products were top notch, there were people all over the country, all over the world, who were developing products. Why choose hers?

He made himself act enthused. "That is wonderful, just wonderful." He smiled a smile to match hers. "It sounds as if it all happened so fast."

"Yes," she said, shaking her head in amazement. "They called me two days before we aired. I can't believe it. But they wanted to get it on television as soon as possible—they said they'd been looking for new skin care products and mine fit the bill. Two days ago we sold as much inventory as we had and they put the rest of the orders on waitlist. And thank goodness for autoship."

Why the rush? Now Dr. Wyatt was sure there was some plan behind it. But he couldn't voice his concerns to Diane. He would just sound like a wet blanket.

"You'll do wonderfully," he told her.

Impulsively, Diane hugged him. Over Diane's shoulder, Dr. Wyatt saw Mrs. Greene watching him and smiling.

57

Ham had always thought that when she finally shed the stifling fat disguise it would be a blessed relief to feel cold again. But the bone-cold shiver she had developed after the slashing attack was not what she'd had in mind. A hot shower, blankets, warm clothing—nothing could drive the chill out of her blood. All she could think of was that the man could have cut higher. If he had aimed at her throat... Her teeth chattered so hard she thought they would shatter.

Where had he come from? Though he had ripped her purse from her, Ham still didn't believe his motivation had been robbery.

Ham hugged the blanket tighter. She had been wrong about Dr. Wyatt. She had been convinced he had taken the Hutching embryo and given it to another couple. But Ham had seen the little Hutching girl herself.

Dr. Wyatt had proven himself over and over to be a completely callous man, who thought himself above all others. But apparently he didn't steal embryos.

Shaking herself, Ham craned her head over the top of the blanket to survey her motel room. She hadn't returned to her apartment. The attack had spooked her. Though she'd told herself repeatedly the attack had been coincidental, Ham had taken it as a sign. For months now she had been prepared to move quickly. She had kept her laptop in her car, along with a packed suitcase. They were all she thought she would need.

So why did she miss those few small rooms of hers? If only for a matter of months, they had been her home. As many times as she'd had to pick up and go in the past, it had never gotten easier. A permanent sanctuary—however simple—seemed the most desirable thing in the world to her.

Huddled on the bed, Ham turned her coffee mug in her

hands for warmth. The room was pleasant enough. But the fact she had been forced out of her apartment made this room just another way station on a never-ending run. She put the mug on the nightstand next to the clock. It was early afternoon; she had lots of time before it got dark.

Still hugging the blanket to her, she shuffled to the window. The sun was shining and the sky was a clear blue. It was picture postcard perfect, but Ham knew it was over 90° in the shade. She shivered. For two years she couldn't go out in the heat because her fat suit would have killed her. Now she couldn't go out because there were people who would kill her.

Ham left the window and shuffled to the desk. Doing some work on her laptop would hopefully take her mind off her troubles and might even relieve the shivering.

It took less time than she'd expected to hack into Connecticut's police computer and search their files. She unfolded the piece of paper containing the license number of the black Mercedes that had chauffeured the pseudopregnant woman in chiffon to Dr. Wyatt's office. Ham had meant to check it earlier, but hadn't gotten to it.

Now she typed in the license number, hoping there was no way for the police to trace this search to her computer. She didn't need to be hunted by them as well.

While she waited, she thought about what she would do if this lead turned out to be worthless. Since the attack, she had had an overwhelming urge to just leave everything behind and run. Though she had always thought people who just wanted a peaceful life were on the unambitious side, right now she would snatch the opportunity to live an anonymous life in any small town in the country.

But even before the police files gave her the information, Ham knew she wasn't going anywhere. She had struggled, sacrificed and worked her way to this point. Now, on the verge of finding out, she wasn't about to give up. Let the bad guys run.

The Mercedes owner's name finally appeared on the screen. It was not what she had expected. Her fault was that she had been thinking too small.

58

Cy was halfway to Ledyard before it occurred to him to question the message he'd just gotten from Ham.

Why had she used an email instead of calling him? Why did they have to meet so far away? And why at a casino?

Cy hadn't had to think twice about going to meet her. Although he now knew she had been wearing a fat disguise when she was attacked—and had had padding to protect her—he was relieved to know she was all right.

He was speeding north on I-95 with such purpose that his hands seemed fused to the steering wheel, and his eyes stared at the highway as if he could see all the way to Ledyard.

Considering she had used him, he was surprised at how much he wanted to see her again.

****

Cy offered the man three one-hundred dollar bills. The man shook his head, motioned toward the green felt table top. When Cy put the bills down, the man fanned them out, then pushed them through a slot in the table.

"Color?" he asked.

Cy shook his head. "Dollar chips." He searched the faces of the other people at the table. She's not here yet, he thought.

The croupier pushed several stacks of chips toward Cy, then said to the crowd at the table: "Place your bets."

Cy dropped several chips onto the nearest square, then circled the room with his eyes. He was peripherally aware of a frenzy of jostling elbows and hands and the clicking sound of chips being dropped into position.

A tiny woman with white hair pushed three purple chips into Cy's hand. "Would you put these on number five, please."

He did; she nudged him again. "The minimum is ten dollars," she whispered, nodding at the sign on the table.

Cy put five more chips down. As the roulette ball circled the slowly revolving wheel, Cy wondered just why he had driven two and a half hours to get here. Did he think Ham needed his help, or did he just want to see her again?

"Place your bets," the little old woman at his elbow said.

Cy looked down at the swept-clean table. He had completely missed the previous spin. He put down more chips. The ball spun again.

"YAY!"

"WAY TO GO!"

"JACKPOT!"

The outburst startled Cy and took his attention to a nearby stud poker table. A young woman was high-fiving her friends while the taped jackpot jingle played. When Cy turned back to his roulette table, he found a young blonde cocktail waitress at his elbow. She was putting a drink down at his place at the table.

"I didn't order anything," he said.

"It's complimentary," she murmured.

"Thank you." He handed her a chip.

When was Ham going to show up? It was noisy, smoky and crowded. He wondered how they were going to have a conversation here.

The people around him were shoving their chips onto the gaming table. Cy lifted his glass out of harm's way, and noticed that the clinging cocktail napkin had something written on it.

Gift shop downstairs — Ham

How had she gotten the message to him? Cy scanned the room, looking for Ham. Why didn't she just come over and talk to him? It finally hit him that he was still looking for the old Ham, the one in the fat suit. He had no idea how she looked without her disguise. She could be sitting right next to him at the roulette table and he wouldn't know.

Cy picked up his remaining chips and put them in his pocket. As he left the roulette area, he asked an employee, circulating with a dust pan and broom, where he could find the gift shop.

"Go to the front entrance and down two flights of stairs. It's on your left."

The clanging of slot machines filled his ears as he passed rows of people sitting mesmerized, pulling handles or pushing buttons. Even though he was intent on getting to Ham, he couldn't help noticing the sounds, the colors, the games. There had to be something for everyone. His eye was caught by a game that challenged the player to rearrange a sequence of letters to form a word: TONIECEPD. In spite of himself, he rearranged the letters of the anagram as he walked.

****

Downstairs, it was almost hushed in the corridor leading to the gift shop. The shop was small enough for him to immediately see it held no one but the cashier. He entered and walked around, looking at the items on the shelves, and watching who entered.

After waiting for twenty minutes, he crossed to the cashier.

"Is this the only gift shop in the casino?" he asked. Why else wouldn't Ham have shown up?

The cashier nodded. She was putting small cigarette lighters in a display case and dropped one of the lighters at Cy's feet. He picked it up, saw it had a piece of paper taped to it.

Don't say anything. Just put this on the counter and buy it.

Cy followed directions, then glanced at the cashier's face. Could she be Ham?

"I'll take this lighter."

"That will be $25 with tax."

Her voice was soft, but Cy recognized it immediately. His heart beat fast and he tried not to stare at her. As he fumbled for his wallet he shot glances at her. She was slim, with blonde hair that brushed her chin. When he caught himself staring at her arms, he realized it was the first time he had seen them bare. How uncomfortable she must have been in the stifling disguise she wore. What kind of motive could have sustained her through the long months she worked at the clinic?

As she took his money, he couldn't help disobeying her note. "Why did we have to meet so far away? Why all the secrecy? I know someone tried to kill you, but he can't even know who you are." He didn't want to say it, but he thought all of this cloak and dagger stuff was going overboard.

She rang up the sale, put his money in the register and made change. When she handed him his money, he recognized the familiar eyes.

"Why didn't he take anything from me?" she said.

"I saw him take your purse."

She shook her head. "He pulled it off so I couldn't use it like a shield. He dropped it when he ran."

That unsettled Cy. An unprovoked attack, and no money motive?

"Dr. Wyatt didn't steal the Hutching embryo," he said.

"I know."

"So you couldn't have been attacked because you'd discovered something someone wanted to hide." It sounded outlandish when he heard these words come out of his mouth. Like a story from a crime drama.

"So why did this man appear as soon as I left their house?" she asked.

"I don't know." How could he know? How could he guess? "Maybe he was on drugs and you were just in his way."

From the change in Ham's eyes, Cy saw that she hadn't considered that possibility, and that it somehow gave her comfort. He reflected that we lived in sad times to take comfort from the fact that an attack had been 'nothing personal.'

Cy could see their encounter was almost over and he wasn't ready to go. There was so much more he wanted to ask her. Why had she come to the clinic? Why did she have such a dislike of Dr. Wyatt? Why had she disguised herself with a fat suit? Where was she staying? How could he get in touch with her? Forget all the grilling questions, an insistent voice inside him said. Just tell her you miss her.

She turned her back to him as she wrapped the lighter in a small bag. "So why did you send the child's DNA sample to the lab?"

Why was she asking him that? What difference did it make? And then he understood. Ham wanted to know why Cy had for a moment entertained the idea that Dr. Wyatt might have stolen an embryo. Did Cy have any reason to doubt the older man?

"I wanted to compare it to another sample from many years ago."

As she handed him the bag, his fingers brushed hers and the light friction made his hand tingle. He leaned slightly toward her and breathed, his nose searching for the familiar fragrance she wore. He almost forgot what he was going to ask her.

"How can I get in touch with you?"

She told him to wait while she got something out of the storage room.

Fifteen minutes had passed before he realized she wasn't coming back out.

So why had she brought him up here?

59

Betty held her breath until she saw the HCG level was a good two times what it had been on Friday.

"You're doing just great." Betty hid her relief behind a big smile. "Now I want you to relax and stop worrying." Betty knew that was easier said than done. But if her patient didn't ease up, she could drive herself to a miscarriage.

"I'm worried about when I leave you and go to the obstetrician," Mrs. Monger said.

Betty saw the worry in the dark circles under her eyes, in the way her face was pulled down. This should be one of the happiest times in her life and she's looking for things to upset her, Betty thought.

There was a knock at the door and Aggie appeared. "Is there anything you need, Dr. Winter?"

What is she doing here? Betty didn't think Aggie ever came in on Saturdays. She was only here when Dr. Wyatt was in. "No. Thank you, Aggie."

"I'll be here for a while if you need anything," Aggie said as she left.

If Betty wanted to be paranoid, she might think Dr. Wyatt sent Aggie to spy on her. But there was no reason for that. What could Betty do that was wrong? It wasn't as if the clinic stocked mind-altering drugs that she could sell or give away. And Betty would never even think of seeing patients off the books. Betty shook her head. What she thought about Dr. Wyatt was starting to color how she saw the world. She didn't like that.

"What's the matter?" The voice was frightened.

Mrs. Monger looked alarmed again. Enough, Betty thought. You've got to stop this or you'll harm the baby.

"Look," she told the woman. "You're a very lucky lady.

You're in good health, you've managed to get pregnant and you're doing just fine. And you have a husband who loves you and who would do anything in the world for you. Those are things that most women would give their eye teeth for. Now you have to do your part—be grateful for your blessings."

The woman widened her eyes.

"Count your blessings every day, several times a day. Feel the warmth of grace surrounding you. And smile. That's what your baby needs from you."

Betty had been writing on a prescription pad as she talked to the woman. Now she handed her the top page.

The woman frowned, then smiled. "That's exactly what you've written down here," she said. "It says three times a day." Mrs. Monger nodded her head. "I can do that."

"I'll do my part," Betty said. "I'm always available, here or at home. You have my numbers. But I think you're going to be just fine."

When the woman left, Betty got her things together. She was surprised when Aggie stuck her head in the office.

"Do you have some time to talk, please?"

That was so unlike Aggie that Betty assumed something was wrong and braced herself.

Aggie got to the point quickly. "Dr. Wyatt never liked Jane. And he's made her into a scapegoat since he lost the money."

That was a lot for Betty to digest. She knew about the cashier's check, of course. And she'd heard the cleaning lady say Dr. Wyatt had been yelling about a sweepstakes and $50,000. But Dr. Wyatt hadn't officially said anything about the missing money or his suspicions. Betty didn't want to give herself away.

"What money is that?" She had never been a good liar, so she didn't know if Aggie would buy it.

But Aggie was apparently preoccupied with her own

concerns. She wasn't watching Betty as intently as she usually watched people.

"Some money was sent to Dr. Wyatt. I don't know exactly how much. But he found out it was missing and he suspected Jane because he said it happened just before she left."

Aggie seemed to have more to say, so Betty waited.

"He asked me to look around the clinic and see if I could find out if Jane had any help."

So Dr. Wyatt had asked her to spy on them. Betty wasn't as paranoid as she'd thought.

"Did you find out anything?" Betty asked.

"Not what he was looking for."

The look on Aggie's face stopped Betty. Until now, she had been hoping to make this short and sweet so she could get home and have part of a Saturday to herself. Betty waited again for Aggie to talk.

"It was in his desk."

Betty couldn't stop the words. "You went through his office!" She couldn't imagine anyone entering uninvited into that holy of holies. Let alone the woman who seemed to carry Dr. Wyatt's train.

Aggie nodded, but her face wore a tormented look. "I just knew something was wrong. With the way he's been acting to us, the way he's blamed Jane. That's not the way he used to be. That's not the way someone who's supposed to do so much good acts. He acts like..." she searched the office walls for help... "like some kind of drug dealer who's angry about someone stealing his money or moving into his territory."

Betty was as startled by what Aggie said as she was by the aptness of the comparison.

"There was a letter from a detective agency," Aggie said. "Dr. Wyatt is still looking for Clea."

Betty frowned. There might be a reasonable explanation for that. "Dr. Wyatt was close friends with Dr. Cy's adoptive parents. He adopted Dr. Cy after his parents and Clea died in the fire. It might have been hard for him to accept that they were really gone since the fire was so consuming." Betty had heard from Cy that only his adoptive father's physical remains had been found in the ashes of the house.

"But looking for her twenty years after a fire that was supposed to have killed all three of them? You don't think that's strange? A doctor who was there at the fire can't accept that those people are gone? He's paying money for twenty years to have someone look for her. Maybe he's crazy."

Betty didn't want to jump to conclusions. "Are you sure the letter was recent? Maybe it was an old letter. There may have been some reason, right after the fire, to look for Clea."

"The date on the letter was last week," Aggie said. "I think there's something wrong with him still looking for her. As if he's hunting her."

Suddenly Betty wanted very much to know the contents of the letter. She was surprised, because normally she wouldn't be curious about another person's affairs. And particularly in this case, since Aggie found the letter only because she had deliberately gone through Dr. Wyatt's desk.

"What did the letter say?" Betty asked.

"That the detective had some information that he would only tell Dr. Wyatt in person."

Well, that takes care of that, Betty thought. She was still mystified as to why Aggie had confided in her. "What do you want me to do?"

Aggie shrugged her shoulders in a helpless way. "I just had to tell somebody."

60

Dr. Wyatt pulled back his arm and swung it with all his force. The ball whizzed over the net and landed just in bounds with a loud thunk.

"Easy! Save some of that for later." His partner, Dr. Pinder, had missed the shot and was already panting and sweating heavily.

What was driving him to push himself so hard? What if he damaged something in his hands or his arms? What would I do if I couldn't practice medicine again? he asked himself. I wouldn't want to live.

Dr. Wyatt stared at the net, thinking about the fire twenty years ago.

His partner, Cy's adoptive father, had died that night. Cy had escaped, but what had happened to Clea and her mother? He had been there that night. He knew no trace of either of them had ever been found in the house. Had their bodies been entirely consumed by the flames, or had they gotten away? He had never been able to find out.

Dr. Wyatt had paid a series of investigators to search for Clea and her mother for twenty years. The fact that in all that time there had never been any trace of either of them had never lessened Dr. Wyatt's hopes. He didn't take the absence of information as evidence that the mother and daughter were dead. He alternately credited the mother's ingenuity or the incompetence of the investigators.

"Heads up!" Dr. Pinder served an easy shot and Dr. Wyatt knocked it back, just out of the man's reach. Dr. Pinder went running for it.

Clea's mother. As far as Dr. Wyatt was concerned, when that woman took Clea away, she stole something that was his. The twenty years that had elapsed had only made him more aware of his loss, not less.

"Your serve." Dr. Pinder stood, his spindly legs spread far apart and braced for Dr. Wyatt's next shot.

Dr. Wyatt tossed the ball into the air. Before it fell within range of his racket, he knew one thing he had to do..

61

Ham stood in front of the mirror, disgusted with herself.

She had wanted a look that would attract little or no attention. Her plan had included cutting the blonde hair she'd worn at the casino, and dying it the most mousy, nondescript brown possible. But she had been unable to do it. After nearly two years of playing a plain-looking, plain-dressing, overweight woman, she never wanted to be deliberately plain again.

Although she frowned at her image, she couldn't help noticing that she made an attractive brunette. Ham sighed; in the past, how she looked had always been beside the point. She had been the only one to notice. Moving from town to town as she grew up, she had never had the time to have a relationship.

At the word 'relationship' Dr. Cy's face appeared in her mind. He had always treated her with kindness and respect at the clinic. He had appreciated her work, told her she was unusually talented. And he had come immediately when she'd sent him an email to meet her at the casino. As if he'd been waiting to hear from her.

Of course he'd been waiting. He wanted to know if she had discovered anything improper about Dr. Wyatt. After all, Dr. Cy was the heir apparent to the clinic. If anything sullied its good name, it would hurt Dr. Cy's future prospects.

Ham immediately regretted her harsh thoughts. She really didn't believe he deserved her cynicism.

In front of the mirror she pulled on a black blouse and a pair of black slacks. Her midriff was bared briefly as she dressed. It almost made her laugh. In two days she had gone from foam rubber rotundity to showing her belly button. She considered the revealing outfit might have benefits—if it kept attention away from her face.

Ham's fingers trembled as she fastened the button on the waistband of her slacks. Even though she no longer bore any resemblance to the blimp who had been attacked, she was still afraid to go outside.

Although Ham now knew Dr. Wyatt hadn't stolen an embryo from the Hutchings, she was still convinced he was guilty of something unsavory. The man was too arrogant, too selfish, too eager to be rich, to be clean.

But how would she prove it? When she lost her job at the clinic, she lost her access to all of the clinic's information. Ham consoled herself with the thought that even if she still had her job, she would likely have accomplished nothing further there. After all, in nearly two years of hunting, the one piece of information she had turned up had only proven to have meaning because of what Dr. Cy had discovered.

Where did that leave Ham?

With one more mission to accomplish. It was crazy, even desperate. But she had waited too long to leave it undone. She grudgingly admired the fool in the mirror, and walked out the door.

62

When Diane opened the door of Betty's office, Betty wasn't prepared for how her friend looked.

From what Betty knew, Diane was living her dream. She was a successful dermatologist. Now she had a skin care line that was being sold—with great fanfare and success—on the shopping channel. But none of that was evident in Diane's face.

"Diane, what's the matter?" Betty regretted her choice of words as soon as she saw their effect on Diane. The botoxed serenity was gone.

Diane walked slowly toward Betty, looking drawn and tired. She indicated the chair at Betty's desk. "Do you have a few minutes?" she asked. "Normally I wouldn't bother you without calling about your schedule, but..."

Betty waved her in. Diane was a friend and didn't have to give advance notice when she needed help—as long as it didn't conflict with Betty's appointments. Betty checked her schedule, made a quick call to Aggie to ask her next patient to wait for a few minutes when she arrived.

For a moment Betty had the urge to lock her office door—she wanted to be able to concentrate on Diane without worrying that Dr. Wyatt was going to interrupt with one of his increasingly frequent and unannounced appearances. But she knew that would be a mistake and only infuriate the clinic head.

Betty motioned Diane to the sofa near her desk, and sat down next to her. Diane was thinner than the last time she had seen her.

"Something's wrong," Diane said.

Betty's heart sank when she thought Diane might mean her health. "You're not ill?"

Diane shook her head. "No, that's not it. I meant something is wrong..." She kept shaking her head and started crying.

Betty's first instinct was to give Diane a reassuring hug. But Diane wasn't a hugger, so Betty just waited, watching Diane's hand tremble as she dabbed her eyes with a tissue.

"At first I thought it was the best thing in the world, the answer to my dreams for my skin care line, when the shopping channel said they wanted to carry my products. But even though it's only been about a week, it feels as if they're invading every aspect of my business. They didn't put any money in, but they're finding ways to stick their noses into everything."

"But how can they do that, if the company is yours?"

"With all kinds of tricky techniques. Like they say they have to have X thousand jars of my night cream. Then they say it has to be a certain jar or a certain printing on the label. Then they say they over-ordered or something is wrong with the label or the jar or the product and I have to take it back and refund their money. So far I've been able to counter everything they've done and keep things straight, but it's costing me so much in accounting and legal fees—not to mention production costs—that it's wearing me down."

"But why would they do that if they like your products so much and they're selling like hotcakes?" Betty asked. What they were doing just didn't make any sense to her. "I watched your first show and you sold out. I bought your whole line myself. I was so impressed by you, I had my order shipped overnight; I couldn't wait. And already I can tell they're the best products I've ever used." Betty's admiration and enthusiasm were genuine; she was glad to see that they seemed to give Diane some comfort.

Diane's face brightened. "Thank you. It means a lot to me to hear you say that." She seemed reluctant to finish saying what was on her mind. She stared at her fingers, that were folding and refolding a tissue.

"I know it must sound paranoid, but I'm convinced they're trying to take my company from me so they can control the manufacturing and packaging. I found out from my manufacturing plant that they've been out there and told them I said it was all right. What were they doing there? My products aren't having any problems. It's like a nightmare."

Betty shook her head. "Why in heaven's name would they want that headache? With all the products they sell, why would they want to get involved with the day-to-day operations of any one of them, when they can just make a percentage by giving the manufacturer an enormous TV audience?"

"I don't know. I can't figure it out. And when I talk to some of the people at the channel, they can't tell me either. It doesn't seem to be something they want to do with every manufacturer. Why with me?"

Betty was mystified. "What's different about your products? Do you have any idea?"

"That's just it. My products aren't different. Sure, I think they're the best, but the channel must carry two dozen lines of skin care."

"Have you considered taking your products away from them? Or does that sink your ship?"

Diane gave a small laugh. "No. I've been miserable enough to consider it. But we have a contract. I can't walk away just yet."

Betty didn't know what she could offer Diane. So she asked her.

Diane became hopeful, even eager. "I have to go on the air for another show late tonight. From eleven to midnight. Will you come with me? You have such good instincts and a cool head, Betty. Meet them, look around. Tell me if I'm crazy. I know it's late and you work so hard. But can you help me?"

Diane looked so lost that Betty said yes immediately. "How do I do this? I don't even know where it is. And how will I get in?"

Relief flooded Diane from her face to her voice. "They're in Stamford. And I can get you in."

Diane got up. She looked years younger than when she had come in. "I feel better just having told you. I'll have a pass waiting for you at the gate at ten thirty. Thank you so much."

Then she surprised Betty by giving her a big hug. "I'll be expecting you tonight."

63

Aggie turned on her heel and bustled away from Dr. Wyatt while he was still talking to her.

She had told him there was someone in his office. When he asked her who it was, she walked away. Dr. Wyatt was stunned. She had never done anything like that before. Why now?

He crossed to his office door, put his hand on the knob. But even before he stepped inside, he knew who was there. It was as if he could sense him, although he had seen him only once before.

Perched on his desk was the detective who had barged in nearly a week ago. What was his name? Horn. He'd horned his way in last week and he was doing it again.

Dr. Wyatt's blood boiled when he saw the man had once again shoved aside the neatly organized items on his desk to make room for a seat.

"What are you doing in my office?"

As before, the man finished consulting whatever—if anything—was written on a pad in his hand before he answered.

"Some new developments in the death of your office manager," he said.

The passage of nearly a week had diminished Dr. Wyatt's compassion. "So? You have to invade my office to bring me an update? Get off my desk."

The detective looked as if he'd expected to be displaced. Dr. Wyatt was sure the man had sat on his desk just to make him angry, throw him off-balance. He was determined not to give him the satisfaction.

"That doesn't sound very sympathetic," Horn said, sliding slowly off the desk. "It's only been a few days since she died. Is it just that life goes on or did she take something from you?" Everything the detective had been sitting on was being pulled to the edge of the desk by his bottom.

Dr. Wyatt had been watching Horn. As the detective stood up, Dr. Wyatt made a dive for his belongings and answered without thinking: "Did you find money on her?"

The detective gave him a long look. "I didn't say that. Why, is some money missing?"

"Of course not." Dr. Wyatt straightened, placed his papers away from the edge of the desk. "You police always assume someone has done something to cause their murder." As soon as he'd said it, he regretted his choice of words.

The detective lifted his eyebrows. "You think stealing from you should be a capital offense?"

That wasn't what he'd said. Dr. Wyatt wanted to snap at Horn, but he clamped his teeth together to give himself time to cool and think. "Why did you come here today, Detective?"

"We thought she was killed during a random robbery, but that's looking less likely."

Why do these idiots always talk this way? Dr. Wyatt thought. Feed you little pieces of information, as if they were leaving a trail of breadcrumbs to lead you in some direction. Dr. Wyatt sighed. "What makes you think that?"

"We recovered a semen sample from her, Dr. Wyatt. And we got a tip that it may be yours."

Dr. Wyatt's head snapped up and he stiffened. He glared with fury at the man now perched on his credenza, his clumsy shoe heels swinging against the beautiful mahogany finish. "Not even you could believe such an absurdity," he said. But Dr. Wyatt thought that wouldn't stop Horn.

Dr. Wyatt felt like crushing this nobody who had the temerity to voice such an accusation. He bit his anger back. This was the way Horn must approach everyone. Fling empty threats to see if he could flush a bird out of the bushes.

"I was never anything less than professional with Jane," he said. He wouldn't have done anything even if Jane had appealed to him. "I am professional with all my staff." Anyone in the office—even Aggie—would have to agree. In spite of Aggie's antagonism toward him since Jane died, he didn't think she had been involved in this accusation—making up some story to tell Horn. Aggie could be unpleasant, but she wasn't vindictive and she wasn't a li...

An alarm went off in his brain as he realized the more likely source of the slur.

Mrs. Greene, his elegant patron. She could have arranged something like this. With money and connections, she could arrange anything she wanted. But why? Dr. Wyatt suddenly knew and winced at the answer: to keep him in line. 'You're like money in the bank, Doctor.' How many times had she said that to him? Well, it seemed she was making a withdrawal.

He was about to say something to Horn, when his analogy took him to an even more frightening thought. What if Mrs. Greene was emptying the account?

His face must have told the detective something. The man began to smile in a satisfied way.

"Something you're not telling us, Doctor?"

Dr. Wyatt needed time and privacy to put some things in order. His office hours were almost over, and he was going to the Greenes' mansion tonight for a party. He wouldn't leave there until he got some answers.

"Get out of my clinic," he said.

64

"You said you had something important to discuss," Dr. Wyatt said. "Make it brief; I have plans for tonight."

Cy had arranged to talk with Dr. Wyatt at his home, after work. During the day he could never seem to catch the clinic head at a good time or in a good mood.

Dr. Wyatt met Cy in the elegant foyer of his home, and didn't invite him in. He apparently intended to stand there while they talked! Cy was unsettled at such a brush-off. He had grown up in this house; his room had been at the top of the stairs that stood behind Dr. Wyatt. Now Dr. Wyatt was keeping him near the front door as if he were a stranger, a salesman. Cy was beginning to despair of ever getting through to the older man.

"The additional patients you gave me," Cy began. "Four of them have left the clinic. Their last IVF cycles were unsuccessful and they couldn't afford any more treatment. If I could use less expensive, but just as effective techniques, I could keep the others who are still our patients."

"The clinic has procedures for a reason," Dr. Wyatt said.

Cy wasn't going to buy that. He had too much pent-up frustration and anger from being put in the position of having to turn away patients in the middle of treatment.

"But these women can't afford them," Cy said. "You knew that when you turned them over to me. You promised me that I could use simpler, less costly methods. You went back on your word and I've had to send away four women we could have helped."

"I don't have to give you or anyone else a reason for my decisions," Dr. Wyatt said. "It's my clinic. I don't answer to you."

Cy had known Dr. Wyatt wouldn't be an easy sell, but he hadn't expected the older man to be so heartless. "This isn't what you said the clinic is about. You've always told me that everyone should have a baby if they want one. But there are only two kinds of people the clinic helps: those who can afford it, and a few others who pay nothing."

Dr. Wyatt's face turned a rapid crimson. Cy's first thought was the older man would work himself into a heart attack.

"How dare you question what I do? Where is your loyalty?"

Dr. Wyatt was looking directly at Cy, and for the first time in his life Cy saw nothing but coldness in the older man's eyes. They reflected no awareness that he knew Cy, let alone that they had shared twenty years together.

Cy shivered inside. How can he cut me off like this? Over some rigid procedures? Where is his loyalty?

Dr. Wyatt turned away, in the direction Cy knew led to his office.

Playing the loyalty card had been unfair, but it had cut. Cy hadn't used the word in a long time. "Dad."

Cy thought he saw a shudder in the older man's shoulders, but he didn't turn around. Walking down the hallway with his back to Cy, he said. "You're a grown man now, Cy. No one is going to look out for you. You make your own decisions, you choose your own loyalties."

That was his answer? Blind loyalty, regardless of a patient's best interests? Cy felt anger fight with aching regret.

"I would have followed you into hell," Cy said. "I would have defended you with my life. You were my hero."

Dr. Wyatt reached the door of his office, opened it and closed it behind him.

****

Cy's hands were tight on the steering wheel. He was driving away from Dr. Wyatt's house, and bitterly regretting the impulse that had brought him there.

Dr. Wyatt had managed to play Cy once again. He had reneged on a promise he had made, and managed to make Cy feel guilty for putting his patients' well-being ahead of his loyalty to Dr. Wyatt and his clinic.

Cy made a quick turn on Maple Avenue, and a bag slid across his dashboard. He recognized the bag. It contained the cigarette lighter that he'd bought from Ham at the casino.

That gave Cy something else to worry about. What if all the hoops Ham had put him through to see her at the casino hadn't been unnecessary? What if she were right, and it hadn't been an accident? What if she needed his help?

Cy told himself that Ham was smart enough to look out for herself. After all, she had managed to get a job at the clinic and fool them all with her fat disguise for a couple of years.

He couldn't comfort himself. And it didn't help that she hadn't given him any way to get in touch with her, not even a cell phone number.

What if she had written something on the receipt for the cigarette lighter? He had never checked.

There was a red light ahead. He slowed to a stop behind another car and reached across the passenger seat for the bag. He unrolled the top, reached in for the wrapped cigarette lighter. When he unfolded the wrapping, he was disappointed to see it held nothing but the lighter and his receipt. He dropped the lighter inside the bag and noticed for the first time that there was another, very small bag inside. Cy glanced up at the light. It was still red.

Cy lifted out the small paper bag, unfolded the top and held it upside down. The sound of a car behind him made him glance in the rear view mirror. There was a car coming up behind him and it wasn't slowing down. Didn't the driver see the red light? Didn't the driver see that Cy was stopped? Cy pumped the brake and hit his horn, but the car behind him kept coming.

Just before the car hit him and his airbag deployed, the contents of the small paper bag slid out. Cy saw it clearly before the collision knocked him out: a tiny pink sock with what looked like an old blood stain on the sole.

65

It wasn't the first time she had broken into a building. It was just the first time she was going to let the occupant know she was there.

She slid inside, her black shirt and pants letting her melt into the shadow. No sense advertising her presence until she was ready.

His house was large. It would have taken too long to find him—doing a room-by-room search—if she hadn't heard his angry voice. Dressing someone down on the phone? she wondered. Taking his work home with him.

In the shadow of his doorway her nerve wavered. She told herself she didn't have to do this. She could leave the way she had come; no one would know. There was no shame—she had put enough of herself into this search. She knew a lot of what she had come to find out. Not everything; but at least she was still in one piece, despite the murder attempt.

The memory of the arcing blade across her midriff swayed her. Her feet were turning away from the door when she had a miserable thought: If not this, then what? What was left for her but more running? Only this time there were more people to hunt her down. More people meant more money and more effort. She had spent most of her life on the run. Did she want to go back to that?

She turned, made herself step into his office. It was a room even more imposing and regal than his office at the clinic. Paneled walls, floor-to-ceiling bookcases, leather sofa and chairs, a massive desk.

He looked up. Surprised, but not alarmed. Her heart pounded crazily.

"What do you want?" he asked. There was no recognition in his eyes, only annoyance.

"Why did you hunt us?" she asked.

His head lifted, like a dog who thinks he hears a familiar voice. "What?"

"Why did you hunt my mother and me?"

It seemed like minutes before he answered.

"Clea?" He didn't take his eyes from her, but searched her face as if he could know by looking at her. Something finally convinced him. "You're alive. You did survive. I was sure you had." There was certainty and relief in his voice. "I've looked for you for years."

How well Clea knew that. It was why she and her mother had been forced to live their lives on the run. Always spending just enough time in any one place to think they could like it or find work. And then something would happen. They would get a call or a strange car would be parked outside or they would hear that someone had been asking about them. Her mother had always known; she'd had a sixth sense about it. Clea had had to learn. And they would pack their few things and move again. They had moved so many times that Clea had been afraid there would be no place that they hadn't been; that there would be no refuge left for them.

Long-suppressed rage erupted from her like lava. It put her fear to shame before vaporizing it.

"Yes, you looked for us," she said. It was a guttural voice she had never heard before.

"You sent people looking for us for years. Driving us out of any small refuge we had. Always making us leave with less than the little we'd managed to put together. Just when we were getting good at a job or at learning something. Forcing us to discard pieces of our lives along the way. You bastard."

She paused. The adrenaline was making her short of breath. How long she had wanted to confront him.

"Why? What could a woman and a baby have that belonged to you, that could have hurt you?" Clea's tension had increased along with her anger; she was tight enough to fling herself across his polished desk, clutch his wiry neck with her fingers.

His response disarmed her. He looked totally surprised. "You really have no idea? After all these years. Your mother never said anything?"

Clea shook her head.

He looked unconvinced. "I find that difficult to believe. You came back here. You got a job at my clinic under false pretenses and spent nearly two years snooping. Why? What were you looking for?"

He was acting as if he were the injured party. If Clea hadn't worked for this selfish and arrogant tyrant for nearly two years, she wouldn't have believed it. Did he really buy what he was saying? Could he be so clueless, so lacking in remorse?

"I came back to find out why you made us run," Clea said. "And to make you pay for it."

She had been carrying that message for twenty years. Clea felt such relief at delivering herself of those two lines that her legs felt wobbly.

"Vengeance?" he asked. He seemed genuinely amused. "How did you think you were going to satisfy yourself?"

"I'll have the authorities audit you," she said. Though she was flinging threats wildly, they gave her courage. She began to advance on his desk, as if her words and her anger could beat down this arrogant man so luxuriously ensconced at the expense of others. "Something won't add up. They'll know something is wrong when you can't account for everything."

The lower part of her body was stopped by the massive desk, but her torso leaned forward and her hand beat the polished wood surface.

"What did you want from my mother? What did she do to you?"

He looked at her again with surprise. "Not your mother," he said. "You were the albatross, the millstone around her neck. I wanted nothing from her. She would have been free if not for you."

It was mental whiplash for Clea. How could she have been responsible for what happened? She had been a baby. Of course, her mother could have run faster without her. But how else could she have been a liability?

"What are you saying? I was her child, she loved me. She told me I was her treasure." Clea remembered something. "My father loved me too. He told my mother I was money in the bank."

Dr. Wyatt's body suddenly froze, while the expression on his face rapidly changed. It was clear to Clea that some calculation was going on in his head, but what it involved, she had no idea. His open eyes, focused on some inner image, mesmerized her and held her at his desk.

Finally he came out of his trance and focused on her. Clea expected him to act in character: to pause after his calculations, then make some pronouncement. So she was totally unprepared when he lunged at her. Before she could react he had grasped her wrist and held it tight.

Clea bitterly regretted that she had come to his house to confront him. But regret escalated to terror when Dr. Wyatt turned the black bag on his desk on its side and slid out a scalpel.

66

Dr. Wyatt shrugged and wiped the blood off his scalpel, then replaced it carefully in his black bag. Clea had given him much less trouble than he had expected. He had thought she would fight back, resist him completely. But she hadn't. She had given in quite near the beginning. After that, it hadn't gone so well. He sighed. He would just have to wait and see what happened tonight.

Now he had to go to a party.

****

The mansion looked as if a convention were being held there. 4TH OF JULY was emblazoned on enormous flags of red, white, and blue. Floodlights in the same colors bathed the mansion. Man-high hedges of sparklers flanked the entrance. Dr. Wyatt stared; he had forgotten the date. Briefly, he recalled the symbolism: red for courage, white for purity, blue for loyalty. In spite of the turmoil the detective had plunged him into, Dr. Wyatt couldn't help smiling at the Greenes' use of these colors to adorn their home.

The long, stately driveway was clear of cars. As soon as Dr. Wyatt pulled up, a valet took his car. He knew they would park it in a remote lot on the immense estate. But close to the entrance three trucks were parked. He passed each on his way to the front door. First was Ratatazzi's Fireworks. That fit in with the sparklers in front. The second truck was from Habit Vineyards. He recognized Habit as one of the businesses Mr. Greene owned, the one which made the irresistible wine he'd drunk at the last dinner party. From the size of the truck, there would be an unending flow of wine tonight.

When he saw the third truck, Amazing Sweepstakes, he chilled. It was the lost cashier's check Amazing Sweepstakes had sent that had caused so much trouble. Why was it here tonight? He paused, had more than half a mind to leave. But he knew there was no avoiding destiny, and if the Greenes had been the ones who created the trouble with Detective Horn, he had better face things head on. It took all his resolution to keep his shoulders from sagging.

Dr. Wyatt walked under the flags, between the sparklers. As he stepped over the threshold, he immediately saw that all of the restraint and decorum reigning at his other visits, were gone. People were laughing, shouting, singing, dancing. Even in the echoing-large foyer there was a crush. Tonight there was no color or dress code—the apparel ranged from obviously expensive to obviously outrageous.

With so many people packed so closely together there was no opportunity to get his bearings. He had no choice but to get swept into the thick of it.

A wineglass seemed to be sloshing in every hand. Dr. Wyatt was determined to drink no wine. He had come here with the purpose of confronting Mrs. Greene and he did not want to be hamstrung by a fogged mind. When a waiter offered him a drink, he shook his head vigorously, but his hand reached for the glass and brought it to his lips. At his first sip, he recognized the ambrosial liquid he had drunk before and vowed not to drink again. He drained it.

In the jostling crowd, Dr. Wyatt recognized a number of people who had been here at the last dinner party. But they weren't dressed or acting the way they had that evening. Tonight dance music vibrated and people gyrated to the beat. A number of people bumped into him as they danced, as they walked, as they swayed in place. Everyone just smiled and nodded. No keeping at formal distances tonight.

Except for Dr. Jagat Singh. With a wince Dr. Wyatt recognized the small doctor from India with whom he had spoken at the last dinner party. Revelers swirled but no one seemed to disturb the small pool of quiet surrounding the man. He wasn't holding a glass, he was just standing, observing. Though Dr. Wyatt's conversation with the Indian doctor had made him uncomfortable, he could still remember everything the two of them had said.

A waiter appeared at his elbow. "When you're hungry, there's a buffet set up in a room down that hall." He indicated the direction with a nod.

He had another glass of wine or maybe it was two, he couldn't remember. He was too busy trying to decide if the attractive women who squeezed past him were trying to get somewhere, or trying to get somewhere with him.

Eventually he identified the light feeling inside him as one of hunger. He put his empty glass on a passing tray and headed for the buffet. Again he made a wrong turn down one of the many marble-floored, wood-paneled corridors, just as he had the last time he was here. He ended up outside the room with the large round table in the center.

Dr. Wyatt couldn't resist entering the room tonight any more than he could the last time. He was drawn directly to the round table; it appeared to be set up for whatever game was being played there.

He had expected to see a deck of cards on the table. But all he found was a large tally sheet in front of each of the five chairs.

Each of the tally sheets consisted of a large grid. Along the left side of the sheet was a list of nine names: of people, companies, institutions, organizations—even of countries. Next to each name, in parentheses, was a one or two letter abbreviation of the name. Across the top of the sheet were the words 'Return on Investment.' The ROI was subdivided into several categories. He saw 'Domestic' and 'Overseas,' with 'Overseas' divided by country.

Each of the squares of the grid was large enough to accommodate a vertical list of nine numbers (all with $ signs), and wide enough so that each of those nine numbers could have up to eight digits, with room left over for two letters.

It took Dr. Wyatt a while (was the wine fogging his brain already?) but he finally figured it out. Apparently the money attributed to each of the names on the left side of the tally sheet was broken down into contributions from the other eight names. Some names had a contribution from several of the other names; others didn't.

At the bottom of the tally sheet was a large star with a number at its center. A grand total, he guessed. He glanced at the other tally sheets. The big star was a different color on each sheet. He looked at the chairs; for the first time he noticed that the chair in front of the blue star was the biggest.

Dr. Wyatt walked around the table, comparing the colors of the stars and the numbers at the centers of the stars. It seemed that the blue star was like a blue ribbon; it had the largest number at its center. A mind-boggling number, even when his mind was already boggled.

And then he saw something on the winning tally sheet that startled him out of his fogginess: his own name.

67

Betty slid out of her air-conditioned car, into the muggy evening. A shower was just what the doctor ordered. She pulled out her house key as she walked to her front door. When she lifted the key to the lock she saw the door was open.

Betty's heart began to pound, both with fear and anger. "Trowe?" she called, pushing the door open with her foot. Had he let himself in again? There was no answer from inside her house. You shouldn't go in, she told herself. Call the police.

She walked in, adrenaline pumping, and flipped on the lights. The interior was ransacked.

As Betty's eyes swept over her home, the sanctuary she had carefully created, her throat constricted and tears poured down her cheeks. It was immediately clear to her that the object of the visit wasn't theft. Whoever had been here had been bent on destruction. There was an unnecessary violence to it—like grinding a heel into a picture after the glass had been broken.

Betty stepped into the living room. It had been a cream-colored oasis; now it was almost unrecognizable. The elegant mirror over the fireplace was reduced to shards crunching under her feet. The marble mantelpiece had been hacked at—someone had to have spent time and energy to do so much damage. Lamps had been overturned and broken, their silk shades soiled and torn. The upholstered pieces—covered in velvet, tapestry, and wool—had been slashed and trailed strips of precious fabrics. Betty staggered at the extent of the destruction.

Though it was as painful as probing an open wound, Betty couldn't stop inspecting the damage. When she saw the dining room was in just as bad shape as the living room, her legs wobbled and she fell into a chair. The gleaming mahogany table top had deep grooves clawed across its surface. The upholstered seats of the chairs had been slashed. Someone had even managed to bring grape juice from the refrigerator and pour it on the Aubusson rug.

Who would have done this? And why?

Betty was having trouble breathing. She felt as if she had been attacked and her assailant had run away, leaving her broken, bleeding and without a word of explanation.

A fear began to make its way through the aching fog in Betty's brain. Did someone know about the help she had given Rose? Or had Dr. Wyatt found out who opened his envelope from Amazing Sweepstakes?

The thought froze her. She sat, hardly breathing, listening for the sound of footsteps. What kind of fool had she been to come into the house? What if someone was here, waiting for her?

Fear for her own safety quickly gave way to fear for others. What if Rose left a message on her answering machine? What if that led to this revenge? Betty's nervous glance reached the mantelpiece, and a small broken vase that had held a red rose. Anger flamed as a suspicion grew in her as to who was most likely responsible.

Betty grabbed a candlestick and quickly probed the rubble, looking for her phone. When she found it under an overturned chair, she tried to play back her messages. Nothing. She had a spasm of anxiety until she remembered *69—the code to retrieve the number of the last person who had called her— and she punched in the digits.

It was the Murray Hill post office—Barbara's branch.

Barbara had promised to find out the owner of Amazing Sweepstakes, who had sent Dr. Wyatt a cashier's check for $50,000.

Betty asked for Barbara, but she wasn't there. The man Betty spoke to had a message for her.

"She told me to tell you something. She said: 'Tell her it was Trowe.' Do you know what that means?"

Betty thought she was going to be sick. "Yes, I know."

Trowe. If he were behind Amazing Sweepstakes, then he hadn't come to tell her he was feeling guilty about AIDS drugs the day he'd broken into her house. He had had an agenda, like always, probably bugged her phones or her house. Or both. He and his ilk had probably listened to Betty's phone calls. Betty turned to ice again as her mind raced back over any calls that could betray Rose. She shook her head; she was sure she'd been careful. Still, something had to have motivated this attack.

What had she done to bring this on herself?

The only thing she could figure was that Dr. Wyatt had found out that she had opened his mail, seen the check for $50,000. But she hadn't taken it. She had put it back in the envelope and put it on Jane's desk. Jane had apparently taken it, used it to finance a vacation.

Jane was dead.

Betty began to shiver until she shook. If Trowe was trying to cover up something, this was only the beginning. What would stop him if he thought she threatened his money or his freedom?

Betty thought she heard something in the kitchen. Though her heart was beating hard enough to jar her chest, she couldn't make herself walk away. She pushed herself to her feet, crossed the Aubusson rug, and opened the door to the kitchen.

Her beautiful, pristine white kitchen was now a melee of stains. Everything from the refrigerator must have been flung around the room. Her large set of carving knives had been used to dig grooves in the cupboard doors.

All of the destruction was making her dizzy. What sobered her quickly was a pair of feet that caught her eye. Betty realized a figure sat in a chair at her table.

68

Dr. Wyatt swayed slightly on his feet. What was his name doing on a game tally sheet? He scanned the sheet. His name code (JW) had made a contribution to all the other names, and in virtually every category. What could he have done to help the other names on the list to make money? Though he recognized the other names, he had no personal connection with most of them.

He began to go over the tally sheets in detail; the one containing his name was the winner, the sheet with the blue star. The other names on the list were: CDC; El Presidente; Apex Confections; Ibis Pharmaceuticals; Medium Media; Habit Vineyards; Estate Oil; and Columbia.

Dr. Wyatt was baffled. Why were these names on a game tally sheet? What role did they play? The only CDC he knew was the Centers for Disease Control and Prevention. El Presidente—President of what? The Spanish form made him think it related to a Spanish-speaking country or company. Apex Confections muse be a candy company. Ibis Pharmaceuticals he recognized; he knew the Greenes owned the company. Medium Media was a media conglomerate. Habit Vineyards was another Greene company, as was Estate Oil. Everyone knew that. But Columbia? Was it Columbia University? Or District of Columbia?

Through the haze in his brain caused by the ambrosial wine, Dr. Wyatt tried to make sense of what he was looking at. I've never regretted that you were on my team. How often had Mrs. Greene said that to him?

He heard someone clear her throat, and turned to find her standing behind him. For some reason he wasn't surprised. As if it was meant to be this way.

"Let's take a walk in the garden, Doctor," she said.

He didn't move. He just stared at her.

"Oh, come along," she said, slipping her arm through his, and pulling him through the door at the back of the room.

Dr. Wyatt followed her through the same door her husband and his friend had used the last time he was here. There was another corridor, which twisted and turned. She said nothing more until they were outside, in a humid night, with the sounds of the party faint behind them.

They were standing in what looked like the center of a maze, a circular area approximately fifty feet in diameter, ringed with hedges at least ten feet high. Dr. Wyatt wondered why she had brought him here. They seemed to be alone. Then something caught his eye near one wall of hedge. He walked over, dread growing in him with each step.

It was a man, lying on his side. Dr. Wyatt knew the bent head. How many times he had smoothed the hair from his forehead while he slept.

Cy.

Dr. Wyatt turned back to the woman with a question in his eyes.

"We don't have all evening for this, Dr. Wyatt," she said.

69

Betty didn't recognize the young woman, all in black, sitting hunched at her table. She didn't have the energy to throw her out and she didn't have the energy to run. She dropped into a chair. At this point, whatever happened, happened.

"Dr. Winter, it's me, Ham," she said.

Betty recognized the familiar voice, but it was coming out of such a foreign body that she might as well have heard a mannequin squeak.

"I had to talk to you and the front door was open. It was all wrecked when I got here—I didn't see anybody—but I had to see you."

All Betty could think to say was: "What happened to you?" It wasn't politeness but weariness that cut her question short. What happened to the rest of you? she had meant to say. Where did it go? Betty could see shoes and pant legs and a long-sleeved top. She has arms, Betty thought.

"It's a long story, Dr. Winter, but please, I'll make it brief. I need your help."

Betty was shell-shocked. The vandals who had destroyed her home had also shaken the peace and order she'd spent years creating in her life. She was too beaten to do anything but listen. She nodded.

OK, Betty thought. Tell me a story.

When Clea was through, Betty's torpor was gone, and nearly all her skepticism.

"Let me understand you," Betty said. "You and your mother escaped from the house the night it burned, and you've managed to elude the private investigators Dr. Wyatt sent after you for the past twenty years." Though such relentlessness sounded unbelievable, Betty thought this part of the story was most likely true. Aggie had told her about the letter to Dr. Wyatt from a private investigator.

"It took everything we had just to stay one step ahead of them," Clea said quietly.

One look at Clea's face and Betty's remaining disbelief dissolved.

Betty marveled at how different Clea looked from Ham—though the only difference was weight and hair. It was hard to imagine that the slender creature in front of her had been an elephant-sized thorn in her side for months.

"You put together the fat disguise and got a job at the clinic so you could find out why Dr. Wyatt had been hunting you," Betty said. She couldn't restrain herself from adding: "How in God's name did you put up with that bulky costume for nearly two years?"

"I had to know why. My life was hell. Not just from living it, but from watching what it did to my mother. She hadn't been expecting a life like that. I was born into it; I didn't know any better. But it destroyed her."

"Did you find out why he did it?" Betty asked.

Clea looked down, shook her head. "My mother and I always figured it was because of something he was doing, that he thought we knew about. But we didn't know anything. And after nearly two years of working for him, the only lead I found turned out to be a dead end."

Clea stood up. She seemed wobbly to Betty. "I have to go back to the clinic. I left something in my desk and I have to get it. I need to borrow your key."

Betty's head was beginning to clear. "Can't you go in the morning? Just tell Aggie that you left something."

Clea's face hardened and for a split second Betty thought she might use force to get the key.

"A couple of nights ago I was attacked on the street. A man stopped me, didn't say a word, just..." Clea stopped. "He slashed a knife back and forth across my stomach. If I hadn't been wearing my fat suit, he would have killed me."

Betty had thought tonight's events had numbed her, but Clea's face looked so young and so hurt. Hadn't this young woman suffered enough?

Clea stepped away from the kitchen table. "I'm still not convinced that it was a random attack; he didn't take my money. I've had enough of all this. I want to leave. There's just something I left at the clinic, and I have to go back there before I leave. Please lend me your key."

The last words were said with pleading. Betty couldn't refuse her.

70

She hadn't called the police.

Betty hadn't even gotten out of the kitchen chair she'd fallen into after she'd found Clea in her house. After she gave Clea her key to the clinic, she had sat like a zombie, staring at the destruction. She hadn't even been able to cry.

What was the point? No matter what she did, there would always be someone or something to drag her back, destroy her progress, take away what she had struggled for. Betty took a long, shaky breath, closed her eyes. She was out at the reservoir again. A small girl, swimming alone and swimming too far. She had struggled to the end of her strength, and she just wanted to stop trying. Just sink and let the water close over her.

Clea called Cy by his first name.

Betty's eyes flipped open. "Why did I remember that? Of all the things to come into my head. With my house in shambles, what do I care what Clea called Cy?" Betty shook her head, sorrowfully taking in the ransacked room.

It was true, she told herself. For nearly two years Clea had called him Dr. Cy. Tonight she called him Cy. Betty reminded herself that Clea had always been Cy's adoptive sister, and now that Betty knew it, there was no reason for Clea to use Cy's professional title.

Betty roused herself to her feet. "If I have enough energy to think about other people's business, I have enough energy to do something here." Make a beginning, she told herself. Find some corner and do something, anything. Betty picked the corner containing her favorite reading chair. She took the shovel still leaning against the fireplace, and began to shovel debris into a pile.

Clea looked so pale.

Why should that surprise her? The young woman had been through a lot before she even got to Betty's. Seeing the state of Betty's house must have been another blow. "More reasonable to wonder how she had the nerve to stay and wait for me in the middle of all this rubble. Besides, that all-black outfit would drain anyone of color."

Clea is going away again.

Betty couldn't help feeling sorry for the young woman. She didn't envy the difficult and stressful life she must have had, always on the run. And what a price she had paid to ensure that she worked at the clinic unrecognized. She had spent two years in a stifling, heavy fat suit. "On top of that, she was nearly killed on the street. No wonder she's had enough."

Betty put down the shovel, rubbed her eyes, then arched her back to ease the stiffness and ache. She couldn't blame Clea for wanting to leave. The only person she had a connection to was Cy, and they hadn't seen each other since she was a baby. Any bonding the two had done over the past two years had to be because Cy was kind to her and appreciated her work—Clea was a gifted programmer. Betty gave a small laugh, surprised to realize she admired Clea's talents.

I wonder how much money Clea has, Betty thought. Will she be able to carry herself until she finds some new place, and something to do?

Betty thought Clea must have saved her money. She had probably made a good salary; computer people were in great demand. What had she had to spend it on? Betty picked up her shovel, went back to cleaning debris.

There was blood in Clea's shoe.

Betty dropped the shovel with a clatter. She had been so shaken by the time she found Clea, she must not have consciously registered the blood. But now she could see it clearly in her mind. It had made a stain on the instep of the black flats Clea had been wearing. And now Betty remembered something else—the message she had found in the Tarot card reading she had done for Clea: DEATH.

The memories coalesced into an idea, and that idea propelled Betty out the front door of her house and into her car. She was going back to the clinic.

71

Cy was lying on the ground, on someone's very expensive landscaped property. His head vaguely ached. He didn't know where he was or how he had gotten here. The last thing he remembered was driving away from Dr. Wyatt's home after the confrontation.

He heard approaching footsteps and voices. His first instinct, one of self-preservation, was to pretend to be unconscious—at least until he knew where he was and why.

When the footsteps stopped next to him, Cy peered out through barely open eyelids. He was stunned to see Dr. Wyatt. What was he doing here? Cy felt Dr. Wyatt bend over him, gently touch his head.

"I'm sorry, son," he whispered.

Cy didn't move. Dr. Wyatt put a tentative finger on Cy's carotid, seemed satisfied that there was still a pulse. Cy watched Dr. Wyatt stand up, smooth his hands over his lower jacket pockets. There's something important in there, Cy thought. Why is he here? Is he responsible for my being here?

"Detective Horn visited my office today," Dr. Wyatt told someone.

Cy saw the red, white, and blue dress of the woman before he saw her face. Dr. Wyatt was talking to Mrs. Greene— Cy had met her on one of her many visits to Dr. Wyatt at the clinic. This must be her estate. The woman smiled ever so slightly. As if the information pleased her.

"So it *was* you who did this," Dr. Wyatt said.

Cy could see the shock on Dr. Wyatt's face. Mrs. Greene had been responsible for the detective coming back to the clinic. Why? Cy thought Mrs. Greene had been Dr. Wyatt's patron. From the distended vein in Dr. Wyatt's neck, Cy could imagine the dizzying burst of adrenaline that must be coursing through the older man.

"You set me up so he would accuse me of having a relationship with Jane," Dr. Wyatt said. "So he could accuse me of murdering her. So I would be so busy defending myself that I couldn't be taken seriously if I pointed a finger at you."

Jane! Why did Mrs. Greene want the detective to think Dr. Wyatt had something to do with Jane or her death? What could Mrs. Greene have done that would need a murder to deflect attention from her?

Mrs. Greene didn't say anything so Cy didn't have an answer to his question.

"Is that what they'll find? My DNA in her?" Dr. Wyatt asked. "Some trail of evidence that proves that I was responsible for her death? Why? Why?"

What kind of person would have the motivation or the resources to set up something like that? Cy began to feel far colder than lying on the ground made him.

Mrs. Greene looked put out. "You're not working out for us."

"I'm not working out?"

Cy heard the incredulity in Dr. Wyatt's voice.

"Why? Because Ham went to see the Hutchings? She found out nothing! One slipup in twenty-five years and you're ready to betray me?"

Cy had heard a quivering in the older man's voice that made him think Dr. Wyatt was going to beg Mrs. Greene to reconsider. In spite of Cy's growing suspicion that Dr. Wyatt was a part of something wrong, something connected to Mrs. Greene, Cy couldn't help feeling embarrassed for him—and resentful at this woman for having such an effect on him.

Mrs. Greene looked at Dr. Wyatt without emotion. "It never happened before," she agreed. "But now that it has, my experience tells me it will happen again. You are a liability."

"A liability!" he sputtered. "How many times did you tell me you were glad I was a member of your team? I thought you were talking about my medical skills" He snorted bitterly. "I provided you with embryos for twenty-five years and I never knew what you were doing with them. Oh, my God." He fell to his knees, staring miserably at the manicured grass in front of him.

He provided her with embryos for twenty-five years? Cy had heard the words, he knew what they meant, but his mind was like a computer that crashed. He was so stunned that he almost forgot to breathe.

Cy was completely incapable of grasping the magnitude of what these two people had done. And for what purpose? He could not imagine how someone could actually fall into that pit and live there. Cy had once just *contemplated* taking an embryo for a desperate patient, and the guilt still goaded him.

The Hutchings had been a false lead. But he and Ham had been on the right track, after all.

While he was kneeling, Dr. Wyatt slipped something from his coat pocket and hid it under a small, flowering rosebush. Cy saw the transfer, wondered what he put under the bush and why.

"Please spare me the bad acting," she said. "Your predecessor..."

"Cy's adoptive father wasn't my predecessor," he said angrily. "He worked for me."

Cy knew there had been bad blood between his adoptive father and Dr. Wyatt. He had gleaned that much from the loud conversations he had heard at home as a small boy.

"Your predecessor wasn't discreet," she said. "He knew where all the transfers went and he made a list. That was why he had a fire. And why we had to search for the child and her mother."

The fire hadn't been an accident! It took all of Cy's willpower not to leap up and grab this woman by her arrogant neck. She spoke with complete indifference about an arson that had killed people and permanently damaged the lives of those who survived. It suddenly struck Cy that she said they had searched for the child and her mother. So she hadn't thought Clea and her mother had died. Cy's heart began to pump so hard he was sure they would notice his body moving.

Dr. Wyatt, who was still kneeling near Cy, nodded slowly. For the first time, Cy thought the older man looked as if he had something on Mrs. Greene.

"Years ago I figured you must have been responsible for the fire," he said. "And I was sure you would search for Clea. That was why I hired my own private detectives, to try to find her first."

"How clever," she said. "So neither of us was successful."

"But I didn't know where the embryos went," Dr. Wyatt said, getting to his feet. "I never saw the list."

She frowned at him. "Don't give me that innocent act. You took the embryos. You knew what I was doing with them— giving them to people who deserved them. People who had more use for them than the ones who contributed them."

At the word 'contribute' Dr. Wyatt's face twisted. "Contribute implies an awareness and a willingness," he said. "Neither was the case. Stole is the correct word. We stole them."

She shrugged. "Call it what you like." She looked around as if she were waiting for someone.

Dr. Wyatt had begun to pace, and Cy sensed an urgency in him. He reminded Cy of someone girding himself for the last lap of a race. What's going on here?

"I figured something else out," Dr. Wyatt said. "About the five chairs at the round card table in the game room."

Mrs. Greene didn't seem at all interested.

"Five of you," he said. "Like devils at the corners of a pentagram."

She gave him a tight smile. "How fanciful of you." She looked around again and Cy sensed an increasing urgency in Dr. Wyatt.

"Each of the five positions at the table had a team of nine. Part of the team consisted of companies you owned; the rest were assigned by lot," Dr. Wyatt said. "I saw your husband

and his friend drawing for one member of the friend's team. He chose from what must have been cards, placed face down. The objective of the game was for each player to make as much money as possible—using the resources of his assigned team to increase the wealth of the companies he already owned—with no holds barred. Your husband's position apparently prospered with me on your team. You won the blue star."

She didn't say anything, but even from the ground Cy could see the twitch at the corner of her eye.

"The assigned team members didn't know they were on your team, did they? They were just resources for you. If you had a company on your assigned team, it was up to you to figure out who in the company to contact and what to offer that person to get what you wanted. If you needed a defense contract signed, if you wanted to buy illegal drugs, if you wanted to make a certain blood test standard, you just had to get to the right person and give them what they wanted.

"What I had to offer you as an assigned team member was embryos," Dr. Wyatt said. "At first you convinced me to give you the leftover embryos that no one had come back for. You said there were so many desperate mothers who would do anything to have a child. The money you paid made it possible for me to expand my clinic. I told myself I was doing more good than harm. Once you had me in your pocket, you pushed for more and more—this kind of hair color, eye color, height, background. Until all I was doing was filling orders."

Dr. Wyatt was breathing hard and his face was red. Cy worried that the older man was going to have a heart attack in front of him.

"You used the embryos I gave you like money," Dr. Wyatt said. "Like currency. But with no paper trail. To buy political favors or votes, to get police to look the other way, to get scientists to print lies in scientific journals...To get people to murder for you. Nothing was too low for you." He shook his head. "Now I understand why your tally sheet shows my name making a contribution to all of the other members of your team. Now I understand why you always said I was money in the bank. Because I was your banker."

Mrs. Greene was obviously trying to control her face, but she still looked to Cy as if someone had walked in while she was dressing. Dr. Wyatt's guess had been on target.

Dr. Wyatt paused to take a breath, but it didn't help Cy. He felt as if the air had been knocked out of him. It had been a *game.* These people had stolen human embryos so they could win a game!

Cy had thought Dr. Wyatt was through, but he wasn't.

"Your husband owns a pharmaceutical company. He paid researchers to falsify test results so that a nonexistent disease is treated with a deadly drug that he manufactures. And his 'team member' in the third world is giving him an enormous market of unsuspecting customers that he'll methodically kill off."

Mrs. Greene ignored him, but Cy saw her hands tremble.

"The word 'Columbia' was on your team's tally sheet," Dr. Wyatt said. "I wondered if it referred to the university or the nation's capital. What a fool I was. Now I understand why your wine is so irresistible. So addictive." He shook his head. "Now I get the design of your bottles. Habit Vineyards has a nun on the label. You and your husband have a sense of humor."

Did Dr. Wyatt mean what Cy thought he did? That the wine had some addictive drug from *Colombia* in it? Things seemed to be getting more and more strange. Cy felt as if he were inside some bizarre movie, watching it from a worm's eye view.

"So that's how it worked," Dr. Wyatt said. "The mystery of the card table and my appearance on the tally sheet."

"Stop it." Mrs. Greene's voice was angry, but she looked as if she had begun to shiver in the hot, humid air.

Cy felt sick at the number of people who were involved, and at their total lack of concern about what they were doing. As if the people they stole the embryos from—as well as the embryos themselves—were some expendable commodity.

"I've known you for so many years," Dr. Wyatt said. "I thought I knew what you were capable of. You didn't need the money—how many hundred million do you need? People's lives were destroyed just so you could *win a game.*"

Cy heard someone approaching. Mrs. Greene seemed to recover. "You've heard the expression 'You can never be too rich or too thin,' haven't you, Doctor?"

A big man with white hair and a white beard who reminded Cy of Santa Claus, walked into the semicircle of lawn. He was followed by two other men. Cy assumed he was Mr. Greene. As the men arrived, Cy saw and heard the opening salvos of a firework display. From his position on the ground, it was impressive.

"I came as quickly as I could, my dear," Mr. Greene said. "The senator is here. He wanted a favor."

Fireworks exploded in the sky, briefly illuminating his face. There was lipstick on Mr. Greene's cheek. Cy doubted that the senator had put it there.

His wife's face tightened. "Well, it won't be embryos." She nodded toward Dr. Wyatt.

The husband looked at Dr. Wyatt with the indifference of someone scanning a magazine rack. He shrugged. "We'll find something else."

For the first time, he seemed to see Cy. "Who is this?"

"Wyatt's adopted son, Dr. Wood," Mrs. Greene said. "He works at the clinic, too."

"Two of them? I only prepared for one."

"That nurse told me he visited the Hutchings. He found out nothing. But he won't let it go."

Cy had always thought Aggie spied on the clinic for Dr. Wyatt's benefit. He couldn't imagine her betraying him, even though she had gotten testy lately. What could the Greenes have done to persuade her? Anything. Cy shot a look at Dr. Wyatt. The older man seemed to have shrunken at the news..

Mr. Greene whistled and a swift dark shape slipped from the portico to stand by him.

The sick feeling in Cy's stomach got worse at the thought of a Doberman killing him and Dr. Wyatt. Not that a bullet from one of Greene's henchmen would be better. Dead was dead. Still, being killed by a *dog?* Cy had been cold. Now he trembled.

An enormous ball of red exploded in the sky, then poured down in a red tail.

In a rush, Cy's memory returned. After he'd driven away from Dr. Wyatt's home, he had been rear-ended at a red light. The airbag had deployed. But before that, something had fallen out of the bag Ham had given him at the casino gift shop. A small pink sock with a bloodstain on the sole.

Cy knew what that meant. Ham was Clea. Clea was alive.

In an instant, Cy was on his feet.

72

It was there!

Clea's eyes strained to be sure she had read it right. Her heart was beating so hard she had trouble keeping her head steady at the eyepiece.

She was in the clinic's lab, perched on a stool in front of the high-powered microscope. She was unutterably grateful now that she had worked out the connections between the microscope, the digital camera, and the computer. She had done it for Cy, for his records and publications; she had never foreseen that she would get any use out of it. But without this setup, she would probably never know...

"I thought you had to get something out of your desk."

Clea jumped, and knocked over the stool. Her heart was pounding like a racer.

Betty walked into the lab, her features struggling between rebuke and curiosity. Curiosity seemed to win.

"What are you looking at?"

Clea had not expected Betty to follow her. Even if Betty hadn't bought her story, Clea figured she would be too busy dealing with the devastation to her home to be curious about her. Or to question her story. What could make Betty drag herself all the way back to the clinic? Did she know something? Clea's heart began to thump harder.

"I came back here to get something that was mine," Clea said.

Betty crossed to where Clea stood, righted the stool. "May I take a look?"

Right now Clea didn't have a choice. Though with all her heart she wanted to, she couldn't snatch what was on the stage of the microscope and make a run for it. Clea shrugged and stepped aside.

Betty leaned over the microscope, adjusted it. Her head

seemed to be glued to the eyepieces, she stayed so long at it, as if she were memorizing what she saw. "It's just a list," she finally said. "People's names and dates."

Clea stepped back, waited for the reaction. She wasn't disappointed.

Betty's head snapped up. "My God. These are transfers of embryos." She stared straight ahead for a long time, then shook her head slowly, sorrowfully. "I knew he must be doing something for that money. I never dreamed it was something like this." She turned on Clea. "Where did you get this?"

Clea took off her shoe and lifted her foot onto a stool. The bloody patch on her sole was visible.

"I don't get it."

"The list was on pieces of microfilm. In a capsule my father implanted in my foot when I was a baby."

Betty looked at her as if she said she received a message from Mars through the fillings in her teeth.

"Microfilm? In your foot? How would a doctor know how to make something like that? Or have the equipment for it?"

Clea lifted her foot from the stool. "It's not that hard. Microfilm can be made by shooting something with an ordinary 35mm camera, using high-resolution film. You develop the film, mount the negative with a light behind it, and shoot the negative. The image you cut from that second negative can be less than a quarter inch across."

Betty's face said clearly that she didn't buy it.

"I figured it out for myself. Nobody had to tell me," Clea said. "It isn't rocket science."

Betty looked as if she were biting her tongue. "All right. How did you know it was there?"

"Dr. Wyatt told me when I broke into his house tonight."

Betty's mouth dropped open.

To Clea, Betty's face showed less of admiration for her courage than incredulity that she could be so stupid.

Betty confirmed it. "How crazy do you have to be to do that? And after the way he treated you at the clinic?"

It's my life and my choice, Clea thought. Funny how people expected you to justify to them things that were none of their business. She might have told Betty that, but not while the microfilm was still in the microscope.

"I had to know why he hired people to hunt my mother and me. There weren't a lot of other ways to find out. In the two years I worked for him, I didn't come up with anything. When he threw me out of the clinic yesterday, there was nothing left but to confront him. In his den."

"Weren't you afraid he would hurt you?"

Apparently, Betty still wasn't satisfied that Clea was telling her the truth. Either that, or she couldn't imagine herself doing the same thing.

Clea knew her knees got weak like everyone else. And like everyone else, she had inner voices that were brave and fearful. Only tonight the brave voice had been louder than the voice that told her to run.

And she had almost been sorry that she'd listened to it. Clea had a sudden impulse to confide in Betty. "Just before he told me about the microfilm he grabbed my wrist and pulled out a scalpel. I thought that might be it."

"Why in God's name did you believe him?" Betty looked dumbfounded. "And how could you trust him to surgically remove the capsule? I would have been so nervous I wouldn't have been able to keep still."

Clea already regretted her impulse. And she was done with trying to satisfy Betty's curiosity about her risk-taking. "I have a pretty good idea what he's capable of," Clea said. "I think when he deals with microscopic embryos and people he's never met, he's operating at a distance that lets him rationalize his actions. But to kill a human being who isn't trying to kill him, and to use a scalpel...I think that's too personal a weapon for him."

Betty let out a long breath and shook her head slowly. "You have a lot more nerve than I do," she said. "Not just because you trusted him, but because you let him cut your foot in his house. What kinds of surgical equipment could he have had at home?"

"He didn't need much," Clea said. "His black bag had antiseptic pads and syringes of Lidocaine. My foot was numb by the time he started. He must be a good surgeon. I didn't feel anything and he was done before I expected him to be."

Betty slowly frowned. "How did you get him to give you this capsule? If he hunted you for twenty years to get his hands on the microfilm, why would he just hand it over to you? Especially when he hadn't even seen it. He must have been wild to find out what was on that list."

Remembering the scene, Clea's knees again felt like jelly and her heart began to pound. That had been an impulsive move, and it could so easily have gone the other way. "He didn't give it to me. After he removed the capsule, he took it to his desk to clean it and take it apart. I knew he would never give it to me, and it *belonged* to me. So I tore off the butterfly bandage and squeezed my foot to make it really bleed and I started crying that I was hemorrhaging. When he came over to look, I shoved my foot in his face and knocked him down. I grabbed the capsule and ran."

Betty's face cleared. Now there was only admiration in her eyes. "I'll bet there are military men who would give their eye teeth for the kind of courage you have."

Clea didn't answer.

Betty moved away from the microscope. "I guess you'll want to make copies."

Clea nodded. She photographed the microfilm, then connected the digital camera to her computer. First she printed out hard copies. One of these she folded and put into her pocket; the others went into envelopes that she addressed and stamped. Then she made a pdf of the list and emailed it with a short note to several addresses she had on her computer.

Betty had watched silently. Now she asked: "Who are you sending the list to?"

Clea had never expected to find anything remotely like the list. She was almost totally unprepared for it. So she had done just the bare minimum she could think of. First, to keep the list safe until she knew what to do next, she had addressed copies to the post office boxes she kept in Westport, Norwalk, and Fairfield. Second, she had emailed the list to contacts at local newspapers, people who had written articles about the clinic. Clea hoped she could trust them to reveal this information—in case she didn't live long enough to do it herself.

Clea told Betty her strategy and watched the woman's face.

"Give me a copy, too," Betty said. "Letting people know what Dr. Wyatt has done is going to destroy this clinic and my job, but it has to be done. If it comes to it and you need me to corroborate, people may believe a doctor who worked here and has nothing to gain from telling the story."

Clea hesitated. There was something she'd wanted to ask Betty since she walked into the lab. "Tell me why you came here tonight."

"After you left, I remembered seeing blood *in* your shoe," Betty said. "I didn't think you'd walked barefoot in my house, so I wondered where it came from. I felt there was more you weren't telling me."

Clea still held a copy of the list. "And why do you want to know what's on the list?"

Betty let out a sigh that riffled the papers in Clea's hand. "In the last few hours, I've had my house trashed and found out I could be an accessory to a theft that is so horrendous...I don't need any more surprises. As bad as it is, I want to know the whole terrible truth."

Clea handed Betty a copy which Betty folded and put in her purse. Clea zipped the capsule containing the microfilm into a compartment in her small purse.

Clea shrugged. "I've got to go."

She was unprepared for what Betty did next. She flung her arms around her and gave her a bear hug.

"I want you to know something," Betty said, releasing Clea. "That Tarot reading I did for you. The five cards that came up? The first letter of the name of each card spells out DEATH."

Clea shrugged, as if she didn't care what Betty said.

"Don't give me that look," Betty said. "Wherever you're going, be careful. The cards don't give idle threats. It doesn't have to happen if you take heed."

Betty opened her purse. "And if you don't take heed and you need my help, you let me know." She gave Clea a card containing all her phone numbers. "Whatever it is. Anytime."

73

Cy's leaping to his feet had narrowly missed getting him knocked unconscious again. For a large man, Mr. Greene proved to be unexpectedly agile. He had held Cy's arms behind his back until the two henchmen had patted him down.

"Why didn't you have them checked for weapons?" Mr. Greene asked his wife. Any semblance to the friendly Santa had vanished.

"What would they carry?"

He ignored her.

"He's figured out...the positions at the card table," she told her husband.

Greene looked briefly at Dr. Wyatt. "So what?"

"He knew it before he came here; maybe he's told someone."

"Again, so what?"

She was looking more agitated. "He must have kept a list of the transfers. What if he gave them to someone? Wipe your cheek," she snapped.

Her husband didn't wipe the lipstick off his cheek. "There is nothing to connect him to us," he said. "That's where Detective Horn comes in. Everyone will be kept busy following the lurid details of that woman's murder. They won't have any interest in any postmortem efforts to involve others."

Cy shot a glance at Dr. Wyatt. They had both avoided looking at each other, though for different reasons, Cy thought. Dr. Wyatt had been exactly right about Mr. and Mrs. Greene and their game. Too bad for Cy's and the older man's sakes his revelation came too late.

"If it doesn't matter what list I may have, why do you want to kill us?" Dr. Wyatt had found his voice.

"Inconvenience, Doctor," Mr. Greene said. "If people start asking questions, looking into various things, who knows what will come to light? We can't afford it."

"Why did you have Jane killed?" Dr. Wyatt asked him. "Clea and Cy didn't even know about the Hutchings when Jane was killed."

Mr. Greene gave a weary shrug. "I thought it might come in handy. And it has."

He nodded toward his two lackeys and they came forward as he stepped back. They both had guns, which they lifted in unison.

Cy went cold. He had been worried they were going to sic a dog on them, and now it turned out to be guns. He didn't know how to prepare himself, or what to do.

Mrs. Greene suddenly lunged in her husband's direction. "Wait!"

Had she had a change of heart? Cy wondered. Had she finally felt regret for her lack of loyalty to Dr. Wyatt?

"He said *Clea.*"

"What does that mean?" Her husband was barely restraining his annoyance.

"He said that Cy and *Clea* found something out. She must be alive. He must know where she is."

Mr. Greene turned on Dr. Wyatt. "Is that true?"

Cy glared at Dr. Wyatt, as if he could burn him into silence. He held his breath, wondering whether the older man would betray Clea or tell them he had made a slip of the tongue.

"She came back to see me," he said.

Mrs. Greene was excited. "Did she have the list?"

He shook his head. "Yes and no."

Rage raced across Mr. Greene's face. "Let's get this over with," he said to the two lackeys.

"No," Mrs. Greene said. "What do you mean?" she asked Dr. Wyatt.

"She didn't know her father had hidden the list on microfilm in a capsule he implanted in her foot."

Mr. and Mrs. Greene seemed frozen for a split second.

"Why didn't you kill her and take it from her?" Mrs. Greene

asked.

Just don't say what's on your mind, Cy thought. To Cy, the look on Dr. Wyatt's face said he was thinking: 'Because I couldn't do it that way. I'm not like you.'

"I planned to bu t it didn't work out that way," Dr. Wyatt said. "She surprised me at my house. She and her mother knew they were being followed and they assumed it was because of me. Clea wanted to know why. I told her about the capsule in her foot, thinking it would stun her long enough for me to grab her." He shook his head. "She was too fast. She ran out of the house."

"Of all the incompetent, moronic..." Mrs. Greene's voice escalated into rage. Mr. Greene looked at her curiously.

"Where is she now?" Mr. Greene asked.

"I don't know," Dr. Wyatt said. "But her first priority is to see the list. And after she does, she'll come here."

74

Clea was ferried across the marble floor of the cavernous foyer by the jostling mass of revelers. She hugged the small purse to her chest, patting it for reassurance. It contained a copy of the list and a syringe of Lidocaine.

She hadn't known she would be coming here tonight. But when she saw that name under the high-powered microscope, she knew where she was going and what she was going to do.

It was the same name she'd seen on the registration of the Mercedes that had brought the 'pregnant' woman in chiffon to the clinic a few days ago. Clea had noticed that the woman left with a smaller stomach than she'd gone in with. A payment? A delivery? Whatever she'd given to Dr. Wyatt, it had to be connected to his commerce in stolen embryos.

When Clea saw the name 'Greene' on the microfilm list— appearing over and over as the person responsible for directing where the embryos went—Clea knew she had to pay a visit. If these people had been in league with Dr. Wyatt, they were as responsible as he was for making her a fugitive for twenty years. It was payback time.

And the Lidocaine? She had no idea why she'd taken it. It had been pure impulse. The extra syringe had been on Dr. Wyatt's desk, next to the capsule. She had swept up both before she ran out of his house. She could have left the Lidocaine behind when she came here. But she had nothing else to use as a weapon, and even if she never used it, just knowing it was there helped to calm her fears.

She had been expecting to break into the mansion just as she'd broken into Dr. Wyatt's home. But she was unprepared for a party, let alone for one of this magnitude. When she heard all the noise, caught glimpses of the guests, she looked nervously at her black slacks and top—would they give her away? *Black can go virtually anywhere* floated into her mind. It was the only fashion rule she knew. She put on her small shoulder bag bandolier-style, and crashed the party.

Once inside, she was in the throes of an event that was not only beyond her experience, but beyond anything she might have imagined. She had never been to New Orleans for Mardi Gras, but she thought the atmosphere must be similar.

Though her black outfit was well within the range of what people were wearing, she still braced herself to be challenged as an intruder. It didn't take her long to realize she needn't worry. The number of revelers, the height of their revelry—not to mention the self-importance of the revelers—were enough to overwhelm any security force. Assuming a confidence she didn't feel, she made her way through the rooms. All that hindered her were the pressing crowds, all the more remarkable to her because the mansion was so immense.

She started out asking discreet directions to find her host, but soon realized discretion was pointless when you had to shout each question several times. Clea finally found Mr. Greene holding court with a bevy of women of varying ages. The lack of inhibition of the party goers, the lack of focus in their eyes, made Clea think they were high on something. She had refused several offers of a glass of wine, assuming that was what made everyone look drugged.

Clea circled the large room, keeping an eye on Mr. Greene. She didn't have to worry about being obvious. Everyone seemed oblivious to what was going on outside their alcoholic haze.

With his white beard and hair and his size, from a distance Mr. Greene had reminded Clea of a Santa. How far that was from the truth. The lipstick smeared on his cheek, and his roving hand told her he was neither immune to feminine charms, nor too discreet to broadcast it. When the current of people swirling around him seemed to ebb, Clea took her chance, and drew to within several feet of him.

"Thank you for inviting me," she said. It was so loud in the room that she had decided simply to mouth the words slowly. But it was soon clear that he hadn't been watching her lips to make out what she was saying. He reached out, took her arm in a strong grip and propelled her through the throng. They went past men and women looking vaguely conscious and vaguely envious, and vaguely trying to pull him into their own circles. But he maneuvered past all of them to a room that was locked until he opened it.

When the heavy door shut behind her like a bank vault, Clea went cold inside. Now that she was alone with him, she was afraid. He was a big man. She wasn't so confident now that she could do what she had come to do and then leave. She didn't want to find herself surprised again, as she had earlier tonight by Dr. Wyatt.

Was that just earlier this evening? The makeshift surgery, her hairsbreadth escape, the crushing demolition at Betty's house, the revelation of the list at the clinic's lab. It seemed surreal. For twenty years she had lived a shoestring of a life. Now in the space of maybe five hours, she felt as if she were in the middle of a fantastic movie.

It was clear to her, despite her lack of experience, that Mr. Greene hadn't brought her here for a conversation.

"Sit down." He motioned to a large sofa.

She went to the sofa, stood uncomfortably by one of the arms.

He opened a cabinet; brought over two glasses of wine. "Here you are," he said.

He drank. Clea took one sniff; knew that a migraine or oblivion was right behind her first sip. She wanted neither.

"Would you turn down the lights?" she asked, feigning shyness. When he turned, smiling, she poured most of the glass between the seat cushions. Ruining their furniture was the least of what she wanted to do to the Greenes.

She watched him walk back to the sofa. She had to get him seated. While he was standing, it would be too easy for him to intercept her when she ran for the door. He needed to sit down, to be relaxed, to be off-guard.

She went behind the sofa, patted the back cushions. "If you sit here, I'll massage your neck."

He shrugged and settled himself on the sofa. With repulsion she surveyed his thick neck, was loathe to touch him. Holding her breath, she began to massage through the fabric of his jacket.

"Wait," he said, struggling to shed his jacket. He threw the jacket over the back of the sofa, pulled his tie loose and tossed it on top of the jacket, and unbuttoned the top button of his shirt.

Now it was worse. More of his neck was visible, folds of flesh that were flushed (she didn't want to think of him aroused). Trying to avoid looking at him, she began to squeeze his skin between her fingers.

Clea could see the top of his jacket out of the corner of her eye. If she could just reach over and slip the list in the inside pocket...She removed one hand from his neck, opened the purse she was wearing, and pulled out the paper, slowly.

"Why are you stopping?" a groggy voice asked. "You have great hands."

How could he still be so alert? She was counting on the combination of wine and massage to put him to sleep. She cursed the fact that he was a large man, and probably had a large capacity.

She put both hands on his neck again.

"Come join me," he said, patting the seat cushion.

Clea had no intention of getting anywhere near his grasp. She had to wrap this up.

"How about another glass of wine?" she asked him.

His jovial attitude slipped. "Forget the wine," he said in a rough voice. "Sit down."

Clea saw too late what he was made of. Saw what was going to happen next. She wasn't going to transfer the list to his jacket and slip out the door. She wasn't going anywhere.

"I said, sit down." He swung an arm in an arc behind him. A beefy hand hit Clea's breast, grabbed a handful of her top.

Clea cried out as he dragged her toward him. She wriggled in his grasp, but she might as well have been a fish at the end of his line. She struggled to pry his hand off her, but couldn't budge even one of the thick fingers. He laughed at her efforts and tightened his grip, drawing her narrow shoulder strap tight and making her purse cut into her free breast

He had just reminded her that she carried a weapon.

Though Clea was trembling so hard her teeth rattled, she unclasped her small bag and pulled out the syringe. As he dragged her head first over the back of the sofa, she shot out an arm and plunged the needle into the side of his neck. With all the force in her thumb, she pushed the plunger to deliver the entire contents into him.

Like a bear stung by a hornet, he let go of her and slapped a hand to his neck, howling in pain. "Bitch!" he bellowed.

Clea pushed herself off the sofa and staggered back, praying the drug would do more than infuriate him.

"Guards!" he yelled.

At least that's what she thought he said. Or what he had intended. What actually came out was garbled. He was already having trouble controlling his mouth, his arms, his facial muscles. Where had she injected him? Her fear that it wouldn't be enough, quickly turned to terror that she had delivered a lethal dose. She hadn't intended to kill him.

His upper body swayed slightly, then he fell over on his side.

Clea waited long moments, then cautiously circled the sofa to see if he was breathing; he was. She watched him as she lifted his jacket and tucked the list in the inside pocket. Then she backed toward the door.

What if he doesn't see the list until later? she worried. What if he puts his jacket away—or sends it to the cleaners without seeing the list?

It was suddenly very important to her that he find the list—the sooner the better. As soon as he regained consciousness. Let it be the first thing that greeted him.

Clea went back to the sofa, pulled his tie from under his jacket. She knotted the tie around the list as if it were a present, then reached out to drape it over his chest.

His hand swatted out and wrapped around her throat.

75

Diane waved at Betty from her seat in front of a large lighted mirror. "Come on over."

Why did I come here? Betty thought today's events must have fogged her mind. Her house had been trashed, and she'd just found out that the head of her clinic was dealing in stolen embryos. She didn't have a home and soon wouldn't have a job. The horrific revelations in Clea's list had made Betty dizzy. Right now she should be trying to put the pieces of her life back together. Not running around the backstage of a television studio. So why was she here?

Betty walked over, stood behind Diane's chair and smiled at her in the mirror. "How are you doing?"

The makeup artist brushed a light dusting of powder on Diane's face. "You look beautiful," she said.

Diane admired her image under the flattering stage lights. "Thank you. You did a great job."

She *had* done a good job, Betty thought. Diane showed none of the stress that she had earlier in the day. She was radiant.

Diane got up and hugged Betty. "Thank you for coming. I really appreciate it, especially after you've put in a long day."

You have no idea, Betty thought. But Betty could already see how keeping her promise to Diane was therapeutic for her. The lights, the nonstop activity at the studio provided the perfect distraction. Tomorrow was soon enough for her to face reality.

"I'm so nervous I have butterflies on top of butterflies," Diane said.

"Why?" Betty was surprised. "I thought the first airing of your line went so well."

Diane nodded. "It did. It was such a success that we sold out. That's why I'm nervous. I don't know what we're doing here tonight. I know my inventory, and it's gone."

A lovely young woman walked over to them. As she got closer, Betty saw she was wearing full stage makeup. Diane introduced her as Tracie, the same hostess who had been on with her at the first airing.

"Whew! What a day." Tracie cast a critical eye over Diane. "You look great."

"Thank you. What's happening tonight? I thought we sold out the first night."

The young woman nodded. "We did. Tonight we're going to bring your skin care philosophy to millions *more* households."

"I brought some of the clinical results," Diane said. She showed them a folder that had before-and-after color photographs of women who had used her products. Betty noticed Diane's hands were shaking; she really was nervous. She hoped it wouldn't affect her, once she was on camera. "I also have some charts showing the increase in skin firmness and suppleness, and other charts that show an increase in hydration."

The hostess interrupted Diane by patting her arm reassuringly and smiling. "Those are great pictures and I'm sure we can fit them and the charts in. But don't worry about tonight. There were so many women who called in during the first show, who were too late. They'll be delighted to have a second chance to order your products."

Diane shivered. "I hope we can produce enough product to fill the orders." She turned to Betty. "I never thought inventory would be a problem."

"Don't worry," Tracie said. "My producer said your partners have deep pockets and lots of connections." Someone called her and she motioned to Diane that she would be right back.

Diane winced. "My partners. I swore to myself that I would never have partners, never give up control of my business. I didn't need their money. Not after people like Cy and others invested."

Betty watched the hostess walk away, remembered the conversation she and Diane had had earlier that day. "She seems pleasant enough."

"She's great," Diane said. "She made me feel so welcome and comfortable the first time I came here. She's not the problem. It's the head of the channel. All the pressure, all the scare tactics seem to be coming from Mr. Peterman's office."

Betty nodded. It was hard to think when so many new and distracting things were going on all around her. All the high-tech equipment and the people running back and forth made it seem as if something very important was going on, and that you must be special to be a part of it. Betty made herself think why she was supposed to be here.

"You said you wanted me to look around and talk to some people," Betty said. "Where can I go and who can I talk to?"

Diane looked so grateful that Betty was rewarded again for coming. "See if you can watch and listen to the producer, that man over there." She nodded toward a balding man with glasses. "If I were paranoid, I'd say that he's the eyes and ears of Mr. Peterman, and spies on me. At any rate, he often plays the middleman. Brings me messages from Mr. Peterman. I'd really like to know what that man wants from me."

Peterman. Betty had run across that name recently. Was it just a coincidence? "OK," she said. "I'll do what I can."

The hostess came by, on her way to the set. "We're on in five minutes. Better get settled."

Diane picked up her folder and her purse. She reached in her purse and her face paled. "My pen! I left it someplace. I need it to make notes so I don't forget what I need to say."

"I've got a pen you can use," Betty said. She opened her purse.

"But it's not my pen. I have to have that pen. It's good luck."

Betty put her hand on Diane's shoulder. "You're your own good luck. Any old pen will do. Take mine."

The hostess called to Diane from the set. "Two minutes. You just have time to come over and sit down."

Diane grabbed the pen out of Betty's hand. "Thank you. I'm freaking out now but I'll be OK."

She started walking toward the set, then turned back. "I need a piece of paper, too," she said. "I'm not usually so scatterbrained. I forgot my notebook and I have to keep notes."

"One minute!" the hostess called.

Betty opened her bag. But before she could get anything, Diane thrust her hand in and pulled out some papers.

Diane shouted over her shoulder as her heels clicked over the floor. "Thanks for saving me, Betty. We'll talk when this is over."

76

Clea pulled up the collar of her shirt and held the ends together to hide the marks on her neck. With her free hand she pushed her way through the throng still filling the mansion. No one in the crush of partygoers stopped her on her way to the front door. None of them looked as if Clea even registered in their consciousness.

Tears and terror raged behind her eyes, threatening. She held them off until she was clear of the mansion and had reached her car, where she'd parked it in some foliage off the long private road.

Clea slammed herself inside and locked her doors, managed to get the key in the ignition despite her shaking. Unshed tears made her eyes ache but now that she had some privacy, she couldn't make them budge. Frustrated, it crossed her mind that the people who had kept her on the run all these years had also kept her from unpacking her emotions. She pulled out and drove away from the mansion. There was no one behind her as she sped along the long private road.

One of the only feelings that she had experienced with any frequency all these years was the one that had driven her—a desire for revenge. So why did she feel nothing after tying the list around Greene's neck? No shred of satisfaction. No sense of accomplishment. Not even a taste of revenge. Why?

Because I'm still a hunted animal, she thought. Only now they know for sure that I'm alive.

What had she been thinking? She could have mailed Greene the list of embryo transfers. She could have gotten it to him in a hundred different ways. But she had had to put it in his face, to let him know she had survived and discovered his secret. Well, she had succeeded. And now he knew what she looked like. She was sure he would recognize her, regardless of what disguise she wore.

Clea thought she was motivated by revenge; well, Greene *ate* revenge. She had seen it in his eyes while he squeezed her throat. Defending herself against his attack had been enough to enrage him. No matter what he had done to others, through God knew what other avenues—no one dared to do anything to him. She knew he would hunt her until she was just bones.

She had to run again. And she didn't want to. She wanted to stay here.

The admission stunned her. She hadn't been in Westport since she was a baby, but she felt at home there. Despite the conditions of her homecoming—the inescapably wretched fat suit, the semi-drudgery at the clinic, the constant vigilance to protect her identity—she had been happy there. She could imagine a life there.

Where would she go now? Where hadn't she been? Where wouldn't Greene look for her? Clea felt empty and weary. She had been running for too long and just wanted to stop. As she drove along the winding drive, her headlights caught lawn and shrubbery, lush in the humid air. What a paradise this estate was. How did a creature like Greene deserve to be sheltered by it?

Off the road, in the distance, her headlights caught four figures. They were the first people Clea had seen since leaving the mansion. Why had they left the party? The partygoers seemed to have everything they could ever want inside the mansion. Instinct told Clea to accelerate past them, but something her eye caught made her slow down.

There were four men. One was Cy! Another was Dr. Wyatt. They all seemed to be hurrying along, deeper into the vegetation along the road.

What was Cy doing here?

Clea stared after the retreating figures. She didn't want to stay here; Greene must have recovered by now and put out an alarm. But Cy's being here couldn't be good, in spite of Dr. Wyatt's connection to the Greenes.

One of the men prodded Cy with an object. There was

something familiar about him. Suddenly Clea knew what it was. He had held a sharp knife the last time she saw him. It was the attacker who had cut large X's in her midsection.

Fear sent a shot of adrenaline straight to her heart, but she wrenched the steering wheel to the right and stamped on the accelerator. Her car bounced from the road to the grass, headed straight for the four men. She lay on her horn the whole way.

All four men turned at the honking and the lights. One of them—her attacker—lifted his arm.

Her windshield *shattered*—what was he shooting? Now warm, humid night air blew on Clea's face. She pressed the gas pedal even harder.

The man lifted his arm again and Clea heard the bullet hit metal.

Did Cy have any idea she was driving the car? How could he?

Clea shot straight into the center of the men. They dove off to either side, hitting the ground. She made a tight turn and a screeching stop. "Get in!" she shouted to Cy.

The look on his face.

In the gleam of her headlights, Clea saw a rapid succession of expressions on Cy's face—what looked to her like confusion, fear, relief, gratitude, and recognition. And something else, that wiped away any remaining doubts. During the long months at the clinic, she had discovered Cy's obsession with finding her. But she had always assumed it had more to do with him than with her. That he couldn't live with himself because he had failed not her, but his *promise* to her. Now she knew there was more to it.

For a golden moment, she was glad she had come tonight. Cy's face shone with redemption. With loyalty, faith, maybe even...

It was a short golden moment. She reminded herself that, compared to her life, his had been one of comfort and peace. He had had the opportunity to grow and learn at his leisure, to form friendships and pursue a career. He had had the luxury to feel pity and regret for her disappearance and to make a project out of looking for her.

Cy ran toward her. The man with the gun was on the other side of the car from Cy; he lifted his arm, aiming at Cy.

"No!" Clea screamed. She swerved around Cy and headed straight for the man with the gun. What am I asking for now? she thought. She had never even hurt anyone, let alone run over them. If he didn't move, she was sure she would take her foot from the gas. Then what? She had no windshield, so there wasn't even a glass barrier between them.

Grace granted Clea a flash of memory, as clear as the original experience. She watched this man as he sliced a large X across her abdomen. There had been no awareness in his eyes that she was even a sentient being, let alone another human.

Clea floored the accelerator.

The man shot. She ducked. He shot again. She ducked again. Thank God his aim is off, she thought. Even under stress, Clea knew you couldn't duck a bullet.

Just before she was about to hit him squarely, he dove out of her path. *Chicken!* But she'd clipped him. Whatever part of his body was hurt, at this point she didn't know or care. All she wanted was for him to be out of commission long enough for her and Cy to get out of here.

Clea sped back to Cy, jerked to a stop so he could get in. But before Clea could step on the gas, a gun barrel followed Cy into the car.

77

The bald producer with glasses came over to greet Betty personally.

"What are you doing here?"

"I'm a friend of Diane's." Betty nodded toward the set. "She asked me to come with her to help calm her jitters." Betty decided not to mention her medical qualifications or anything else.

Though he didn't move his stare from Betty's eyes, she could feel him looking her up and down. For a brief moment she was actually worried that he wouldn't find her acceptable.

"OK," he finally said. "But you'll have to wait over there." He pointed to someplace far off-camera. "I don't want any distractions during the presentation."

I don't like him already, Betty thought. But that isn't very definitive.

Betty found a vantage point that allowed her to watch Diane and the bald producer. Diane was right; he watched her like a hawk, made notes on his clipboard and frequently talked into a headset. Betty got the impression that every bit of information about Diane's presentation was being fed live to someone—maybe Mr. Peterman.

Thankfully, Diane was fine. She had quelled her nervousness and was confident and charming on camera. Betty was watching someone who knew she had a great product and knew how to get that across to an audience. A couple of times during the presentation, Betty caught herself reaching for her cell phone to call in an order.

Despite the excitement and her intention to help Diane, Betty was getting drowsy. She fought it, stood up and walked back and forth. Looked at her watch. She hoped the presentation was almost over, so she could go home and to bed.

At that thought, Betty was both fully awake and fully depressed. Her home. What was there to go home to? No home; soon, no job.

Betty's attention was grabbed by a loud voice rising in volume. She found the source—the bald producer. He was talking rapidly and loudly into his mouthpiece, at the same time gesturing wildly to the people on the set. What was he trying to tell them?

Betty walked closer to the set to see what was happening.

At first, the scene looked perfectly normal to Betty. The hostess and Diane were talking about Diane's skin products. Diane was holding up another chart to show the benefits of using her skin cream. Betty scrutinized every element of the set—the people, their clothing and makeup, furniture, even the props.

The only thing that could be at all out of the ordinary was the chart Diane was holding.

Now Betty looked more closely, and it seemed that what Diane was presenting on camera wasn't a chart. What was it? Betty scanned the set for a television monitor, and walked to one that was far away from the agitated producer.

Betty peered at the television screen. What Diane was holding didn't look like a line graph, a bar graph, or a pie chart. Maybe it was a table of results. Betty walked closer until she could read the writing. She froze when she realized what she was looking at.

When Diane had grabbed some papers out of Betty's purse, she had inadvertently taken the embryo transfer list. Diane was holding up one page of that list on national television.

78

"You sent the list where?!"

Cy hissed the question to Clea as they sat huddled on the floor. They had been returned to the mansion and were imprisoned in the game room—Dr. Wyatt had given them that bit of information before lapsing again into a catatonic state. The room had no windows; Cy guessed it was soundproof as well. Though it would probably do no good to scream for help, that didn't mean the room wasn't bugged.

But what point was there in trying to hide anything? Greene had made it clear he planned to kill them. Clea's appearance had only delayed his plans, not changed them. Greene was probably regrouping, as he toasted his guests with another glass of wine.

Cy had been rapt as Clea told him about the capsule, what it contained, what she had done with the list, why she had come to the mansion. He didn't realize until she was finished that his mouth was open. Now Cy sat staring at her, overwhelmed by her courage and presence of mind.

A keening sound startled Cy. Its source was Dr. Wyatt, who was now lying on the floor in a fetal position and rocking himself back and forth. Why did he have to fall apart when they needed another clear head?

"I sent emails to local papers," Clea said. "Because I wanted to make sure that everyone knew what he did. Even if I..."

Cy knew what she meant. She had no illusions about tonight, either. Helpless anger raged in him. Just when he'd found Clea, they were both scheduled to be killed. Cy had been cheated out of twenty years with Clea. Right now he would give anything for another chance.

"So you tied the list under Greene's nose?"

Clea nodded and looked away. It had been a foolish thing for her to do. But Cy could understand why she had done it.

It was a small bit of revenge taken on the man who had robbed her of peace for twenty years.

"When I tell him that I sent the list to so many places, he won't dare to hurt us. People will know who did it."

Cy nodded, though he had more confidence in being able to stop a rhino than Greene when he was high on rage. He studied Clea. Though he believed everything she had told him, she looked so vulnerable. He wanted to be strong for her, to protect her.

"He isn't afraid of anyone. He has the money and contacts to make anything go away."

It was Dr. Wyatt. Since they had been herded into this room, he had been silent and withdrawn, curled up in a ball in a corner. The events of the past few hours must have shattered him. The older man had thought these people were his friends...Cy stopped when he realized he was feeling sorry for the man who had made all the embryo transfers possible.

"It's like in Congress. If you can keep the motion from reaching the floor, no one can vote on it," Dr. Wyatt said. "It's very effective. Greene always manages to pull strings so nothing he does ever comes to light."

As if on cue, the door opened and Greene walked in, followed by two men carrying body-sized plastic bags.

In spite of his resolution, Cy thought he was going to be sick.

79

How could I have let Diane take the list? Betty agonized.

Betty knew she had been traumatized by the sweeping vandalism of her home. And she had been stunned and devastated by the revelation that a commerce in embryos had been taking place under her nose, in the clinic where she worked. A lot had conspired to unhinge her tonight. But she should have had enough presence of mind not to let that list out of her hands.

Betty was staggered by the implications of what she had unintentionally allowed to be broadcast across the country.

Surely, with all the millions who watched this channel, there must be people who were touched by that list. Maybe they knew someone on it. Maybe their own names were on it.

Betty's heart was racing and she had to clasp her hands together to keep them from shaking. She tried to tell herself that maybe it wasn't as terrible as she'd first thought. Would anyone looking at that list know what it represented? There were no headings for the columns. And Betty was sure that the 'donors' had had no connection with the 'receivers.'

Betty's attention was drawn back to the bald producer. It was clear from the red color of the man's face and his wild gestures that the list meant something to him. More than something. The list seemed to have at the same time upset him and paralyzed him. Why was he having such a reaction to it? Why didn't he just yank the list off-camera and go on with the show?

Betty couldn't stand still any longer, eating herself up over the damage that might have been done. She had to get the list back in her possession. But first she wanted to know what the bald man was saying and who he was saying it to.

Betty circled behind the producer and positioned herself close enough to pick up parts of his end of the conversation.

"Both names are on it. There's no question..."

Betty's glance alternated between Diane and the producer. Diane still didn't seem to realize that the paper she was holding up wasn't one of her charts.

"It's not just any list of names," the producer insisted. "There are two columns. Right next to each other."

Good Lord, Betty thought. He sounds as if he has some idea of what that list is.

Someone must finally have gotten a message to Diane. The camera was on the hostess, and Diane turned over the paper to look at it. She frowned, looked completely blank. Then her eyes widened, and she searched the set. Betty felt like shriveling up on the floor.

Betty heard the producer say: "The names are..."

The rest of his pronouncement was cut off by a scream from the set.

80

"What's going on here, Greene?"

A man stood in the doorway but kept his hand on the doorknob, as if he was unsure about coming in. Even though this house was enormous and well-constructed, through the open door Dr. Wyatt could hear faint sounds of revelry. The party must still be in full swing, he thought.

"What do you want, Peterman?" Greene's voice was harsh.

Dr. Wyatt was alert again. He was ashamed and embarrassed now for having panicked. He had allowed his fears—and betrayal by the Greenes and Aggie—to overwhelm and weaken him, to make him crawl into himself. And he had found that too small a space. Another revelation.

He knew the new arrival; twenty-odd years ago he had helped this man and his wife have the daughter they just lost in a car crash. And he had seen Peterman in this room just days ago, seated at the round game table with Greene. Now Dr. Wyatt understood the game he had watched that night. Peterman had drawn a card to select a new member of his team. Skin Man. Dr. Wyatt still didn't know what that referred to.

Peterman's glance fell uneasily on the man-sized plastic bags. "What are you going to do with those?"

"Nothing you have to concern yourself with," Greene said. "This is private."

Peterman didn't budge. It occurred to Dr. Wyatt that Peterman had expected Greene to be alone, was still hoping to see him alone.

Thank God he came, Dr. Wyatt thought. They needed someone rational to balance Greene's blind rage. Dr. Wyatt reluctantly shot a glance at Greene. He looked like a hyena ready to drip blood from his jaws. The simile surprised and frightened Dr. Wyatt; he had never been so fanciful. He couldn't help wondering if the closeness of death heightened all one's faculties.

"I'd still like to know what's going on," Peterman said.

Stay, Dr. Wyatt thought. Talk him out of acting like a madman. The damage is done. All he's doing is being vengeful. While he had been curled in a fetal position on the sofa, he had overheard Clea tell Cy what she had found in the capsule. He heard what she had done with copies of the list. With the list made public, his career was over. If they could prove his involvement in court, his freedom would be over, too. He pushed those thoughts away. Staying alive was his first priority.

Dr. Wyatt glanced at Clea. He couldn't read her face. Belatedly, he wondered if it would have been better if he'd killed her before removing the capsule. His shoulders sagged; he knew it was something he was incapable of. Steal embryos, yes. Slice open a human being's jugular, no. He didn't know if that meant he was a timid pawn or still barely human.

Greene stood by the round table. "I have business to conclude. Whatever you came here to talk about, it can wait until later. Go away."

Peterman's ears laid back. He stepped into the room.

Dr. Wyatt didn't know whether to be hopeful that Peterman was staying, or anxious that there was likely to be a confrontation.

"What are you doing here?" Peterman asked again.

Dr. Wyatt didn't think Greene would deign to answer, thought he would tell the two thugs to throw Peterman out. But Greene told the two men to wait outside. When the door closed, he gestured dismissively toward Dr. Wyatt, Cy, and Clea as if they were so much furniture.

"Twenty years ago her father hid microfilm in her foot. That microfilm contained a list of the embryo transfers that he and Wyatt did. I have that list, but it will be made public if I don't stop them. To save our interests and keep our business private, I have to stop these three."

A strange look briefly distorted Peterman's face.

"What do you mean, list of transfers?" Peterman asked. "How many were there?"

Greene shook his head with irritation. "What difference does that make? The point is we have to do damage control."

"But what if the list has already been made public?" Peterman asked. "What will you do then?"

Greene shot a wary glance at Peterman. "If these three aren't around to open their mouths, we can squash any reports. I have people who know what to do."

Dr. Wyatt's heart spasmed at the cold delivery of Greene's words, but he still managed to hear Peterman say:

"I'll bet you do."

There was something in the way Peterman said this that didn't give Dr. Wyatt any comfort.

Greene must have read something in his fellow gameplayer. "What do you know about the list?"

Peterman hesitated for a beat, then said: "It's been broadcast nationally on my station."

Dr. Wyatt gasped, whether with hope or despair he didn't yet know.

Greene looked like a mad bull, as if he could kill Peterman. "You had the list."

Peterman put up a hand. A hand won't stop him, Dr. Wyatt thought. You'd better have something else.

"I didn't broadcast the list," he said. "It was done by that dermatologist you had me draw."

What is he talking about? Dr. Wyatt wondered. Then it hit him. *Skin Man.* A slang term for a dermatologist. That was the card Peterman drew. The newest member of Peterman's team: Diane and her face products. How had she gotten the list so quickly, if he had just taken the microfilm out of Clea's foot earlier tonight?

"I don't believe you," Greene said. Then his head slowly swung toward Clea. "You."

"I gave a copy of the list to Dr. Winter, who works at the

clinic. I also sent copies to newspapers. Big papers. Nothing of what you did is going to be a secret anymore."

Greene glared at her as if he could kill her with his eyes. Dr. Wyatt wondered what the man was thinking. He was always capable of murder. How would his mind work after an evening of his own stimulant-laced wine?

Finally Greene turned back to Peterman. "If these three aren't around, there isn't anything to prove the list is linked to us..."

"To you," Peterman corrected.

"...and nothing to threaten our game," Greene finished.

Peterman glanced at the three captives, then turned back to Greene. "There's nothing in the rules of the game about murder."

"It's in your best interests to protect the game," Greene said.

Peterman jerked his head to indicate outside the room. "But there are rules out there about blowing people up in a car to cover your tracks."

"What are you talking about?" Greene asked, but his face said he already knew.

"I found out something tonight about my daughter. She was one of those embryo transfers."

Greene seemed to relax. "You already knew that,. You knew where those embryos came from and you still wanted one."

"I also found out that her husband was the result of an embryo transfer."

Greene didn't say a word. His eyes didn't leave Peterman.

"And I found out that both of them came from the same donors."

Oh my God, Dr. Wyatt thought. He was feeling sick.

"They were on their way to Wyatt's clinic when their car blew up," Peterman said. "It wouldn't have been good for your business if it got out that a brother and sister were married thanks to your efforts."

Greene still didn't say anything.

"That was why the fire had to be so thorough. And why the police told me the DNA evidence said it looked as if there had been only one person in the wreck."

Peterman was reaching in his pocket. Dr. Wyatt prayed that it was for a gun.

"It's time for you to pay up," Peterman said.

Greene found his voice. "What do you want?"

Peterman's pupils seemed to dilate. His gaze swung to the round table and he stared at it as if it were the Holy Grail.

"The first seat at the table," he said.

"No," Dr. Wyatt moaned.

Greene visibly relaxed. "Done," he said. "There's an Amazing Sweepstakes truck parked out front. Tell the driver to bring it around the back."

81

Betty walked up to the bald producer and yanked off his wireless headset.

Extreme circumstances call for extreme measures, she thought. The producer swung an arm at her to take it back. Betty held up her hand. "Don't even think of it."

She put on the headset, spoke into the mouthpiece. "Mr. Peterman? I'm at your television studio and I've just seen the list that was broadcast. That list does not belong to Diane and she had no idea she was showing it on camera."

Betty waited for an answer. Silence.

"The list was mine and I inadvertently gave it to her," she said.

"Who is this?" a voice said.

"Betty!"

It was Diane. Betty swung toward the set, saw Diane gesturing to her. Here it comes, Betty thought, bracing for Diane to explode at her. Diane has a chance to make it big and I mess things up for her. Betty gave one backwards glance at the producer, who was scurrying away toward the wings. No doubt going to get security. She hurried toward Diane.

The set was in chaos. Faces aghast, a babble of voices. People running everywhere.

"They went to commercial so they can figure out what happened," Diane said. "Someone named Rose called in and said she knows you. Do you know who that is?"

Rose! What could make her call? And why hadn't Diane asked her about the list? What had happened that could be more upsetting than that? Betty nodded. "What did she say?"

Diane's face was pale and she was white around the lips. "She said she ordered my face cream. When it arrived and she opened the jar, she said she found a small packet of white powder in the bottom of the jar."

Betty's mind raced in horror over the range of toxic chemicals that could exist as a white powder. And the reasons why someone would send it.

"Cocaine. She said she knows it's cocaine," Diane said.

"WHAT!"

The loud voice in her ear reminded Betty she was still wearing the headset. "You heard correctly," she told the voice. "Mr. Peterman?"

There was such a long delay Betty thought he had gotten off the line.

"Yes," he finally said.

"Someone found cocaine in a jar of the cream," Betty said. Her tone had changed; now she wasn't apologizing. She was on the offensive. "How can that be?"

"Maybe they're a crackpot like you," Peterman said. "Who are you?"

"I'm a doctor at Dr. Wyatt's fertility clinic," Betty said. "And a friend of Diane's."

"If something is wrong with her products, ask Diane; her company fills the jars," he said.

Betty's gut instinct told her not to trust this man. She suspected that he did know about the cocaine in the jars. Was that why he had been horning in on Diane's business? So he could use her as a courier? The thought made Betty's blood boil.

"You must know something about this," she told Peterman. "You've been pushing your way into Diane's manufacturing facility, trying to take over her production and packaging. Now you say you don't know why cocaine is in the jars? Maybe that's why you've been trying to take over her business."

As soon as she said the words, Betty regretted them. She didn't even know this man. He was the head of the shopping channel and could probably get rid of Diane and her products in a heartbeat. Not to mention the legal consequences of an illegal substance being shipped in Diane's jars of cream.

Betty was sure she had gone too far this time.

"Who's been going to her factory?" Peterman demanded. "When? On whose authority? I never gave any orders to do that."

Betty was surprised by the vehemence of his denial, but she had heard good liars before. "It's your shopping channel," she said. "Who else could give approval? And if you're not so obsessed with her business, why is that producer hovering over her every second and keeping a headset glued to his ears so he can give you minute-to-minute reports?"

"I don't owe you any explanation for how I run my business."

There was silence and Betty was now sure he had hung up on her. She closed her eyes. Where did she and Diane go from here?

"But I can tell you that I didn't authorize anyone to go to Diane's factory. And my producer tells me the person who called in said she knows you. How do you fit into this?"

Betty had been wrong. The producer hadn't run off to get security; just another phone line to call his boss.

Betty didn't know how Rose had managed to be one of the people who got a jar of cream with cocaine in it. A plastic packet of cocaine didn't sound like an accident; it wasn't like finding something in a jar that was an impurity or represented a flaw in the manufacturing or packaging process. Betty suspected that many other people had found cocaine as well.

As if to confirm her thoughts, there was a commotion on the set once again. Betty was close enough this time to see and hear what was going on. The shopping channel took live testimonial calls from customers, and two more women had called in to report that their cream contained a small packet of white powder. This must be the tip of the iceberg, Betty thought. How many others had found the small white packet and not had the nerve to call in to report them? Who would believe someone who said they possessed cocaine because it came that way in their face cream?

"I think your people treated the first caller as a crackpot, but now it looks as if there are a lot of women who found cocaine in their jars," she told Peterman. "Is your producer telling you about the additional calls?" Betty knew about five second delays. She was sure there would be no more live testimonial calls—at least not tonight.

"What do you know about the list that was broadcast?" Peterman asked.

Why was he grilling her about something that had nothing to do with him?

"What is it about the list that interests you, Mr. Peterman?" Betty asked.

Besides being twenty years old, that list was probably indecipherable to anyone who saw it for a few seconds on a television screen. A sudden thought. How had she been so stupid? Betty shook her head. The destruction of her home was still reverberating in her head, giving Betty her own delay.

"Your name is on that list, isn't it?" she asked.

Betty figured Peterman would answer that question; it would be easy enough for her to confirm.

"Yes, it is," he said. "Did you know that before you put it on the air?"

"No. And I didn't put it on the air. It was an accident that the list was broadcast."

The disbelieving sneer was loud in her ear.

"Before tonight I didn't know that list existed," Betty said. "I took it for safekeeping. I work at the clinic that was involved." Betty's heart dropped and she nearly collapsed on the floor as what she was saying to him sank in. Her life had been devastated over and over again tonight. How was she still standing?

Betty made an effort to pull herself together. "I had no intention whatsoever to use that list in any way to harm anyone," she said. "This has been an unnerving night for me for many reasons, and that is the only reason I can give for accidentally letting that list out of my hands. My being here tonight was solely to give moral support to Diane, who is an old friend and colleague."

Betty paused. She had come tonight to try to find out why Peterman's people seemed to want to take over Diane's company. But Betty had had no reason to suspect any connection between the shopping channel and the list—nor would she have used the list to get to Peterman had she known the connection.

"Seems like a lot of unexpected coincidences," Peterman said.

"The unpleasant ones are always more plentiful than the pleasant ones, in my experience," Betty said. It could be her life's motto.

Betty could hear Peterman breathing on the other end of the line. Finally he spoke.

"So you work at Dr. Wyatt's clinic?" he asked her.

"Yes." Though for how much longer, Betty didn't know.

"Well, Doctor, it may be in your interest to make one more trip tonight."

82

When Peterman left the game room, Greene wheeled on Clea, his face crimson. He lifted huge hands toward her.

"You bitch!"

Clea faced him squarely and didn't back up. Cy lunged to her side and grabbed her arm, intending to yank her out of Greene's path. She shook him off.

"Because of you and your greed, our house was burned down, my father died, and my mother and I spent twenty years on the run," Clea said. "You should rot in hell."

Greene stopped, but the look on his face stayed. He strode to the door, opened it. Cy heard him give orders to the goons outside.

"Get rid of them."

Then the door slammed shut behind him.

"It doesn't have to end that way," Dr. Wyatt said. He was standing behind Cy and Clea.

Cy spun in surprise to face the older man and for the second time tonight was amazed by his appearance. Dr. Wyatt had finally pulled himself together. Cy expected the shock the man had suffered would have changed him, but he wasn't prepared for the kind of change. Dr. Wyatt now had a sense of purpose about him that Cy didn't recognize.

"I'm sorry, Clea, that I had you and your mother hunted. Cy, I'm so sorry for having hurt you. I never meant to."

Cy didn't know how to answer him. Dr. Wyatt's face said he was aware—probably for the first time in his life—of how he had affected others, and he regretted it. Cy found it unsettling to think this could be the man's death bed confession.

Clea completely ignored Dr. Wyatt. Cy was sure an apology from him couldn't begin to make amends to her.

Cy tried to shake off the fear that was clutching him. How did Clea look brave and collected in the face of death?

Cy shot a glance at the closed door.

"I have an idea," he told her.

"Save it," she told him. "You're 0 for 2."

Cy opened his mouth to explain himself.

"There are no windows and there's no large duct work," she said, almost sobbing. "What are you going to do, hide under the furniture or behind the books?"

Cy saw she was hanging on in spite of her terror. He could, too. "I just thought we have a better chance of getting out of here when Greene and his thugs aren't in the room with us."

"And do what?" Clea asked. "Threaten to break a priceless Chinese vase?"

"Maybe you could use this," Dr. Wyatt said. He drew an automatic pistol out of his pocket, laid it on the table between them.

Cy's eyes widened. Dr. Wyatt had performed the gesture as if he offered a gun to Cy on a daily basis. It must be the item Cy had watched him hide under a bush in the garden. How had he managed to retrieve it? Cy looked at Dr. Wyatt's face. An entirely new persona was there; this one confident and calm. Maybe he's even a better actor than a doctor, Cy thought. Greene's men had probably dismissed Dr. Wyatt as a spineless wimp when he had his first panic attack, and didn't watch him closely after that. Now Cy wondered if that had just been an act. Which was the real Dr. Wyatt?

Cy touched the gun. He felt the way he had the first time he'd picked up a dead crab on the beach.

"There's one full clip," Dr. Wyatt said.

Cy picked up the gun, looked down at the uncomfortable weight in his hand. His head snapped up when he heard a series of explosions from inside the house, then screams. Cy was turning around, trying to figure out from what directions the explosions had come, when a shattering of porcelain fragments filled the air inside the room.

Dr. Wyatt was throwing Chinese vases at the door.

The door to the game room flew open and Dr. Wyatt flung himself to the floor. "He's got a gun!" he yelled.

83

Now Betty knew the warning in Clea's Tarot cards had not been idle.

At first, Betty had assumed that Peterman was lying to her. When he said Mr. Greene was planning to kill Dr. Wyatt, a woman and another man, though Betty immediately thought of Clea and Cy, she didn't believe him. It was crazy. Betty knew Dr. Wyatt was arrogant and infuriating, and virtually anyone who worked with him had at one time felt like wringing his neck. But what would one of the richest men in the country have against him?

A thought had finally struck Betty in the middle of her conversation with Peterman, and she realized how slowly her mind was working tonight. Mrs. Greene had been a patron of Dr. Wyatt's. It was a small clinic; even without Aggie's public service announcements, Betty had known about her visits. She had noticed how the woman's perfume clung to Dr. Wyatt after each visit. Maybe Greene was getting revenge on Dr. Wyatt for having an affair with his wife. But how did Cy and Clea fit into that?

When Peterman told her of the Greenes' involvement in the list of embryo transfers, Betty was staggered. But when he told her what had happened to his daughter and her husband, Betty was sick.

Betty made herself take one deep breath, then another. As if she had been in a soundproof bubble while she talked with Peterman, now the noise and activity of the television studio inundated her. Betty got her bearings, then looked for Diane. She found her leaning against one of the columns in the studio, shaking her head in a way that scared Betty.

"Diane, what's wrong?

"Nothing. That's what's wrong. Nothing. Women call up to say they've found cocaine inside my jars of cream, and now they're selling lawn sprinklers."

Diane nodded toward the set, where a smiling host stood on astroturf enthusiastically demonstrating a sprinkler.

"I don't know what's going to happen to me and my company," Diane said. "They pushed me to make all these presentations, they muscled their way into my factory and now you'd think they'd never heard of me. At least until the DEA and the lawyers get involved."

Diane was pale and looked as if she were going to drop. Betty reached out a comforting hand.

"Diane, I'm so sorry. And I'm sorry that you got that list."

Diane looked as if she'd already forgotten about it. "It threw the producer into a panic. What was it?"

Betty figured the entire country had seen it, she might as well tell Diane. "Dr. Wyatt was involved in stealing his patients' embryos and selling or giving them to other people."

"Oh my God." Diane blinked her eyes. "What's going on?"

Betty had no answers and she was nearly drained by her own losses. "I don't know. Not yet." Betty took a deep breath. "I have to leave."

Diane's eyes slowly widened. "You came here to help me when you had troubles of your own." She hugged Betty. "If I can help you in any way, I will." She picked up her purse with shaking hands and pulled out her cell phone. "I'm going to call my lawyer and then I'm going home. I can't take any more tonight. If it all goes to hell in a handbasket, so be it."

Betty thought that she herself needed refuge and sleep, but she couldn't think about them yet. She had promised to meet Peterman at the Greenes'.

****

"Detective Horn?" Betty was on I-95, heading north to the Greenes' estate. She had decided to heed the Tarot's warning, even if Clea hadn't.

"Who is this?" He sounded tired and annoyed on his cell phone.

Betty reminded him of his visits to the clinic, when he was

investigating Jane's death, and that he had given them his cell phone number. Then she told him as concisely as she could what had happened since then and what Peterman had told her.

"You've got to be crazy, Doctor."

Betty was ready to hang up on him. "If you don't believe me now, you will when copies of that list end up on the front pages of the newspapers. Then you can explain why you didn't help."

"Hold on. I didn't mean I don't believe you. You're just crazy to be going there by yourself. After what you've told me, I wouldn't go there alone if they were throwing a banquet for me."

The beating she'd taken tonight was taking its toll. Betty's energy and her resolve were flagging. "All right. How do you want to handle this?"

"Where are you right now?" he asked.

"On I-95, just past Bridgeport, heading north."

He was silent for a while.

"You're going to get there about twenty minutes before I do," he said. "There's a long driveway leading to the main house. Wait for me at the bottom of that drive. Don't go in without me."

"You know where it is?" Betty was surprised.

"Oh, yes."

84

The two goons took one look at the three bodies on the floor and ran. Thank God for small brain pans, Dr. Wyatt thought. His heart was pounding so hard with adrenaline that he had had trouble keeping his body still.

He managed to pull himself to his feet before his left leg collapsed under him. He glared at his foot as if it had betrayed him; saw blood running out of his shoe. With shaking hands, he untied the laces and tugged off the shoe. Then he pulled off the blood-sticky sock. He felt queasy as he looked at the bloody groove and gingerly probed it with a finger. Just a nick; blood but no real damage. He let out his breath, wrapped the sock around his foot. He picked up his shoe and stuffed in into his jacket pocket.

Dr. Wyatt stood up and limped across the room to retrieve his gun from Cy's hand. This time he didn't reach for Cy's pulse; he didn't even look at his face. He limped out of the room and down the hallway, leaving the game room and the sounds of explosions in his wake.

Though he had no idea why fate had offered him a reprieve, perhaps even a 'get out of jail free' card, he felt he had risen to the occasion. This thought made him smile.

Hobbling quickly along paneled corridors he had never been in, listening for footsteps or voices, he chose a path that took him further away from both. He looked back once at the bloody trail he was leaving; decided that was the least of his worries.

Before he expected it, he saw colored lights dancing on a marble floor, and he realized he was near the rear of the mansion. Cautiously, he shuffled closer, and saw a bank of French doors letting in light from the fireworks display. Right outside must be the terrace and the circle of hedges he had earlier been escorted from at gunpoint.

He limped slowly toward the French doors. Some sixth sense made him pull himself into an alcove, and within seconds he knew why. A security guard with what looked like a walkie talkie ran by, opened a French door and ducked out onto the terrace. He then came back to wave to a disheveled Mr. Greene. Greene lumbered heavily past Dr. Wyatt, through the French doors and onto the terrace.

"Stay here," the security man said. "Until I get back, don't go anywhere. OK?"

Dr. Wyatt didn't hear the reply, but the security guard ran back the way he came.

Though he knew he shouldn't stay, Dr. Wyatt could no more tear himself away from the scene on the terrace, than he had been able to resist going into the game room. By the intermittent light of the exploding fireworks, Dr. Wyatt could make out two figures on the terrace: Mr. and Mrs. Greene. Something muffled their conversation, so he edged closer to the open door.

Dr. Wyatt made out the tone of their conversation from their body language before he could hear their voices. Mrs. Greene stood stiffly on the terrace, hugging herself. Mr. Greene paced back and forth like a caged bear.

Dr. Wyatt heard new, larger reverberations of explosions somewhere in the depths of the mansion.

Greene snatched up potted flowers and smashed them on the stone terrace. "Who is doing this to me?" he roared.

Mrs. Greene stumbled backward on the stone terrace, out of range of flying fragments.

Greene was wild. His voice was furious. "It can't be Peterman. He found out about his daughter and son-in-law. And he knows about the car crash. But I gave him the first seat at the game table." Greene spun around as another explosion boomed inside.

His wife leaned against a column. Her breathing was shallow and rapid. Dr. Wyatt wasn't surprised; she must be terrified of him.

"Why do you think *he* did it?" she asked.

He ignored her. There was a loud crash and he shook a pedestal and knocked it over onto the terrace.

"Why don't you blame it on me?" she asked.

"Where is my security?" he roared.

Overhead, fireworks lit up the sky in red, white, and blue. In her gown of the same colors, Mrs. Greene looked as if she might be in some kind of patriotic commercial.

Mrs. Greene began to move agitatedly, a step or two toward her husband, then back. What's going on? Dr. Wyatt wondered.

"Why don't you blame me?" she asked again.

Greene ignored her.

"You blame everything on me, but you don't give me credit for anything."

"Shut up!" Greene shouted.

Her agitated pacing stopped and she uncrossed her arms and clenched her fists.

"It was my idea to work with Dr. Wyatt, to use the embryos to get things done. I arranged everything with him, I arranged for the transfers, the payments..."

Greene turned on her. "You nothing! You can barely arrange to have your hair done or your face lifted. I make things happen."

Her face looked white. She swayed a moment, then opened her arms.

"I made this happen."

Greene snorted and continued pacing. Then he stopped. When he spoke, his voice was guttural.

"You made what happen?"

Dr. Wyatt heard her take a shaky breath, then Mrs. Greene said: "The destruction of your fiefdom."

The words made Mr. Greene stagger. As if she knew she wouldn't have much time, Mrs. Greene spoke rapidly.

"*Your* house, *your* furniture, *your* artwork, *your* guests, *your* whores. All yours and all going up in smoke. On your special occasion."

An enormous firework flag exploded in the sky, served as a backdrop for an immobile Mr. and Mrs. Greene, who faced each other as if in a tableau. Finally:

"You're crazy and ugly," he said.

Mrs. Greene dropped her voice so Dr. Wyatt had to strain to hear her.

"Do you want to know how I did it? Explosive devices in your closet, in your study, in your game room, in your bedroom, everywhere I could think of. It was the only way I could live with you. With your cheating—in my house, in my face! As if I..." Her voice cracked.

"As if I didn't matter. As if I had no feelings. I hated you so much. But divorcing you wouldn't take enough away. You would just crawl off and start over. And then I figured out a way. Something I could control. So whenever I wanted, I could bring you to your knees."

Mr. Greene swayed on his feet. It seemed to Dr. Wyatt the man still didn't believe his wife. Believe her, he thought. She's capable of anything.

Mr. Greene's voice was a harsh whisper. "Why tonight?"

She held something up. Dr. Wyatt couldn't make it out, but Mr. Greene must have recognized it. He lunged and grabbed his wife and she collapsed like a folding chair. He followed her to the ground. On her back, she made futile attempts to push him away.

Dr. Wyatt dragged himself to the open door and looked down on Mr. and Mrs. Greene, just a few feet away. He pulled the pistol out of his pocket.

As if they had rehearsed it, Dr. Wyatt bent to his knees and gently slid his pistol across to her. The grating sound of metal on stone was like a cue to her. She turned her head as the pistol reached her hand.

Now Greene was squeezing her throat. She closed her fingers around the gun, groped for a handhold, then lifted it to her husband's head and pulled the trigger.

Mr. Greene collapsed like a bear rug on his wife.

Dr. Wyatt waited, watching and listening. Then he hobbled out to the two figures. Shakily, he lowered himself to kneel beside the mound of Greenes. He held his breath as he felt for one carotid pulse after the other.

Nothing. He sighed with relief.

Then he retrieved what Mrs. Greene had been holding. He pushed it into his pocket and limped into the maze of hedges.

85

Betty followed Detective Horn's car along the long, winding drive to the Greenes' mansion. How big is this estate? she wondered. How do bad guys manage it? Trees, shrubs and mown grass stretched for long distances on both sides of the drive When she came over a crest and saw the house, it took her breath away.

The immense Georgian-style building was illuminated by a colossal display of fireworks and a myriad of red, white, and blue spotlights. The house seemed to go on forever as Betty drove parallel to the front, looking for the entrance.

As she pulled to a stop and parked her car, Betty saw smoke wafting out of broken windows. Oh please, not fire, she prayed. Cy, Clea, stay safe. Betty saw people straggling out of the house. Something seemed to be wrong with them. Though they had sense enough to get out—and their clothes and faces looked untouched by smoke—they were milling around in front, staring vacantly at the house and each other.

Detective Horn had parked ahead of her. He took one look at the partygoers faces, then spat out orders to the men in the three squad cars that had come with him.

"You, call for backup, the fire department and ambulances. Get these people away from the house. Don't let anyone back in the house. You, go inside and herd the others toward exits. As high as this bunch is, there have to be others who won't know to come in out of the rain. There have to be a lot more exits like this one. Find them. Fast. You, come with me."

He turned to Betty. "I don't think you should come in, Doctor. I'll find Greene and Peterman myself."

How quickly he forgot who gave him the lead, Betty thought.

"No way." Betty shook her head. "Cy and Clea are in there. And I'm a doctor. You need me."

Horn shrugged. "It's your funeral."

Betty wished he had chosen just about any other words.

By now the flow of disoriented people out of the mansion had dropped to a trickle. Betty easily followed Horn as he walked between the large sparklers and crossed the threshold.

Though her mind was on Cy and Clea, Betty couldn't help being overwhelmed by the vastness of the place. The foyer reminded Betty of the inside of St. Peter's—large, opulent, and remote. She turned around, marveling at the marble, the wood, the crystal—until someone bumped into her and she stepped aside, out of the way of a string of partygoers being guided to the front door by Horn's men.

Horn took a look around and shook his head. "This is too public a place for Greene to be doing anything violent—even though most of these characters probably wouldn't notice if a bomb exploded under them."

Horn headed back the way he had come, with Betty hurrying to keep up with him. Outside, he swept his gaze left and right, then started at a trot to the left.

"Where are we going?" Betty asked.

"The back. There's a formal hedge garden and a large terrace. Two wings of the house enclose it. I'm guessing that's a better entry point."

Betty couldn't help asking the next question."How do you know so much about this place?"

Horn's face was tight. Betty didn't think he was going to answer her.

"We've been staking out this place for a long time."

Horn nearly ran into a man who suddenly stepped out of the shrubbery in front of him, The detective had his gun ready.

"Who are you?"

The man lifted his arms. palms facing the detective. "Brett Peterman. I called Dr. Winter." His eyes swung to Betty.

"What's going on here, Mr. Peterman?" Horn asked.

Peterman slowly lowered his arms. "Greene is in the game

room with Dr. Wyatt and two other people, a man and a woman. He plans to kill them. He sent me to the front to the Amazing Sweepstakes truck to tell the driver to bring it around the back. I think he plans..."

Detective Horn cut him short. "I think I can figure that out for myself." He told one of the policemen with him: "Bring that truck around the back." He motioned to another policeman. "Go with this officer," he told Peterman.

"But I told Dr. Winter to come. You need me to take you there."

Horn waved him aside, hurried on with Betty right behind him. "I know the way," Horn told her. "And that one isn't looking to help anyone but himself."

They ran past a large hedge and onto a broad expanse of terrace. Horn almost stumbled over the bodies, which he identified as Mr. and Mrs. Greene. Betty knelt beside them, feeling for a pulse. She sat back on her heels and shook her head.

Two large booms shook the house, followed by deafening, crashing sounds. Horn put his hand on Betty's shoulder. "It sounds like the upper floors are caving in. We're not going inside."

Betty didn't have time to digest what he'd said before a policeman ran up to Horn, motioned for him to move apart from her. She watched him whisper to Horn. What now? she wondered.

Horn came over to her and helped her gently to her feet.

Oh God, not Cy and Clea, Betty prayed.

"I know you've had a traumatic evening, but I've gotten word that there was a break-in at your home. Do you know anything about that?"

Betty was almost relieved, except it alarmed her the way Horn held her gaze. His understanding attitude scared her, too. Her old mistrust of the police resurfaced and she worried that he was trying to trick her into something. She hadn't reported the break-in. Was that a crime? She was too tired, though, to be guarded.

"Yes, I know there was a break-in. No, I didn't report it. I found Clea in the kitchen and I ended up following her to the clinic after I lent her my key. Then I went to the television studio to see Diane. Then I came here. Why?"

"How much of your house did you examine?" he asked.

What in the world does that have to do with anything? Betty wondered. "Just the living room, the dining room, and the kitchen."

"You didn't go upstairs?" he persisted.

Betty was exhausted and at the end of her rope. "No. They destroyed my home. I had enough after I saw the downstairs. Why? Was there something special that they left me?"

Horn got a funny look on his face.

"Upstairs, in your bedroom," he began. "There was a man's body. We think from the ID he carried that his name was Trowe..."

Betty sucked in her breath, felt light-headed. Her eyes and throat pinched from tears that wouldn't come. "Trowe," she said. "My ex-husband."

"We'll investigate this, of course," Horn said quietly. "Right now it looks as if it was a suicide. Though I don't think it will stay that way."

Betty thought about the last thing she had said to Trowe: 'What happens when they decide they have one more black man than they need for their conspiracy?'

Betty stood blinking at nothing. After everything, after all these years, he was finally gone. Trowe had always managed to be a destructive force in her life. Tonight he had ransacked her home and gotten himself killed in her bedroom—he had stayed true to form to the end.

86

Dr. Wyatt limped slowly to the Amazing Sweepstakes truck. Though Greene had ordered it around back—to take away three bodies, including his own—Dr. Wyatt thought it was his best bet for an escape. Greene and his wife were dead. The goons had run to save their own skins. And the Amazing Sweepstakes people owed him. The $50,000 Trowe had insisted on sending him through the mail had been stolen and there hadn't been a replacement.

He calculated that he could make it, even limping. There was no one in the truck—all those stupid storm troopers were running around the mansion on Horn's errands. He patted his pocket and smiled. He had kept only one of the items he'd taken from Mrs. Greene's lifeless hand. The two plane tickets to Switzerland he had discarded after a cursory glance. One had been for Mr. Greene; the other for a woman whose name Dr. Wyatt didn't recognize. But the remaining item he had taken and clutched to his heart. It was a small leather wallet containing the name of a Swiss bank, and a numbered account at that bank. It was all he needed for a new beginning.

In spite of the wound on his foot, in spite of the betrayal and loss he had suffered tonight, he felt no pain or tiredness as he pushed himself to hurry to the truck.

He was almost at the door of the cab when some idiot shouted: "He has a gun!"

****

Dr. Wyatt was lying on the ground, feeling knives stab him when he tried to breathe. His eyes were half-closed against the pain, and wet from the sharpness and surprise of it. Through the haze he saw a form bending over him, heard a voice at once familiar and strange.

"I am a doctor. Let me help him."

Of all the people in the world to minister to his needs!

It was that Indian doctor, Dr. Singh. The one he had talked to at the dinner party here days ago, the one who ran a fertility clinic in India. Dr. Wyatt had seen him earlier in the evening. Why was he still here? Why hadn't he run like the others?

Dr. Singh seemed to be applying pressure to his chest.

"There is not much I can do to help you, Dr. Wyatt," he whispered. There was such gentleness in the man's hands, and his voice was full of regret.

He was feeling cold now. He must have shivered, because Dr. Singh took off his own jacket and put it over him.

"I will wait with you until the ambulance arrives," he said.

The significance of those words made their way slowly to Dr. Wyatt's brain, and he felt a chill that didn't come from loss of blood. Slowly and painfully, Dr. Wyatt slid his hand from under the jacket and reached for Dr. Singh's hand.

"Please hold it," he whispered.

There was a small, quiet circle around them, for how long, Dr. Wyatt didn't know. He went in and out of consciousness, but he always found Dr. Singh's hand holding his own.

Then there was the sound of a vehicle racing to a stop. Doors opened and slammed, and the sound of wheels and metal bouncing over the terrace. My ride, Dr. Wyatt thought.

The paramedics were almost upon him, by the sound of their voices. A thought, at once so unexpected and so right, came into Dr. Wyatt's mind. He squeezed Dr. Singh's hand. "Come closer," he said.

Dr. Singh bent over. With an effort that made him gasp, Dr. Wyatt pulled his other hand from under the jacket and pressed something into Dr. Singh's chest.

"Take this," he said. "For your clinic."

He pushed the small leather wallet containing a numbered Swiss account into Dr. Singh's hands.

"With my compliments," Dr. Wyatt said.

87

Pain crammed so tightly in Cy's skull that there was no room for thought.

He groaned on the floor like a wounded animal. Pain kept exploding in his head, until he had trouble seeing. Cy tried to contract away from the pain, and rolled on his side.

He saw the other body. The small red pool she was lying in. His brain made space for the thought that it was Clea; she was wounded and needed help.

Cy didn't move toward her, not an inch. The pain gripped all of his awareness in a vise. He listened to it, grimaced at its screaming volume.

His brain was firing randomly now, giving him unconnected images and words. Into the middle of this chaos was dropped a whole memory: Cy was lying outside a flaming house, rolling in pain from the burns on his chest, forgetting about a tiny child in her crib.

That thought dragged him across the carpet, and drew him to all fours over Clea, though the effort made him so sick, he wanted to throw up.

He weaved over Clea, feeling for a pulse, trying to stop up the newly made exits for her blood. He pulled off his jacket and pressed it to her, but blood kept filling up the fabric. Finally, idiotically, he realized part of that blood was running from his head. They both had to get out.

Whether he had become accustomed to the pain or it had lessened, he was able to pick up Clea's limp body and stagger to the open door of the room

The explosions in the house were closer. He felt the building shudder, saw large plates of ceiling in the hallway shake free and crash in clouds of dust. The hallways looked the same to him. He didn't know which way led out.

This is the second chance you prayed for, he thought.

A shock of adrenaline sent loud echoes of pain through his skull. Cy leaned against the door frame and slid down, eyes closed. Such pain. It shrank him into a tiny unmoving point of consciousness. There was no wanting to go anywhere or do anything. Just to have the pain stop, even if it meant dying.

A burst of depressing, weakening thoughts rained down on him.

She's not Clea, he told himself. It's not a second chance. You can't step twice into the same river. She's not the little girl in the crib. She's someone else. Who didn't need me for twenty years...

Cy could feel something shoving aside these thoughts, until only one thought filled his mind: She won't get out without you.

He opened his eyes, saw a smeared blood trail in the hall-way. It was a direction and he staggered as he followed it. His worries made better progress than his feet, and sucked at his strength. What if she didn't make it? What if she didn't want him? What if she left again?

Anger and pain made him shut that voice down. To hell with what ifs, he thought. There is only here and only now.

He couldn't ransom anything. Not with promises or good acts or suffering. He could get her out or he could stay. Take it or leave it.

Cy decided to take it.

He dragged himself down corridors, following a smeared, bloody trail that seemed to go on forever. Until he saw the colored lights on the marble floor.

He clutched Clea to his chest and dragged one foot after the other toward the lights, until he reached the French doors.

As he swayed in the doorway, someone outside looked up and cried out, then ran toward him. It was Betty.

With a lot of police. And a wailing siren.

Later

There were palm trees and a blue sea in the background. A full moon hung in the sky.

Cy held Clea gingerly as they danced. He could feel the bandages on her back through her dress. Her hair smelled of flowers when he kissed the top of her head.

"I'm sometimes sorry I found out about that list," she said. "And made it public."

His regretful exhale ruffled her hair. When would they leave all that behind them?

"I was trying to find out why Dr. Wyatt hunted my mother and me. It turned out to be more than I wanted to know."

"I was trying to find you," Cy said. "And if that's what it cost, it was worth it."

"That's cavalier of you. The list didn't change your life." But she didn't pull away from him.

"Right. I just lost the man who raised me, my job, and my good name."

Cy could feel Clea smile against his chest. "No one blames you. You weren't involved," she said.

"The lawyers do and it doesn't matter," he said. "They'd sue my office desk if it helped them."

"You weren't that cynical when I met you."

"And I'm probably not half as cynical as I'll be when it's all over. If it ever is."

Cy held Clea tighter.

"If Betty and Diane are any indication of how things will turn out, there may be hope for us," he said. "The cocaine scandal is making Diane's jars of cream sell like crazy. It's like when a restaurant has a mob killing and gets a boost in popularity. And Trowe's bosses at the CDC paid Betty a settlement to spare them the embarrassment he caused. She's going to move to a house she's dreamed of owning."

Clea didn't say anything.

"I know it was stressful, but what you did was brave. A lot

of lawyers will make out, but a lot of heads will roll, too. It will clean up businesses. Government too."

Clea tensed in his arms, and Cy did a dramatic, sweeping turn to take her mind off it. He came too close to the palm trees. A tear appeared down the middle of a paper trunk.

"Hey, buddy!" the bar owner shouted. "Watch what you're doing."

"It wasn't the whole list," Clea said.

"Sorry," Cy shouted to the man. "I'll pay for another back-drop."

Clea had stopped dancing. Cy stopped.

"It wasn't the whole list."

"Of course it wasn't," Cy said. "The transfers they did twenty years ago weren't the last of it. Who knows how many they did since then?"

"The list I made copies of," Clea said. "There was another page. I didn't show it to anyone."

"Why?"

"There were different kinds of transfers on that page. Not to individuals. To countries."

Now Cy was silent.

"Groups of transfers. Sent to each country. A lot in the Middle E

ast."

"Why didn't you turn that list over to the police?" Cy asked.

They were alone on the dance floor, but Clea pulled him to the side.

"Because of who delivered the embryos. He wasn't any-body twenty years ago. But he is today."

Cy knew what she was afraid of. "If that person is power-ful, you don't want to live another nightmare of being hunted."

"No."

"So we'll go higher than that man. As high as we have to go. We can't let this pass. The safety of the country could be involved, Clea. If we have to, we'll take it to the President."

"Then we'll have to wait for the next election," she said.

ACKNOWLEDGMENTS

With love and gratitude
to my father,
Metro Spewock,
for everything.

With much gratitude
to Anke Gray,
for her friendship,
help, and encouragement.

You can write to the author in care of:

Thornwood Publishing Company LLC
830 Post Road East
Suite G-4
Westport, CT 06880
phone/fax: 203-226-5312

or by email:
tentrees@earthlink.net

You may order copies of
One of My Own
online, or at your local bookstore

Visit
ThornwoodPublishing.com
to:
See our other books—fiction, non-fiction, and audiobooks
Read first chapters and reviews
Sign up for the free newsletter
Download free articles and recipes
Email us
Order books at discount.